SECONDS FROM REVENGE

Seconds from Revenge

A Murder Mystery

Dr. L. Jan Eira

To order additional copies of this book, contact:
Xlibris Corporation
1-888-795-4274
www.Xlibris.com
Orders@Xlibris.com
70570

PREFACE

As a physician and educator, I have attempted to utilize my murder mysteries as a teaching tool for common topics in heart disease. In the background of the fictional stories, there lie nonfictional lessons about cardiac and electrophysiology matters. The distinction between the fictional and nonfictional is, I believe, clear and straightforward. These heart-related topics are explored in more detail in my Web site, www.janeirabooks.com.

Though this book stands alone, it is the second volume in the saga that has become Dr. Jack Norris' story. The first book, titled *First, Do No Harm*, recounts the events that so affected the protagonist's life. *Seconds from Revenge* puts the final touches on the tale.

I hope you enjoy reading this medical murder mystery as much as I loved writing it.

ACKNOWLEDGMENT

I want to express my gratitude for the moral support and editing contributions from the many people who have helped me through the conclusion of this book, as well as *First, Do No Harm*, its first volume. Thank you.

Special thanks to the main contributors, including Adam Janeira, Jim and Louanne Davis, Kevin and Kelly McCarthy, Adalyn Schillaci, Judie Tasch, Anne Crawford, Dan Adams, Tina Murphy, and Lori Adams. Others providing editorial assistance and encouragement include the lovely ladies of the Baby Brigade Book Club in Noblesville, Indiana. They are Ellen Hostetler, Kristen Boice, Kerri Haffner, Rochelle Meisner and Soma Dey. Thank you.

Jane, my magnificent wife, has provided everlasting support. Her endless love and encouragement have helped to define our beautiful relationship, one where we each can flourish in our pursuits. Moreover, to Jane and my daughter, Ellie, I also owe my deepest appreciation for the family time from which they were deprived while I endeavored to pursue my passion to write. Thank you.

Finally, I am indebted to the countless people, too many to enumerate here, who have helped with efforts to expose my books by word of mouth, advertising my work to those in their circles, near and far. Dissemination of unknown novels by first-time writers is always a difficult task. Their assistance is particularly valuable and appreciated. Thank you (and please keep up the good work!).

DEDICATION

I dedicate this book to my three amazing children – Brian Andrew, Adam Joseph and Lauren Elizabeth (Ellie). I hope you know I love you very much, and how proud I'll always be to have you as my children. May you always find the strength to conquer the struggles and tribulations of life. Always believe in yourselves as I will always believe in you. May all your dreams come true.

INTRODUCTION

Heart disease is the number one killer of Americans, taking, on average, one of us each minute. Death often comes rapidly in the form of sudden cardiac arrest. The afflicted individual is unexpectedly robbed of life due to the abrupt emergence of an exceedingly rapid heartbeat that causes the pumping chambers to quiver uncontrollably. This often occurs during the night, leaving loved ones to discover the lifeless body in the morning. Electrophysiologists are doctors trained in and devoted to the study of heartbeat disorders.

Once sudden cardiac arrest occurs, the game is practically over. Within ten minutes, the brain, devoid of blood circulation, will become irreparably and permanently damaged. The secret to winning this game is to be proactive.

Over the years, multiple factors have been identified which place individuals at risk for sudden cardiac death. Once these develop, it is of extreme importance to initiate crucial classes of medications and avoid certain others. When medications alone are insufficient to ameliorate the risk, the patient is fitted with a small device that monitors the heartbeat and delivers a lifesaving shock in case of a cardiac arrest. This apparatus, an implantable cardioverter-defibrillator, or ICD, takes relatively minor outpatient surgery to insert.

Many drugs increase the risk of heartbeat disorders, including sudden cardiac arrest. The propensity certain medications possess to cause catastrophic racing heartbeats is termed proarrhythmia. Before research brought this to light, only ten to fifteen years ago, many of these potentially harmful medications were prescribed routinely. Although this iatrogenic problem is becoming less common, every few months, electrophysiologists at busy medical centers are asked to evaluate such a patient, who typically present with fainting spells. These are the lucky ones, as others simply unexpectedly depart this life while performing routine activities of daily living or, more commonly, while they sleep.

1

Two months earlier

Right outside the house, a dark sedan drove by slowly. Calculating. Scheming. The car stopped for a few seconds in front of the mailbox bearing the words *The Norris Family*, then continued. The car and its driver remained unnoticed under the cover of nightfall and disappeared into darkness. This was one of several surveying trips.

Inside the home, the dinner table was cleared, the dishwasher still churning away. The beautiful sunny day had been replaced by a calm dark evening and the time to relax was quickly approaching. All was tranquil. All seemed right. Jack and Claire were putting their son, Nick, to bed.

Dr. Jack Norris was a handsome tall man in his late thirties with mysterious dark eyes but a bright, friendly smile. Despite pushing forty, Jack refused to give up on his youth, alternating three-mile runs with trips to the gym for muscle toning. On Sunday evenings, he captained and organized the Heartbeats, a coed indoor soccer team, where Jack starred as the right midfielder. His other passion was flying. He owned a Beechcraft Bonanza, which he piloted not only when he needed to get somewhere far and fast, but also when he required a bit of peace and solitude to collect his thoughts. Flying was as relaxing for Jack as a blankie is to a toddler. He tried to fly at least an hour a week. This wasn't always possible since Jack was the head of the Cardiology Department at Newton Memorial Hospital in Evansville, Indiana.

Dr. Claire Norris was a cardiac psychologist. Now that she was a *mommy*, she worked on a part-time basis, seeing patients two, sometimes three, mornings a week, while Nick frequented preschool. She was a beautiful woman in her early thirties with blond hair and blue eyes. It had been these characteristics that attracted Jack to her the instant they met years ago. At that time, she was a psychology student, and Jack, a doctor in training. The rest, as they say, is history. They now had a spirited three-year-old boy, Nick, who was being groomed by dad to become a soccer star with the United States Men's National Team. As such, Jack would often point out the need to eat all one's carrots and green beans. Jack explained to Nick that at this very moment, there were many three-year-old boys in Brazil, Spain, Argentina, England, and Italy eating all their veggies, hoping to one day join the national team of their respective soccer-powerhouse countries. It would be with these boys that Nick would have to clash during their international matches some twenty years from now. And so little Nick would eat his vegetables, convinced of some vital higher purpose, one he did not yet quite comprehend.

At bedtime, the habitual toothbrushing followed the customary inevitable whines of protest. Pajamas on, it was time to read a bedtime story or two and say good night. At Jack's side throughout the nightfall drill was Trinity, the family dog. She was a purebred Vizsla, a Hungarian hunting dog. "If ever Hungarians move into the neighborhood, we're going hunting!" Jack would joke as he introduced the light brown canine companion to welcomed visitors.

Earlier, when the evening was younger, Trinity suddenly, and seemingly without reason, growled. Motionless, she stared at the wooden front door, as if to survey the dark beyond with her extra senses. Jack petted the dog and looked out a front-facing window. All appeared calm.

"What is it, girl? Do you hear something?" solicited Jack, intrigued with the dog's uncharacteristic behavior. Trinity stood still then wagged her tail, giving the all-clear sign. Maybe it was the indication of a false alarm. The Norris family would carry on, unaware of the mysterious occupant of the dark sedan and his repeated trips in the shadows.

2

Present time

Doctor Jack Norris was buckled in the Beechcraft Bonanza. Moments earlier, soon after landing at Spirit of St. Louis Airport, Claire and Nick had deplaned. At their side now, Jill, Claire's cousin, and her daughter, Lauren, stood waving, watching the airplane preparing for departure. Goodbyes had been punctuated by embraces and adorned with I love yous and I'll miss yous. Now alone, Jack made final arrangements for his flight back home. He read over the pretaxi checklist and noted that all items had been addressed. Outside the airplane, the day was gloomy, a significant chance of rain forecasted for St. Louis. With the headphones tight around his ears, he jotted down the important weather facts, as he listened: "Spirit of Saint Louis Airport, automated weather observation 22:05, Zulu; wind, 350 at 05; visibility, 10; sky condition, overcast 3,000; temperature, 28 Celsius; dew point, 17 Celsius; altimeter, 3009."

Before leaving home, Jack had filed his flight plan via the Internet with the FAA. That essential information was now accessible by the clearance controller's computer.

"Spirit of Saint Louis Clearance, Bonanza, 98-gulf-kilo, requesting clearance to kilo-echo-victor-victor," requested Jack, his microphone nearly touching his lips, to guarantee optimal transmission of his communications with the tower.

"Nine-eight-gulf-kilo, standby," returned the controller.

"Standing by," said Jack, waiting with pen and paper in hand. He knew he was about to be provided with several important data points necessary for his flight.

"Bonanza, 98-gulf-kilo, cleared to Evansville as filed, fly to altitude of four thousand feet, expect nine thousand in ten minutes, departure frequency 126.4, squawk 6441." Jack repeated the information, acknowledging it. In no time, the Bonanza taxied to runway 26-left and took off.

This was the first time he flew to this small airport. As his aircraft gained altitude on autopilot, Jack took in the moment, admiring the picturesque monuments that were the magnificent city of St. Louis. In awe, he observed the breathtaking Gateway Arch, the winding Mississippi River, the Busch Stadium, and the vast sea of tall buildings, as they progressively diminished in size, now viewed from two thousand feet in the air and climbing. Moments later, the aircraft punched a hole through the cloud layer at three thousand feet as it sped heavenward. Once Jack reached four thousand feet, the sky was clear and sunny, beautiful light blue visible for as far as the eye could see. There were wisps of clouds here and there, decorating Jack's picture-perfect view.

"Bonanza, 98-gulf-kilo, climb to nine thousand, direct to Evansville," commanded the departure controller.

"Climb nine thousand, direct Evansville," acknowledged Jack.

The trip would be about fifty minutes of bliss. The calming nature of flight was well-known to Jack. At nine thousand feet, the air was still, allowing for a perfectly smooth ride. He had a lot to think about and the journey would give him an opportunity to clear his mind and reflect. The events of the last few months, particularly the last few weeks, were very much on Jack's mind. One thing was for sure: his nemesis was back.

Three years earlier, the small city of Evansville and surrounding counties were assaulted, suddenly acquiring national notoriety. Notoriety for all the wrong reasons—the kind of reasons no one wants. Several heinous murders had been committed at Newton Memorial Hospital. The carnage was the outcome of a moneymaking scheme involving three executioners. Of the three terrorists, one was killed, another was incarcerated for life, but the third villain was still at large. The fugitive went by many pseudonyms, but his real name, Jack eventually learned, was Simon Lagrange. Lagrange, now prominently displayed on the FBI's Most Wanted List, had been the mastermind behind the dreadful bloodbath that so profoundly devastated the community. The country. The world. Jack Norris had helped the police disrupt the murderous plot and bring the homicidal activities to a halt. Having escaped the law, Simon Lagrange was now back, looking for revenge, or so Jack truly believed. There was no clear-cut evidence, but Jack had sensed something was wrong for months. A growing sensation of doom loitered within his every fiber, as if his body was a massive raw nerve. This feeling was now erupting, causing a volcano of emotions. The mere thought of the dreadful events of three years ago stirred a soup of feelings in Jack, a sinking feeling in the pit of his stomach. His heart would race, his muscles would tense, and his palms would become clammy. Jack felt uncharacteristically anxious and helpless, topped with a hefty measure of despair and rage. Trying to compose himself, Jack endeavored to halt his musing and took in the beautiful vast light blueness accentuated by fluffy white islands here and there, as the airplane effortlessly raced to its destination.

The first step was to protect the most important people in his life and get them out of harm's way. This trip had accomplished that goal. Claire and Nick deplaned in St. Louis a few minutes earlier. The second step was to face the problem. To face the problem, Jack had to understand it first. More relaxed, he continued to gaze out of the cockpit. Surrounding the airplane, there was peaceful serenity. Six thousand feet below his flight path, at three thousand feet, a pergola of thick clouds prevented visualization of the ground, no doubt giving those living in the area a sense of a murky day. From Jack's vantage point, nothing could be farther from the truth.

"Nine-eight-gulf-kilo, contact Evansville Approach on 127.5." The words emanating from the headphones broke Jack's thoughts.

"Evansville Approach, 127.5," he responded as he inputted the new frequency in the transmitter. "Evansville Approach, 98-gulf-kilo with you at nine thousand." Jack spoke calmly into the microphone, a moment later.

"Nine-eight-gulf-kilo, Evansville Approach, good morning, altimeter in Evansville 3002."

"Three-zero-zero-two," repeated Jack, acknowledging the information. He changed the settings on the altimeter to reflect the updated figures. His mind went back to deep reflection.

It was likely Simon Lagrange had changed his physical appearance. There were many eyes looking for him. Lagrange had escaped with a lot of money and he was cunning, intelligent, cruel, and, no doubt, dreadfully bitter. Three years was a long time to plot revenge. With time and cash aplenty, Jack could ill imagine what Lagrange's vengeance plan would be. Jack had to be prepared and match—no, exceed Simon Lagrange's ingenuity and smarts. Jack knew he himself could not even come close to the killer's malevolence. Or could he?

The shift had been unusually quiet at the Evansville Air Traffic Control Tower. One of Jason Fuller's jobs was to watch over the corridor of airspace currently utilized by Jack Norris' aircraft. All synchronous blips on his radar were accounted for and widely separated, allowing for a relaxed posture, feet up on the desk, a cup of coffee in his hand, and pleasant conversation with the new controller sitting nearby. Tiffany was young and pretty, definitely eye-candy material.

"Hey, Tiffany, wanna hear a good one?" uttered Jason, breaking the monotony and securing the woman's attention.

"Sure." She nodded.

"Did you hear the one about the woman who met a man in a bar? Having already downed a few power drinks, she turned around, faced him, looked him straight in the eye, and said, 'I screw anybody, anytime, anywhere; his place, my place, in the car, front door, back door, on the ground, standing up, sitting down . . . it doesn't matter to me. I've been doing it ever since I got out of college and I just love it.' Eyes now wide with interest, he responded, 'No kidding, I'm a lawyer too. What firm are you with?'" Both controllers laughed.

"That's a good one, Jason. Where do you hear these jokes?" she asked. "You have the best—," her words were interrupted by something she spied on Jason's screen. "You got bogey." Her right index finger pointed at a dot blinking rapidly in bright yellow. Both sat up straight. Jason quickly assessed the situation and mentally prepared for what he was about to declare.

"Evansville Tower to unidentified traffic twenty-four miles west of the airport, please respond," requested the air traffic controller. An uncomfortably long moment of radio silence followed. No answer returned.

"Bonanza, 98-gulf-kilo, unidentified traffic at your twelve o'clock, twelve and a half miles out, moving fast toward you," warned a voice with a smidgen of apprehension in Jack's headset, interrupting his reflection. The air traffic controllers' main role was to provide for adequate aircraft separation. Having a new unidentified blip on his radar in the path of and so close to the Bonanza made Jason exceptionally uncomfortable. He put the mug of coffee down on the counter and shoved it aside, his eyes fixated on the blinking dot.

"Looking for traffic," replied Jack, as was customary. Almost reflexively, Jack turned his attention to his radar screen, where a yellow blinking light corroborated the information. "Evansville, Bonanza, 98-gulf-kilo, I have traffic on my screen," said Jack after a few seconds.

"Evansville Tower to unidentified traffic thirty miles west of the airport, please respond." Nothing. Radio silence. This message was repeated in several other frequencies commonly used by air traffic controllers and airplanes in the area. The longer a radio response failed to return, and the closer the dots on the screen became, the higher the apprehension, which by now was palpable both in the tower and in Jack's cockpit.

"Have you been able to contact that traffic on any frequency, Evansville?" asked Jack, waves of dread escalating.

"Negative on contact, 98-gulf-kilo," said Jason. "Turn ninety degrees to the right and descend a thousand feet. No delay." Save for computer learning drills during training, never in his six years of service had Jason come across anything even closely resembling what he was facing now.

"Roger, turning ninety degrees to my right and descending a thousand, 98-gulf-kilo," responded Jack, a hint of worry in his speech pattern.

Another moment of silence ensued as all eyes focused on the dot blinking rapidly on the screen. The other plane mirrored Jack's moves and soon was again flying toward the Bonanza, descending to his flight level.

"Evansville Tower to unidentified traffic thirty-three miles west of the airport, please respond." This message was repeated several more times in multiple frequencies but no response.

To Jack's continued astonishment and horror, the airplane continued to encroach on his position. The radar screen displayed the yellow light, now blinking more rapidly, indicating the other aircraft was within eight miles, the distance between them diminishing fast. The yellow blip soon became orange on the screen, signifying an increasing danger of collision. A beep now emanated from the unit, adding an auditory warning to the visual alert. Jack tensed up in his pilot's seat. He tried to tighten the seat belt, but it was already snug. He sat up straight and held the controlling yoke tightly, ready to make changes to the airplane's flight direction and altitude, as might become necessary.

"This guy is coming right at me," he whispered to no one. "It has to be Lagrange." The warning symbol on his screen suddenly turned red, loudly proclaiming that the bogey was dangerously close to his airplane, now within four miles off his nose and at the same altitude.

"Gulf-kilo, take evasive maneuvers," yelled the controller into Jack's ears. A bead of sweat appeared on the young doctor's forehead. Then another. Jack took steadying and calming breaths.

"Have you been able to communicate with traffic, Evansville?" asked Jack.

"Negative. No communication at all, Gulf-kilo. Fly at your discretion. I recommend a quick change in altitude and heading."

One thing is for sure, thought Jack, *you're faster than I am; I have to be smarter.*

"Taking evasive action," announced Jack, this time purposely being vague in case malevolent ears were monitoring the transmissions. *Is this my last flight?* mused Jack, sickened by the prospect. *Is this son of a bitch crashing into me?* Horrified, he glimpsed at the approaching airplane less than half a mile outside his windshield, flying at his altitude. *Am I ever going to see Claire and Nick?* he brooded, nearly suffocating with terror. Jack saw the other plane. It was coming fast, and it was right there. Right outside his cockpit. *Oh my god! We're going to crash.* In a last act of desperation, Jack turned and pushed hard on the yoke to quickly drift the nose of his aircraft to the right and earthbound at two thousand feet per minute, hoping this last-ditch effort would avoid a midair collision. As the Bonanza sunk hurriedly, Jack glimpsed the other plane flying rapidly in the opposite direction and only a few feet away. The proximity to this near kamikaze caused Jack to tremble horribly and feel an emptiness in the pit of his stomach, adrenaline pouring into his veins. Sweat beads cascaded down his eyebrows onto his face.

Jack's airplane had acquiesced to his commands, and soon it hurled toward the ground. This generated a new warning buzzer, loudly competing with the proximity alarm already in progress. The racket increased the tension of the moment. Red warning lights flashed wildly from the instrument panel. Jack pulled back on the yoke to resume leveled flight. The bogey slowed down, turned around, and was now again speedily chasing the Bonanza from behind and at the same altitude.

He didn't want to collide with me. He would have done it, if that was his intention. He just wants to play chicken up here, the crazy son of a bitch, sensed Jack, following the other aircraft's moves on the screen. *He's chasing me again. There's more to come. Oh great!* The throttle was at maximum, but the faster airplane would soon catch up.

"Nine-eight-gulf-kilo, he went by you fast but he's back on your tail; he's closing in fast," shouted the headphone. "We've alerted Homeland Security, but it'll be—"

"Hello, Dr. Norris," Jack barely heard. These words, coming out of nowhere, interrupted his concentration. Though the whisperlike sound was delivered in a mellow and calm tone, it roared above all other noises in the cockpit. "Hello, there. Dr. Norris, are you there?" reiterated the soft voice.

Where is this coming from? thought Jack apprehensively, his head turning side to side, hoping to locate its source. The words were strange. Out of place. Unanticipated. As such, they continued to capture Jack's full attention, above and beyond the background of loud cacophony of warning clamor and the much-louder air traffic controller's agitated voice. Jack looked all around the cockpit. He was alone.

"Gulf-kilo, fly one-one-zero, descend to—," persisted the excited controller. Jack took off his headphones, trying to hone in on the barely audible eerie voice in the distance.

"Hello. Are you there, Jack?" the quiet, serene words murmured again.

It has to be him. It has to be Lagrange, reflected Jack. He placed the headphones on the right passenger seat. Doing so allowed Jack to realize the remote sound arose from that direction.

"Can you hear me, Jack?" the man's voice continued calmly, a hint of rancor barely discernible. "Hello, Jack!" One thousand five-hundred feet had come and gone, as the Bonanza hurriedly approached flight level 7,000. Jack pulled back on the yoke to continue leveled flight at that altitude. He reengaged the autopilot, ascertaining that the present speed and heading would be maintained. He spied the bogey on the screen. He was now a half mile behind and 1,500 feet over him, descending and closing in on him fast. Jack's body trembled and his heart hammered in response to the massive outpouring from his adrenal glands.

"I know you can hear me, Jack. Check under the right seat," proclaimed the mysterious hushed voice. Jack released his seat belt and reached under the passenger seat. Despite the uncontrollable hand tremors, Jack found a solid object and carefully retrieved it from its resting place. It was a walkie-talkie. He placed the device on the seat as he buckled up. Jack looked outside the cockpit but realized his vision was useless and unhelpful as the approaching aircraft was behind and over him.

"I wish I could see your face right now, Jack, but I have to settle for your voice. If you'd be kind enough to use the walkie-talkie," said the unruffled voice.

"What do you want, Lagrange?" responded Jack, fuming.

"Come, come, Jack. What do I want? I want revenge. Payback. I had it all, glory and fame. You saw fit to take it all away. For that, you will pay."

"You are a sick man, Lagrange. You need help. Let's land the airplanes and talk about this. I will get you all the help you need."

"What will help me is to see you squirm."

"You want to kill me? Okay! Let's land the airplanes and you can have me. People on the ground don't have to get hurt. Land, and I'm all yours," Jack spoke nervously into the walkie-talkie, a hint of panic in his voice, rivulets of sweat dripping down his forehead. His grip on the yoke resulted in white knuckles.

"Kill you I will. I will get my revenge," emphasized the rogue airman, fury and wrath now accentuating every syllable of his words.

The faster airplane was now parallel with the Bonanza. Out of the corner of his eye, Jack briefly glanced and studied the aircraft. He could not identify the pilot, who maneuvered his plane to match speeds perfectly.

"Speaking of revenge, look behind you," said the scoundrel, endeavoring to get a glimpse of the struggling doctor whose cockpit suddenly flooded with dense smoke after a small explosion arising from behind and underneath the pilot's seat.

Several moments later, the Bonanza stalled, forcing the aircraft to dip downward. The airplane entered a spiral, plunging earthbound at six thousand feet per minute. The aircraft's structure shuddered uncontrollably as it sped to its inevitable doom, dense smoke emanating from the small cockpit window located to the left of the pilot. The plane sank rapidly, striking hard through an opaque cloud layer at around three thousand feet. The strong arm of gravity yanked the aircraft downward, now out of sight, spinning faster and faster, out of control.

The tension at the Evansville Tower had become unbearable, filling the air and the hearts of all witnessing the events unfolding, as depicted on the radar screen. All personnel on duty had joined Jason, all eyes fixated on the computer display. The blinking dots representing the two airplanes they had been following were too close to make a clear determination as to whether a collision had occurred over the last several seconds. The two blips had merged on the screen and from them continued to emanate a blinking red circle labeled *Imminent Danger of Collision*. An earsplitting beep proclaimed the urgency of the message.

"Bonanza, 98-gulf-kilo, Evansville Approach, over," said Jason nervously into his microphone, praying for an answer. "Bonanza, 98-gulf-kilo, please respond," he repeated after what seemed to be an eternity but was, in fact, several seconds of radio silence. Jason noticed his right hand was shaking, creating mini waves of ripples through his coffee. He put the mug down on the table. Gloomily and slowly, he scanned around the room at all present. Their faces and demeanor spoke volumes. All eyes poignant, overwhelmed, devastated, all hoping for the best but preparing for the worst.

The radar screen and its accompanying deafening blare persisted with the loud declaration *Imminent Danger of Collision*.

"I can't take it anymore," said Tiffany, sitting down. "I'm going to get sick to my stomach."

"Bonanza, 98-gulf-kilo, Evansville Approach, over," radioed Jason again, gloomily looking into Tiffany's eyes, in understanding. He too felt waves of nausea. Several seconds later, he keyed the microphone again. "Bonanza, 98-gulf-kilo, Evansville Approach, please respond." Nothing. "Bonanza-gulf-kilo, over." Zilch. No reply. "Bonanza gulf-kilo, please respond."

3

Three months earlier

"It was three years ago that the harrowing events took place," continued Mr. Paul Adams, Newton Memorial Hospital's chief administrator. "These events left us in turmoil and robbed us of our innocence. We lost friends. We lost family. But through our loss we have gained strength and so we've endured. We survived. We are stronger now. Tonight we gather here, to celebrate just that. Our facility is now 100 percent back to full functioning. We are on course to continue our healing, and we look forward to a bright, thriving future once again. All of this was possible only with the guidance and hard work of many. These people can only be considered one thing—heroes. Heroes here tonight among us. Most prominent among them is Dr. Jack Norris. Today's ceremony, besides allowing us to give remembrance to those we lost in the past atrocities, helps us look ahead to our bright future. Today, we congratulate Dr. Jack Norris, as he is our newly appointed chief of cardiology and electrophysiology. Jack, will you please come up here?" gestured the administrator, wearing a full-sized smile.

Jack got up and walked to the stage while all rose and applauded. Like all the other men at the event, he sported a black tuxedo with a bowtie, making him look elegantly debonair. Claire, sitting at his side, was wearing a beautiful long gray gown, accentuating all her stunning features. Her blond hair was stylishly pulled up in a bun, adding to her spectacular appearance. Jack walked up to the podium. He manipulated the microphone resting on the stand, establishing its proper distance from his mouth.

"Thank you, Mr. Adams." The applause simmered down after a long moment, then, little by little, stopped completely. "Thank you." Jack directed his appreciation to the crowd. All had retaken their seats. He proceeded, "Three years ago, we were assaulted. Newton Memorial Hospital was assaulted. Evansville was assaulted. Money-hungry thugs dared to carry out research on innocent men, killing many of them. With the help of the Evansville Police Department and the FBI, the assassins were stopped." As he spoke these words, Jack winked in Susan's direction. Detective Sergeant Susan Quentin wore a blue sparkly evening gown that accentuated beautifully her long curly blond hair. She was in her midthirties. She was pregnant, highlighting a radiant face-glow that told it all. With a smile, she acknowledged the remark. She and Jack had been most instrumental in bringing to a halt the carnage of three years earlier. Sitting next to Susan was her husband, Dave Hamilton, who gently squeezed her hand, resting in his.

Jack's touching and inspirational speech lasted but a few more minutes. As he stopped speaking, all got up, applauding. Mr. Adams returned to the podium to introduce the next speaker.

"Thanks, Jack. I would now like to recognize a gentleman you have known for the last several months. Soon after the heinous crimes, we realized it was of paramount importance for us to have the best security system money could buy. Newton Memorial has spent a great deal of time, money and effort to do just that. We need our patients, our employees, staff and visitors to feel as secure and comfortable as possible. A thorough search led us to Mr. Nai Trepur. He needs no introduction to most of you. Nai came to us with the best of recommendations. He is a retired officer of the French Secret Service, with many years of experience. In a relatively short time, he has put into place numerous procedures and policies that have significantly increased the level of security at Newton Memorial. For that, I am immensely grateful. Nai, please come up here." Nai Trepur was an older but well-built man with graying temples. His physique demanded constant trips to the gym. He appeared to be in his midforties, but was probably closer to sixty than fifty. In his tux, he looked exceptionally elegant, and youthful.

"Merci. Thank you. Merci," repeated the distinguished man with a thick accent and a hint of embarrassment for all the attention directed at him. "It has been my privilege and honor to provide security services for Newton Memorial Hospital," he said shyly. "I'm sorry for my Engleesh is not too good," he smiled. As he continued to struggle through his speech, all listened intently, trying to decipher the meaning of his words. "It ees my opinion that the eennocint lives lost are the real heroes we ceelebrate tanight." The address was difficult to follow precisely, but touched many hearts and inspired many souls, nonetheless. Once finished, the head of security confidently and unhurriedly walked back to his seat while the room stood and applauded.

Several other speakers took turns at the podium. Afterward, all of the guests in the great hall mingled, as drinks and hors d'oeuvres were offered. In the background, soothing live chamber music added style and elegance to the ambience.

"It's always a pleasure to see you, Mr. Trepur," said Susan Quentin, smiling. She approached, accompanied by Jack and Claire.

"The pleazoore is all mine, madame," declared the Frenchman, taking her hand and gently kissing it. "Bonsoir, Dr. Jack. Good eeveening to you too, Dr. Claire." She curtsied, smiling. She too had her hand kissed ceremoniously. "I have to call her Dr. Claire and him Dr. Jack," he explained for Susan's benefit. "They have the same last name, no?" Nai took an hors d'oeuvre from a passing tray as he spoke, nodding at the waiter. Smiles all around.

"We appreciate all you've done for the security here at the hospital," declared Jack.

"Yes, I have heard about your security measures. Very impressive," agreed Susan.

"Merci. I beleeve we must put into place procezures to evoid the problemes of the past, huh?" said Nai. "We can never be one hondreed percent safe, but we should get as close as posseebel to that, no?"

The four conversed for several minutes with pleasant exchanges. Jack felt safer, much more so since Nai Trepur took the job. He had seen the security force increase, with phones strategically placed on campus to allow access to a security guard at a moment's notice. Security officers escorted the night-shift nurses to their cars. Staff, visitors, and patients were searched through metal detectors as they entered the facility. The whole place seemed more secure. It felt good.

Only one minor detail bothered Jack about Nai Trepur. He had icterus, a slight yellowish discoloration of his sclera, the whites of the eyes. It can be a sign of liver dysfunction, alcohol abuse, maybe hemolytic anemia, a condition where the red blood cells in the circulation are destroyed. Rarely, the condition can be associated with severe cardiac problems, such as valvular heart disease. *Or maybe it can be a normal thing for the French. It's faint, barely noticeable,* thought Jack.

"The man is brilliant. He's done so much in so little time," declared Claire as they settled into the Lexus, interrupting Jack's musings. It was time to go home.

"Yes, he's done a lot. I know I feel better. Safer," said Jack, starting up the car. *I hope it's not alcohol,* he thought. *These Frenchmen do like their alcohol and liver pâté. That could lead to a fatty liver and icterus.* They drove on.

"So, how do you feel, honey? Today was your big day. Your chiefhood was finally announced. You are now the new chief of cardiology at Newton Memorial Hospital. Can I say I knew you when?" asked Claire after a long moment of silence.

"You can even say you slept with him when," Jack smiled. Claire slapped his knee.

"You men, is that all you think about?"

"The species must live, on and on."

"So, how does it feel to be the chief of the department?"

"Great, but nothing in comparison to the day I met you," answered Jack. A grin.

"Ohhh! That's sweet, honey."

"Or the day Nick was born."

"Ohhh, that's even sweeter!"

"Or the day I found out I was alive. Alive after getting Rat Poison." The mood in the car changed. Silence reigned. The couple locked eyes for a moment.

"Yes, those were much more significant days in both our lives," said Claire, breaking the hush, squeezing Jack's right hand.

"I can still remember when I first woke up and saw your face. You had tears in your eyes. I so wanted to wipe your tears, but I was still paralyzed. I couldn't move. All I could do was lay there," recollected Jack.

"It must have been scary for you," whispered Claire.

"By then, it was awesome. I was alive. The last thing I could remember before that was when I was drugged." Jack stopped to gather himself and swallow the choking knot in his throat. This was still exceedingly emotional for him. The wounds had long healed, but the psychological scars would not fade away. Not anytime soon.

"The Rat Poison drug," said Claire somberly.

"So many people died. And for what? Money!" A pause. "I miss John," said Jack after a long moment.

"I miss him too. He was a great friend," agreed Claire.

"Yes, he was." Jack's eyes moistened as tears appeared one by one. Silence again. Claire fished a tissue from her purse and gave it to Jack. She used another to wipe her own tears. They drove on. Wordlessly. Mournfully remembering those lost. The sacrifices. The wounds.

4

The waiting room was full—standing room only. Matt Lauer discussed today's news on the wall-mounted TV. It seemed like any other morning at the Newton Memorial Outpatient Cardiac Clinic. This portion of the building, attached to the main hospital, served as doctor's offices. The cardiac patients were seen on the first floor. Beyond the waiting area, the cardiology and electrophysiology fellows worked as fast as their level of expertise allowed. The young doctors in training would see patients in the small rooms and formulate an opinion as to what the problem was and what to do about it. They would then come out and confer with the attending physician assigned to the clinic that day. Today, the task was allotted to the chief of the department, Dr. Jack Norris. The attending physician, an older and more experienced doctor, would review the facts and enter the room with the trainee to visit briefly with the patient. The situation would be discussed and plans made. The trainees would then dictate a note reflecting the conversations and order the appropriate tests and medications. A return appointment would be given the patient and on to the next case.

"I just saw Mrs. Ana Janheri, who is a forty-three-year-old woman with a history of supraventricular tachycardia. Here's the EKG," said Dr. Frank Hanes. Frank was an attractive tall man in his late twenties, this being his first year of cardiology fellowship. He had completed three years in internal medicine but decided to continue his training to become a cardiologist. Today was his office day and he had been assigned to Dr. Jack Norris. Jack looked at the EKG briefly and handed it back to Frank.

"What is it?" he asked of the young man.

"SVT," he replied.

"What does SVT mean?" asked Jack.

"Supraventricular tachycardia. It's a rapid heartbeat where the impulses that force the pulse to quicken are located in the top chambers in the heart," answered Frank.

"That's right. But there are several types of SVT. Which type do you think this one is?" persisted the teacher.

"I don't know."

"Do you know the definition of a double-blind study?" asked Jack, a serious tone in his voice. After a short pause, he continued, "An orthopedic surgeon and a medical student looking at an EKG." Jack smiled. Frank reciprocated, nervously at first.

"Good one. That's good." Frank was now in a full-blown laughter. "I gotta tell Kate that one."

"See the QRS shape?" Jack pointed to the wave on the graph with his pen, getting back to business. "The P wave is at the end here, making this SVT more than likely AV node reentry. This is one of the most common rapid heartbeat disorders in this patient's age group. What is the most common in patients over sixty?"

"Atrial fibrillation," answered the young doctor confidently.

"That's right. Approximately one out of twenty Americans over sixty has atrial fibrillation. One out of ten in the eighties age range"

"Mrs. Janheri has tried different medications. We've given her beta-blockers, calcium-blockers and now sotalol, but she continues to be symptomatic with multiple recurrences. Should we try amiodarone?" asked Frank.

"No. Let's talk to her about an ablation procedure, explain the potential risks, benefits, and alternatives and see what she wants to do." The two doctors walked into room 7. When they emerged from the room a few minutes later, the patient accompanied them.

"We'll get the ball rolling. Call if you have any questions. Otherwise, we'll see you on the day of your procedure," said Dr. Norris.

"Thank you both." Mrs. Janheri smiled and exited the area.

"Frank," said Jack, "I have one for you: You have a wolf, a rabbit, and a carrot on one side of a river and you're trying to get them to the other side. But you have to do it one by one. If you leave them alone, the wolf will eat the rabbit and the rabbit will eat the carrot. Wolves don't eat carrots. How do you do it?" asked Jack.

"First take the rabbit across," started Frank.

"Good. That works, since the wolf and carrot are left alone and they're safe together. What's the next step?" asked Jack.

"Hmm," murmured Frank pensively. "Which should I go get next?" he said, thinking of the possibilities. "Not sure."

"Okay, think about it. Let me know the answer when you know it. Go finish the report. Hey, if you'd like, plan on assisting me with the ablation procedure." Frank nodded and disappeared into the dictation room, a smile on his face.

"Ready for another patient? I have a case to discuss with you, Dr. Norris," said a young woman wearing a white coat, seeing Frank depart the director's side.

"Go for it, Maria." Jack stood by the counter where Dr. Maria Butler, a second-year trainee, had set down her paperwork. She was a thin brunette wearing blue scrubs under her white coat. With her was Sundeep Singh, a third-year medical student. He was Eastern Indian, intelligent, and driven to succeed. His cardiology rotation had begun a few days earlier.

"This is Mr. William Stoops. He is doing extremely well. He's a sixty-eight-year-old man with an ischemic cardiomyopathy. His last EF was 38 percent." This said, Maria's gaze turned from the paperwork to Jack.

"Sundeep, tell me more about his ischemic cardiomyopathy; what caused it? And tell me what EF represents," interrupted Jack.

"He had two large heart attacks, the first two years ago and another more recently. He developed arterial blockages in two large coronaries that made the walls of his heart weak. After the heart attacks, his left ventricle was only pumping 20 percent of blood with each heartbeat. That's his ejection fraction or EF. He was started on all the right meds but his ventricle only improved a bit. He then received a defibrillator which has brought his EF to 38 percent, where we measured it to be last month." Sundeep was confident about the medical facts.

"What are his medications?" inquired Jack, looking back at Maria.

"He is on Coreg CR, 80 mg a day; Altace, 10 mg daily; Aldactone, 25 mg every morning; Crestor, 20 mg daily; and aspirin, 81 mg daily. Excellent combination and dosages," she offered.

"What about the implanted defibrillator? What does it do? Tell me more about it," asked the older physician of the med student. This type of questioning of medical students is a commonly used tool in teaching. After all, repetition is a good way to learn.

"The implantable cardioverter-defibrillator or ICD was inserted to shock his heart to normal if he has a deadly rhythm, called ventricular fibrillation," he answered.

"So, if the rhythm is normal, the device is just on standby?"

"That's right. The patient has not had any shocks for the last nine months."

"But the heart is working better since the device was implanted. If it's mostly on standby, how did it help strengthen the heart muscle?" asked Jack, as he looked through some pages in the chart. "See here? This graph confirms that the device has not given any therapy for rapid heartbeats. He's been clean for nine months. Why is his heart stronger?" challenged the professor. Dr. Maria Butler and her student were bewildered and deep in thought. A moment of silence ensued.

"The medications had more time to work on the heart muscle," interjected Maria.

"That's true. But the other important factor in how well Mr. Stoops is doing is CRT or cardiac resynchronization therapy, which this device also offers," said Jack. "The device constantly paces the right and left ventricles together. Before the implantation, his right heart was contracting before the left. His heart was out of sync. Now things work more efficiently since the ventricles are synchronized. This translates into better quality of life and greater longevity, statistically speaking. Notice how many times he was hospitalized before the implantation and afterwards." Maria and Sundeep listened intently to every word.

"He says he feels much better. He has more energy, can walk longer, and do things he enjoys doing. Thanks for that explanation, Dr. Norris." Maria smiled and gathered the records as they both walked into room 9.

"Dr. Norris, the man, the myth! Dr. Butler, this man saved my life. But even more importantly, he improved my golf game by several strokes," said Mr. Stoops excitedly.

"Good morning, Mr. Stoops. Dr. Butler says you're still doing well and having no problems." Dr. Norris shook the older man's hand and all sat down.

"I'm a new man, doc. I feel great. My wife says I'm back to being a pain in her ass. Oops! Sorry," said Mr. Stoops shyly, looking at Maria.

"I'm familiar with the word. I've used it once or twice myself," she said, putting the older man at ease with a big grin.

"Well, you get out of this office. This is for sick people, not for normal pain in the asses like you," said Dr. Norris, smiling and shaking the patient's hand again as he opened the door. The three walked out into the hall.

"Thanks, Dr. Norris. I owe you my life. If you ever want to learn a real sport like golf and give up soccer, let me know. I'm your man; I can teach you how to play."

"Golf isn't a sport. It's hardly a pastime. Soccer is the only real sport." The two men smiled.

"Thanks, Dr. Butler," said Mr. Stoops as he left the area. "Good luck to you," he wished, looking at the med student. Maria took the chart and walked to the dictation room.

"Dr. Norris, Mr. Kyle Johnson got here late. His appointment was two hours ago. He's out in the waiting room yelling at everybody. I've called security," said Shelley with a concerned look. "I've tried to reason with him, but he's drunk and crazed." Shelley Simms, the newest secretary and medical assistant, was thin, doe-eyed, dark haired, and perky. She began working at the outpatient clinic only a few months earlier and, despite her vivacious demeanor, was the last person who should be dealing with good old Kyle, a frequent flyer at the office, who often caused a ruckus.

"Not again. Where is he?" asked Jack. Shelley walked to the waiting room with Jack in tow. She opened the door leading to the large room. Several people were sitting, witnessing the ongoing exchanges, in disbelief. An older man was standing arguing loudly with Kathryn Fanning, one of the seasoned, though young, nurses. Kate, as everyone called her, played a pivotal role in the outpatient clinic. She was a young woman with dark brown hair and brown eyes and, like most nurses in the clinic, sported pink scrubs with a white T-shirt underneath. The tipsy man's balance was obviously suspect as his torso moved slightly to and fro. In the background near a broom closet, Jack spied the new janitor. Cesar Madera held a mop and water bucket and looked on in dismay.

"Thanks, Dr. Norris," whispered Kate when Jack approached.

"It's okay, Kate. What's going on, Mr. Johnson?" asked Dr. Norris loudly to distract the patient from his persistent screaming at the young nurse. He stopped talking in midsentence and looked in Dr. Norris' direction. The patient was in his sixties, unshaven, disheveled, and scruffy. As Jack approached him, it was quite apparent he had been drinking as he reeked of alcohol.

"I'm here to see my doctor. Hey, you're my doctor, ain't ya?" blurted out the intoxicated man.

"Yes, I am. You are disrupting the office," stated Jack firmly.

"This bitch says I'm too late and you won't see me," he stated, pointing at Kate.

"We don't allow that kind of language around here, sir. You need to apologize to Nurse Kate." The man looked at Jack with some intimidation. He stumbled side to side. His words were slurred and unclear.

"I just want to see the doctor for my heart. I don't want no trouble," he said.

It was then that security stormed into the room. There were three men dressed in blue, one of whom Jack recognized.

"Good morning, gentlemen. Mr. Trepur, how are you? Good to see you this fine morning." Jack wasn't in the mood to deal with drunks.

"Bonjour, Dr. Norris. We will take care of thees," said Nai Trepur with a thick French accent. The two guards held the inebriated patient under the armpits and gently escorted him out of the area. All other patients in the waiting room sat in their chairs quietly, mesmerized by the activities. "Is everyone fine heere?" asked Nai Trepur.

"Yes, we're okay. I have never experienced a security team respond so fast. Thank you, Nai," said Jack, appreciatively. "Will you take him to the Emergency Department? I'll call there. We'll try again to see if Mr. Johnson will agree to inpatient detox. He really needs help, if he'd only accept it."

"You and thee nurses are for takeeng care of pations who want your help, not drunks," he said with a smile. "We'll take him to eemerguncee room now. Call if you need soometheng." Nai left the waiting room. The ongoing discussions on TV could be heard again but no one was paying attention to the wall-hung unit, as Matt Lauer went on and on about something or other. Jack and the nurses returned to the back office.

"Thank you, Dr. Norris," said Kate. "Thank you for getting Dr. Norris for me, Shelley."

"No problem," said Shelley, her frowned face now relaxed and smiling.

"I wish we could help Mr. Johnson with his alcohol addiction. When he's sober, he's actually a pleasant and kind man," said Jack somberly. "Unfortunately, he's almost always drunk."

"Is there nothing that will help him?" asked Kate.

"Not until he's ready. There's a drug called disulfiram or Antabuse that could help him, but he has to want to quit," said Jack.

"What's the drug do?" asked Kate.

"It helps people quit booze by making them vomit if they consume alcohol. It's used in conjunction with regular counseling.

We'll try again this time, and see if he'll agree to restart the process of drying out and staying sober. First, he'll need to cool off and sober up a bit. I'll have the addiction people talk to him in the Emergency Department. Hopefully, he'll agree to get help this time."

"Will you please sign this incident report?" asked Shelley, as she re-approached the group, having stepped away for a short moment. "I have to fax it to security ASAP." Jack took the paper and scanned it.

"Don't forget to practice safe fax," he said, signing the document. Jack called the Emergency Department doctor on duty and explained the situation, then hung up the phone.

"Does this sort of thing happen a lot around here?" asked Shelley, reviewing the incident report she had prepared. "This could be a dangerous place to work."

"No, not really. Security is so much quicker and efficient these days," stated Jack.

"Yes, I agree. I was here before the Rat Poison murders," added Kate. "I had my car broken into. It took almost an hour to get someone to report to the parking lot just to write up the incident."

"Do you think the murders wouldn't have happened if we had a better security force?" asked Shelley.

"No. Only Superman could have prevented those murders." With these words, Jack recalled the events of three years earlier, the events that led to the assassination of his best friend, John. Jack's demeanor changed. He became quiet, fighting back tears.

"How horrible it must have been," voiced Kate sympathetically.

"What happened exactly?" asked Shelley, not quite in tune with the sadness displayed by Jack.

"Don't make Dr. Norris relive that brutal ordeal all over again," supplicated Kate. By then, Frank and Maria had approached the team. They sat and listened.

"That's okay, Kate. It actually helps to talk about it. It certainly still is a source of deep sadness. But it's getting better and better as time goes on," said Jack, noticing his heartbeat and breathing pattern involuntarily quickening. The sinking feeling in his chest and abdomen had begun to materialize. Jack persevered, "There was a doctor here who was a brilliant researcher. He discovered a drug for heart failure patients, which turned out to improve symptoms but increase the chances of dying from heart disease. The FDA never approved the drug for use in humans. During the initial investigations, he discovered that the drug induced intense paranoia, confusion, and combative behavior. He was experimenting with rats. The rats treated with the drug mutilated the other rats in the cage to death, then destroyed themselves. Many rats perished, and the project became known as Rat Poison."

"Wow," said several of them, realizing the atrocity of it all.

"It wasn't all bad," continued Jack with a forced smile. "They invented a drug delivery system involving tiny bubbles. The bubbles were filled with a medication, any drug such as chemotherapeutic agents, cardiovascular medications, and so on. The subjects breathe the bubbles into their lungs but nothing happens until the bubbles are destroyed by a remote ultrasound device." Jack paused abruptly. Hearing himself utter these words, Jack experienced deep emotional and physical changes that choked him deep in the throat, a typical display of post-traumatic stress disorder. Jack became anxious and diaphoretic. His breathing quickened. His pulse sped up and his heart thundered inside his chest. He spoke slowly and hesitantly when he could speak again. "Please forgive me. I need to take a moment." Jack retreated to a bathroom nearby.

"When Dr. Norris was poisoned with Rat Poison, it almost killed him," said Kate, breaking the long moment of silence when Jack was out of earshot. "Dr. Norris was one of the people who stopped the bad guys from continuing their research and killing more people."

The group stood there, still, wordless, feeling Jack's pain and agony. Somberly and quietly, one by one, the doctors, nurses, and secretary disbanded and went back to work.

5

Jack tried to put it all behind him. Again. It surprised him with how much more healing he still required, even though the incident had occurred three years before. When he awoke, Claire was already up and about. The intense emotional turmoil inside Jack from the discussion at the office the day before had dissipated almost completely. By now, he could fake complete normalcy. Jack had been on call the night before. This morning, he took the opportunity to sleep late.

"I slept like a baby," proclaimed Jack, slumber still covering part of his face. He stretched his arms wide then sat up in bed.

"Okay. Let me change your diaper now," said Claire mockingly. "No time to dillydally," she exclaimed. "We're going to be late. It's almost ten o'clock. We're supposed to be there by noon. I need your help gathering Nick's toys? Put them in that basket and then stick it in the van. Jack, get in the shower. Hurry up." Claire was going over last-minute details in her head. The Norris family was going to a barbeque picnic at Newton Memorial Hospital to welcome the new cardiology fellows.

"Are we taking Trinity, Claire? Can we? Please?" asked Jack as he arrived in the kitchen half-dressed, postshower.

"Please? Mom?" echoed Nick.

"Did they invite dogs?" came the reply. The boys looked at one another. In silence, and simultaneously, they shrugged their shoulders.

"Yes," lied Jack hesitantly, buttoning up his shirt.

"Okay. She can come along." The boys smiled.

"Come on, girl. Get your leash," said Jack to the overly excited dog. She obliged and showed up moments later with a leash in her mouth. "Good girl, Trinity," said Jack, hooking up the leash to her collar.

The four got into the van. Claire started up the vehicle as Jack helped Nick to buckle up. The trip to the hospital was uneventful. When they arrived, the parking area was full. Beyond it, many people gathered around several large outdoor grills, smoke, and appetizing aromas emanating from the area. Farther back, there were several people playing volleyball, basketball, and soccer. Jack and Claire gathered their stuff and walked to the party area. It was a beautiful sunny day with a slight, cool breeze.

"Hey, you party animals!" shouted Jack as he approached one of the groups. Several people nodded and waved, welcoming the newly arrived.

"Hi, Dr. and Dr. Norris," said Lori. Lori Hughes was a nurse in her forties, heavyset and wearing a yellow summer dress. "Did you hear the news?"

"No, what is it?" asked Claire.

"Frank, Kate, come here, please," yelled Lori, gesturing at a couple to approach. Shelley was with them. She came too. As the group was drawing nearer, Kate raised her ring finger, displaying a beautiful engagement ring. Claire took her hand and gawked at the diamond.

"Wow. This is beautiful. Good job, Frank. I assume you picked the ring?" asked Claire, eyes on the young man.

"Yes. He surprised me this morning," interjected Kate, beaming. Frank nodded, wearing a million-dollar happy face.

"Did you say yes, Kate?" asked Jack.

"No, but I thought I'd keep the ring anyway." She smirked jokingly. "Yes. I said yes," answered Kate, now smiling brightly. She kissed Frank.

"Can we borrow Nick and Trinity, Dr. Norris?" interrupted Peggy Snyder excitedly. "I brought my black lab."

"Sure. Go have fun, Nick," said Claire.

"Let's play. Come on, Nick," said Peggy. "Come here, Trinity." Peggy, Nick, and Trinity ran off as Jack and Claire nodded in the affirmative.

"I'm very happy for both of you," said Jack.

"You make a lovely couple. Picture time," announced Claire, fishing her camera out of her purse. Frank and Kate kissed for the picture.

From the hospital's main building approached Nai Trepur. "Gud morneeng, everybody," he said, announcing his arrival.

"Hello, Nai. Let's get a cheeseburger. I'm hungry," offered Jack, walking toward the grills. The group followed as Nai greeted the others.

"Did you play soccer in France, Nai?" asked Jack after swallowing.

"I never played," answered Nai.

"A Frenchman who never played soccer? No way!" said Jack.

"Come on, honey. We can talk about something other than soccer, can't we?" interjected Claire.

"Speaking of significant others, where's that boyfriend of yours, Shelley?" asked Kate, trying to change the subject.

"Oh, he couldn't come. He's tied up," said the young secretary.

"You haven't told me anything about him yet. Do tell. When can we meet him?" asked Lori.

"I don't know. Sometime soon."

"Bring him in to work. We all want to meet him," said Kate.

"I will," promised Shelley.

"What's the schedule like on Monday, Dr. Norris?" asked Kate.

"Frank and I are performing an ablation. Right, Frank? Are you ready for it?"

"I'm ready, Dr. Norris. I've been reading up on it. I'm all keyed up," answered the young doctor.

"That's all he's talked about the last couple of days. I think he's a bit nervous about it," said Kate.

"Don't be nervous, Frank. I got you covered," said Jack with a smile. As Jack spoke, the smile on his face faded and wrinkles appeared on his forehead. In the distance, Jack saw a figure standing by a tree, looking in the direction of the group. Between the sun in his eyes and the distance between them, Jack could not be certain as to the identity of the man. He was average height and a bit scruffy looking. It looked like the new janitor.

"Hey, who's that man over there in the shade?" he asked of the group, temporarily taking his eyes off the figure.

"Where?" asked Nai, then Claire, all looking in the direction Jack was spying.

"I can't see him any longer. He was there a second ago," said Jack, perplexed.

"Probably some guy wishing he was here eating one of these delicious burgers," joked Frank. Jack continued to look in the vicinity of his mysterious vision.

"He's gone now. You may be right," agreed Jack.

Behind a large group of trees, Lance Lantz hid from view. He was thin and tall and in his midtwenties. He was a true believer in love at first sight. Ever since he met Nurse Kate, as he called her, he became irreversibly hooked. She was all he could think about. Her eyes were enchanting, and he would not live without her. Unbeknownst to Kate and the whole world, he had acquired a large collection of pictures of her, taken by him clandestinely. He was hoping to add several images to his collection today. Kate's photographs were prominently displayed on a corkboard in his apartment. This compilation was Lance's most precious possession. She would become his, no matter what. He would find a way to win her hand.

From a distance today, he realized that Kate Fanning had become engaged to Dr. Frank Hanes. This drove a dagger through his heart, freezing it, draining color from his face. He climbed up a large oak tree and sat back on a branch about eight feet off the ground, remaining unnoticed. From that vantage point, Lance removed his camera from its pouch and attached the long zoom lens. He photographed Kate multiple times, concentrating on her awesome face and sparkling eyes. As the click-click-click sound resonated softly and repeatedly, rivulets of tears flowed down his face.

"You will be mine, Nurse Kate," he promised himself, sobbing. "One day, you will belong to me."

The BBQ party proceeded uneventfully. The group of friends and coworkers ate, played, and conversed until it was time to go home. Nick and Trinity were exhausted, and bedtime tonight came without fanfare. Jack and Claire, completely worn-out too, sat on the couch in front of the TV, winding down after such an exciting day.

"Who knew?" said Jack.

"Who knew what?" asked Claire, intrigued.

"A Frenchman who doesn't love soccer." Jack was hit on the head with a pillow from the couch. "Thanks, I needed that," said Jack, grabbing the pillow and placing it under his head, augmenting his comfort. "That's better. Much better."

"I did notice the whites of his eyes have a yellowish tinge, just like you said," remarked Claire.

"Did you notice the scars?" asked Jack.

"No, what scars?"

"There are four scars on his abdomen. I saw them when we were playing basketball.

"I didn't notice any scars. What are they from?" asked Claire.

"Who knows? They're probably knife wounds. They're thin, like puncture marks. They must be battle wounds," said Jack.

"He was in the French Secret Police or something like that, wasn't he?"

"Yeah. Something like that."

"Vat else deed you noteece about Monsieur Nai Trepur?" asked Claire, imitating a French accent.

"He's got tiny scars on his face too," said Jack, disregarding Claire's attempt at humor. "Those are hard to see. He must have been in a bunch of fights during his lifetime."

"What I noticed most of all today was how much Frank and Kate are in love. They make a great couple," Claire uttered, sitting back in the sofa next to Jack.

"Yeah! They do seem happy. Like us," agreed Jack, placing his arm behind her neck. Claire smiled, agreeing. They kissed.

6

————————

Jack and the cardiology fellows were about to start ward rounds. The young doctors gathered the patient charts on an ambulatory chart rack, consulting a list of patient names as they went.

"That's all of them," said Dr. Gary Lewis, a second-year fellow.

"Thanks, Gary." The group walked toward room 801.

"We were consulted on this sixty-two-year-old woman who has a diagnosis of multiple personality disorder," commenced the young doctor just outside the patient's room. "I spoke with her a few minutes ago. Right now, her name is Sarah. When she's Sarah, she is pretty normal, including a heart rate that ranges from high sixties to low eighties at rest. When she's Nanette, she becomes agitated and anxious, and her heart rate is in the thirties and forties. She feels faint and weak. So, in short, Nanette needs a permanent pacemaker, but Sarah does not. Sarah does not want a pacemaker, since she doesn't need one. Nanette does need one but won't consent because she's crazy. What should we do?"

"We'll need to talk to her psychiatrist about who and how we should get consent for the pacemaker implantation surgery. Do you think the slow heart rate is the cause of the multiple personalities or a result of it?" inquired Jack of the group.

"Good question," admitted Gary. "I don't know."

"I guess if we put in a pacemaker and Nanette never comes back, the multiple personalities were caused by the slow heart rate, maybe due to decreased blood flow to her brain," said Jack. "This is an interesting case. Let's talk to her psychiatrist. Please page him. Meanwhile, tell me about the next patient, in room 802."

"This is a seventy-year-old woman with chest pains and atrial fibrillation," began Gary. "She did not have a heart attack, but—" The young doctor's words continued, but became increasingly distant and undecipherable, then were interrupted by a clatter of a man running in their direction from the elevator, located on the opposite side of the corridor. He looked like the new janitor. Hispanic. Mysterious. Malevolent. The guy was wild-eyed and crazed. He yelled something unintelligible. The man removed a small unidentifiable instrument from his pocket as he approached the group of doctors. He attempted to spray its contents into Jack's nose. From behind, Nai Trepur stepped in, quickly disarming the demented man. Nai kicked the spraying device from the man's hand, causing it to slide several feet down the hall. Nai and the intruder faced each other, ready to engage in hand-to-hand battle. As this posturing progressed, the Hispanic man pulled out a knife. Nai remained calm and alert. The man advanced, rapidly sinking the knife into Nai's chest. Blood spurted out of the wound. The man located the spray device, picked it up, and swiftly directed its deadly mist of molecules toward Jack. Instantaneously, Jack felt the stinging sensation down his respiratory tree. With this came an uncontrollable feeling of confusion and terror. Jack started to perspire and breathe deeply and rapidly. *"Rat Poison. Not again. Not Rat Poison!"* yelled Jack, reliving the horrid sensation of three years back. His heart hammered loudly and forcibly inside his rib cage. Jack grabbed the trespasser with both hands and threw him against a nearby wall. The man fell on the tile, unconscious. Jack then turned to the students, feelings of rage beginning to percolate inside his being. He had a strong yearning for blood and annihilation. Insurmountable desires within him compelled Jack to destroy all those men and women. Jack, the strength of ten men sustaining him, effortlessly snatched the assailant's knife now embedded deep in Nai Trepur's corpse. Armed and dangerous, with acid running through his veins, Jack advanced toward the terrified group of innocent doctors and students, prepared to cut and squish them to death, one by one.

It was then that Jack took a deep breath and sat up in bed. He perspired profusely as he looked at his hands, his mind still confused over the nightmare he had just experienced. The commotion woke Claire up from deep sleep. She turned on the bedside light and looked at Jack. He was sitting in bed, short of breath and dazed.

"You had another nightmare, honey. You're okay." Claire hugged Jack, helping ease him into reality. Little by little, Jack's mind began to accept the passing phenomenon.

"Another nightmare. I'm okay," Jack told himself. He was calming down. He could feel his breath slowing. His heartbeat was gentler and less hurried now. "When will this be over? Why can't I shake this?" asked Jack. Claire continued to hug him. She remained quiet. How she wished she could give him a firm answer. The truth was, he probably would never be able to shake it. The two sat in silence for a long moment.

"Maybe, when Lagrange is brought to justice," hoped Jack, breaking the stillness of the night. Claire remained wordless, supporting him with her presence.

"We'll get through this, Jack. Together, we'll conquer this," she finally spoke.

7

Bad nights were fewer and fewer now, but still coming unpredictably.

It was Monday morning. Jack was assigned to the Electrophysiology Laboratory. Today, Jack was doing an ablation.

"Watch and learn, grasshopper," said Jack as they began. Dr. Frank Hanes was at his side. Vijay and Tracy, the EP lab nurses, had administered sedation and the patient lay comfortably on the table in the center of the room. Jack inserted long tubes or catheters first into the right femoral vein in the groin, then up the vena cava, the largest vein in the body, guiding them into the right atrium and ventricle. In no time, Mrs. Ana Janheri's cardiac electrical system was hooked up to the lab's computer. Different electrical structures displayed different signatures on the computer. These were analyzed for timing and shape. Frank took it all in, understanding most of it, but not all. Some of it would have to come in time. Jack promptly induced the rapid heartbeat disorder as he pushed different buttons on the electrical stimulator.

"This is the clinical tachycardia," he informed Frank. "The morphology is identical to the rapid heartbeat she had when she visited the Emergency Department last month." The doctors analyzed the tracing. Frank nodded. "This is what we thought she had, AV node reentry. I'm going to map it in the triangle of Koch."

"I read about it this weekend. This is cool," said Frank in astonishment.

"Follow what I'm doing on the fluoro screen and on the mapping display," instructed Jack. Frank complied.

After several applications of cryo to the appropriate area, the rapid heartbeat could no longer be induced. A freezing burn had been delivered in the area that previously short-circuited Ana's electrical system. She was now cured, forever rid of this problem.

"This is cool," repeated Frank in awe. "Thanks for letting me watch. May I come back sometime?"

"Of course, grasshopper. As many times as you'd like," said Jack, removing his surgical gloves and snapping them into the garbage can. "Thanks, Vijay and Tracy. I'm going to talk to her family." The two doctors exited the lab, finished the paperwork in the dictation area, and walked out to the waiting suite in search of the patient's relatives.

"I'm assigned to the outpatient office. I should have been there ten minutes ago. I'll see you there later today," said Frank as he ran ahead to the clinic. Jack had a few stops to make first. He was due at the office, but not for another twenty minutes. He walked toward room 309 to speak with a patient he had seen earlier and whom he promised he'd visit later in the day. While walking there, he passed a door labeled SECURITY. He had noticed this area before but had never entered to see what was beyond. He welcomed a chance to rethank Nai for his help with the inebriated man in the outpatient clinic a few days earlier. He crossed the threshold to find a small waiting area. No one was around. Another door was ajar. A sign on it announced *Nai Trepur, Director of Security*. He knocked. No answer. He pushed the door open and entered the director's office. There was a desk with a computer and many plaques on the walls.

"Impressive," reflected Jack, admiring the wall decorations as they told the story of Nai Trepur, the French law enforcer. He walked around to the plaques and stopped at the computer. Internet Explorer was on. The Internet address tabs were familiar to Jack: *www.FlightAware.com* on one and *www.FltPlan.com* on the other.

These were Web sites often used by pilots. The first allowed tracking of flights; the second permitted pilots to check the weather and file information with the FAA.

Jack's beeper went off loudly, its display showing the phone number of the office, followed by 911.

"Gotta go," said Jack to no one there as he departed the area briskly. He soon arrived at the outpatient clinic. The place was like a zoo. That is to say, everything was normal.

"Can I present this patient to you, Dr. Norris?" asked Dr. Gary Lewis, who had just exited one of the clinic rooms.

"Sure, Gary. Did you page me stat?"

"Yeah, that was me. This sixty-four-year-old woman moved here from Ohio recently. She called the office on Friday to be evaluated for several episodes of fainting. She was seeing a cardiologist in Ohio for a while, but since she was stable, only her family practitioner followed her up. She had a heart attack two and a half years ago. She had atrial fibrillation and was put on quinidine. She is also on digoxin and Lasix. A week ago she went to a family picnic, and soon thereafter started herself on over-the-counter Advil for muscle aches. She's been having dizzy spells and increasing shortness of breath with activities. On Thursday last week, she fainted unexpectedly. On Friday, she fainted again and three more times over the weekend."

"What are your thoughts? What do you plan on doing for her?" asked Jack.

"When she arrived here, I put her on the monitor." He paused for a moment, searching the stack of papers in the chart for the rhythm strips he had collected. "I don't like her meds. Quinidine is not a good idea in a patient with known coronary artery disease; she's on Lasix without potassium or magnesium supplementation. I'd like to stop all these drugs, get some blood work and a stress test to evaluate her for ischemia and assess her heart function. Ah, here it is." He handed Jack a strip showing the patient's heart rhythm.

"No question," said Jack, looking through the graph. "She should be on a statin, aspirin, ACE inhibitor, beta-blocker. I don't think quinidine is a stellar idea for her either. What do you think of this?"

"This lady is lucky to be alive. These are runs of torsades." Gary appeared apprehensive and distraught.

"Runs of what?" asked Samantha Shuman, a medical student passing by who overheard the exchange between the two doctors.

"Torsades de pointes," offered Gary. "This is a sometimes deadly heartbeat disorder. In this situation, it is iatrogenic."

"Ia whata?" she inquired, even more puzzled.

"Iatrogenic. That means her medications are causing it." Drs. Frank Hanes and Maria Butler, along with several nurses and medical students, had arrived and were now listening in. The tone was tense, attracting medical passersby.

"Frank and Maria. Look at this rhythm. What is it?" asked Jack, using the situation as a learning tool.

"Torsades," they both said almost in unison.

"Very good. Let's go talk to her." Both doctors and their growing entourage entered the room. Mrs. Josephine Winterman looked uneasy and troubled.

"You didn't know you were going to be a pop quiz today, did you?" asked Jack to put her at ease. "I'm Dr. Norris, one of the cardiology attendings." He extended his right hand and she shook it with a forced smile. "Your pass-out spells are due to a rapid heartbeat. This can be dangerous, but we're going to take care of it for you. We will need to put you in the hospital right away."

"Can I go home first and come back later?" she inquired.

"Oh no!" Gary piped in. "This is potentially life threatening. We need to transfer you to ICU at Newton Memorial right away. We'll get a wheelchair and take you there from here," explained the young doctor.

"Okay, if you think that's best," she acquiesced. "What's causing this problem?"

"We suspect that when you started Advil for your aches, you threw off your kidney function. This is rare but happens sometimes. When your kidneys malfunctioned, your blood levels of quinidine and digoxin increased and caused this rapid heartbeat. Your potassium and magnesium may be depleted from taking Lasix. We'll need to do blood work, stop your medications, and check out your heart function. Don't worry, we'll straighten all this out for you." Jack gave a reassuring smile.

"May I call someone for you?" asked Shelley, noticing the patient was alone.

"Yes, please. Will you please call my son?" said the older woman, looking through her purse to locate the phone number. The group of doctors exited the room with a plan, leaving Kate, Shelley, and the patient alone.

At the insistence of the head of security, the process of transferring people from the outpatient to the inpatient areas involved, in part, summoning the ever-vigilant Security Department. Nai Trepur had put this plan into being as a safety precaution. Since the clinical personnel were often short staffed at the clinic, having the security people help with the patient transfer was a welcomed change to the modus operandi. Soon, Trepur and another guard arrived.

"What's going on?" asked one of the security officers.

"Ees all okay?" reiterated Nai Trepur.

"We're okay. We have a patient that needs to be transferred to ICU," said Jack, easing the tension of their arrival.

"What ees the name of thee pationt?" asked Nai. He proceeded to write it down for his report. "Oh, by thee way, Dr. Norris. I was askaed to reemind everybody about thee hepatitees blood test. You weell do test soon, no?"

"The dreaded blood test. I hate to have my blood drawn," said Jack.

"What kind of blood test?" inquired Ellie Singer, a med student.

"The hospital is having all employees get hepatitis B vaccines. For those who have been vaccinated before, we have to get a blood test to see if our antibodies are protective. If not, we have to be revaccinated. And that's me. I need to have blood work. I hate that. Can I skip it?" said Jack rhetorically.

"You doo surgery. You are at reesk of needle stucks. You, of all people, should be prootected against hepatitis, no? Eef I can doo eet, you can doo eet," said Nai Trepur reassuringly, proudly showing a Band-Aid on his forearm.

"He's a big chicken when it comes to having his blood drawn," voiced Shalyn Ayer, the office nurse practitioner, with a grin. "Everybody's gotta do it. Don't worry, Mr. Trepur. I'll keep reminding him until he gets it done," said the nurse, looking at Nai Trepur, who returned a nod of understanding.

"You call it reminding. I call it death by nagging. And you'll do it over and over and over," said Jack, hopelessly.

"You betcha. If you don't want the reminders," returned Shalyn, putting emphasis on the word *reminders*, "get the blood test quickly." With that, Shalyn exited the area, smirking.

Soon the paperwork and wheelchair were ready, and the patient was transferred to the hospital's intensive care unit.

"Gary, write her admission orders and get her labs. Call me later to go over everything," instructed Jack, happy that the subject of blood drawing was over.

"Got it, boss." The concerned look on the young doctor's face for the patient had begun to fade, gradually replaced by Gary's typical demeanor.

"Come with me," said Kate, taking Jack's arm, towing him toward the exit door.

8

―――――――

"Hi, Kate, did you come down to the dungeons just to visit me?" said the lab tech shyly. Lance Lantz was the poster child for geek. He wore heavy-rimmed glasses and thick lenses. On his face, there were nests of acne here and there painted on an incurable canvas of unspoken lovesickness for the nurse. Lance was a smart guy but had been an underachiever. He was now the shift supervisor at the main laboratory at Newton Memorial, a position he held with pride. He had met Kate when she first began working at the hospital and required blood work for the preemployment process. For him, it was love at first needle. He found her beauty irresistible and alluring, her eyes enchanting. Alas, his social ineptness did not permit him to express his sentiments. Near her, he felt nervous, a sense of panic looming about his wits, tying knots in his tongue. He attempted to disguise it all with hopeless cracks at quick wit.

"Lance. I need a favor. Have you met Dr. Jack Norris?" she forged ahead.

"We've seen each other around, but I'm not sure I've had the pleasure." Both men shook hands. "How can I help?" Lance asked.

"I need a blood draw. All employees are required to test for—," started Jack.

"The hepatitis B titers," interrupted Lance. "Have a seat. I'll take care of it myself. Get you out of here in a jiffy." Gathering his things,

Lance momentarily and imperceptibly blushed. How he wished it were Kate he was tapping. Blood draw, that is. Well, at least she was present to see him work. See him at his best. In his element.

Dr. Jack Norris sat in a chair equipped with a small side platform specifically designed for venipuncture. The phlebotomist tied a tourniquet around Jack's forearm. Pretending to concentrate on a vein to draw blood from, Lance surreptitiously appraised the beautiful young nurse out of the corner of his eye. The perfect woman. The perfect life companion.

The next thought caused wrinkles to appear on Lance's face. *Was she really engaged?* he pondered, *to that doctor?* The notion was difficult for him to accept. *Just because he's a doctor doesn't mean he'll make her happier than I will.* He looked at Kate, who was staring at the needle hovering just above Jack's skin. Noticing his gawk, she locked eyes with Lance's. He smiled as his gaze quickly returned to the doctor's arm in search for a good vein. *She is so beautiful,* he continued to reflect. *What will it take for you to be mine, Ms. Kate?* A good-enough vein became easily palpable under his index finger. Lance steadied his right hand as he prepared to guide the needle into the vessel. *What if I had something you needed?* An almost imperceptible tremor appeared on his hand. He was sure Dr. Norris didn't see it. He was looking away. Who cared about him anyhow? Did Kate see him shake? He needed to prove to her that he was better than her doctor fiancé. A steady hand while doing his job was imperative. The tremble was unusual, and it wasn't happening because of the blood draw. It was occurring because of where his mind was. *I bet you'd give yourself fully to me if I gave something very important to you.* It was time. The vein was prepped and ready to be tapped. *Would I be your hero if I gave you something you couldn't live without? Or someone?* Despite the indiscernible hand quiver, it was time to advance the needle. Kate was watching and the blood draw had to be faultless. One shot. No room for error. No chance for weakness. *What would it take for you to give yourself to me, Kate?*

"Ouch," yelped Jack, squirming in the chair. "Ooh, that hurts."

"Don't move," spat Lance firmly, still trying to enter the vein, having punctured the doctor's skin with the needle. "Stay still."

9

It was dark out. Most people were getting ready to go home and enjoy the evening. It was Kate Fanning's turn to close shop, after yet another busy day in the outpatient cardiology clinic at Newton Memorial Hospital. She still had paperwork to finish, charts to file, examination rooms to tidy up, last-minute phone calls to make to patients, and other miscellaneous items. This quotidian would take the better part of an hour, after which she would exit and lock up the building.

Kate was in her twenties, but exceedingly conscientious and proud. She was born in a small town in southern Illinois to hardworking farmers. She picked nursing as a career, but almost anything that would get her out of Dykersburg, Illinois, would have done. Her life was now running smoothly, better and better each day. She left home at eighteen to attend nursing school in Evansville, leaving behind mom, dad, and two younger siblings, one of whom was Maggie, a beautiful six-year-old girl with Down's syndrome. Maggie had brought joy as well as sorrow to the Fanning family. Her congenital heart defects and necessary open-heart surgeries had been costly, both financially and emotionally. Despite having a dream job and life now, as the eldest, she felt obligated to the family. She sent home at least one hundred dollars each month, though this was harder and harder to achieve. Kate made $34,000 a year working as a nurse at the clinic, barely enough to pay rent, food, and utilities. On a positive note, a very positive note, Kate met Frank, with whom she immediately fell in love. He had proposed and the wedding date was set. She looked at the engagement ring on her left fourth finger and beamed. She stood there for a long moment, a smile on her face.

Earlier that same day, seventy miles to the west, the Fannings had been scheming. Barbara and Bill, recently aware of Kate's engagement to Frank, were eager to hold their oldest daughter in their arms and congratulate her. Frank was such a wonderful young man. They could not be happier. Secretly, the Fanning family had driven to Evansville to do some shopping, and then surprise Kate in the evening for dinner.

"Amelia, get Maggie's new coat and hold on to your sister's hand," barked Barbara at the girl, some tension in her voice. Shopping at the mall was stressful. Going to the big city was stressful. All the traffic. All the people. She had a love-hate feeling about the mall and the city. Although she loved the ability to shop for almost anything she needed in one place, she detested the crowds that inevitably were present. Having to watch over her two daughters, especially Maggie, made things more difficult. Nevertheless, surprising Kate and seeing the expression on her face at their arrival would make it all worthwhile.

"Relax, Mom, everything is taken care of," reassured Amelia in a soothing voice. Bill looked at her and smiled understandingly. He knew his wife would be stressed, but he also knew the older girl would help take care of her younger sister. Amelia, now fourteen, had become quite a beautiful, precocious young woman, nearly capable of running a household by herself. Bill stood pensively. Smiling, proud.

The family walked deeper and deeper into the guts of the large mall. Out of the corner of her eye, Amelia saw a familiar face. It was larger than life. The entrance of a sports apparel store proudly featured an oversized poster of soccer icon David Beckham. Amelia paused and smiled for a few seconds, reflecting about the sport she adored and the eye candy displayed on the placard. During this short stopover, Maggie peered at the establishment next door and spied Simba, the Lion King, her favorite movie. Just like Beckham, the large doll stood pompously advertising the many items for sale in the toy store.

"Hakuna Matata," she muttered, pointing at the window proudly displaying the lion. "Can I have Simba? He's my best friend." Amelia smiled. Barbara and Bill looked at one another, each studying the other's body language.

"What do you say?" whispered Barbara.

"Is it expensive?" Bill adjusted his glasses, attempting to see the price tag. "Let's go inside," he resolved, boosting Maggie's beaming smile.

"You go. I'll sit out here. Hurry up. We don't have much time." Barbara gathered the bags she was carrying, placed them on the large mall bench, and sat down. Her gaze followed her family as they entered the Walt Disney store, but soon they were all out of sight. Blankly, her eyes fixated on the passersby. Millions of people came and went, or so it seemed. A man approached from the opposite side of the mall and sat on the same bench, but his back to hers. He opened up the *Evansville Courier* and began reading. Barely aware she had company, Barbara fished her cell out of her pocketbook and opened it up. She couldn't wait to call Kate, but preparing to dial the phone, she thought better of it. She would make the call when the family was together in the van. She grinned at no one in particular and put the Motorola on the bench, next to her. Several minutes later, she looked at her watch.

What's taking them so long? she thought. It was at that time that Maggie exited the store, loads of excitement and contentment written all over her face. Barbara stood up and approached her daughter.

"Look, Mommy. Look." Maggie was energized. Ecstatic. Holding Maggie's hand and slowing down her forward progress was Amelia, who also carried a large bag. Barely visible inside was Simba's proud mane. Barbara grinned. Taking advantage of the commotion, the stranger, still sitting on the bench, turned and with one swift move stole the cell phone, got up, and departed the area inconspicuously. The Fannings gathered the packages and started toward the parking lot.

"This is the best present I ever got, Mommy," declared Maggie.

"I'm happy for you, Maggie," said Barbara. "Let's go show Katie."

"Amelia, grab this bag and Maggie's other hand," ordered Bill. The family walked out Green River Mall to their van.

"Kate is going to be so surprised," exclaimed Amelia. "Let's call her."

"Who wants to do the honors?" asked Bill.

"I do. I do," said Barbara with waning enthusiasm as she searched for the Motorola in her purse. "I can't find my cell phone," she finally announced, disappointed, checking all her pockets yet again. "I think I left it on the mall bench. I had it in my hand but put it down on the bench. I can't believe I did that."

"I'll go get it," said Amelia. "I know exactly where the bench is. I'll be right back." Amelia exited the van, closed the door, and walked rapidly back into the crowded mall.

As she walked away from the family vehicle, a small dark round object was operating from its hiding place under the rear bumper. The covertly installed unit supplied the necessary signal to allow GPS tracking of the Toyota Sienna.

"Be careful, honey," exclaimed Bill.

Like a homing pigeon carrying a vital message home, Amelia walked briskly toward the bench. She weaved in and out of small groups of people strolling about the mall. She reached the David Beckham poster and halted her progress briefly. Looking at the picture gave her a chance to smile and ponder. The irritation of the situation quickly melted away. Feeling refreshed, Amelia resumed her hurried walk, and several yards later, she reached the bench. She stopped. The seat was empty. She looked all around. She got on her knees and glanced underneath.

"Can I help you, miss?" inquired a man's voice. "By any chance are you looking for a cell phone?" Amelia looked up to see who had spoken.

10

Kate, Lori, Shalyn, and Shelley departed the outpatient clinic building together, bound for the employees' parking lot.

"We're still waiting to meet your man, Shelley," said Lori. "Can you at least show us a picture?"

"Yeah, we're starting to think this boyfriend of yours is imaginary," joked Shalyn.

"You'll meet him someday. He's been busy, is all," said Shelley.

"By the way you speak of him, you two seem to be very much in love," interjected Kate. "And that's all that matters. We'll meet him whenever you are ready for us to meet him."

"I have to stop at my in-laws. I gotta run, girls. See you tomorrow," interrupted Shalyn. She walked off in a different direction. "Have a great evening."

"Good night, all," said Shelley, the phrase repeated by the others. Each of the ladies sauntered in different directions deep into the parking lot, each in search of their own vehicle.

A few minutes later, Kate arrived at her Honda Civic. She plucked out the keyless remote from her pocket, and in an instant, her car chirped with joy. She opened the door and sat behind the steering wheel. What she didn't notice was the small device attached to the underside of her car, exactly like the unit located under the bumper of her family's van. Just like them, she was being tracked by GPS. In addition, behind the headrest of the rear seat, a small camera had been mounted, allowing spying of her actions. Both of these hidden devices remained undetected. Kate took a deep breath. She placed her purse on the passenger seat and, in so doing, noticed a cell phone on the seat. A strange cell phone, one she had never seen before. It wasn't Frank's, and it certainly wasn't hers. No one else had been in the vehicle for the last several weeks. The device was not on the passenger seat earlier that morning. She was sure of that. For a second, she sat motionless; then she abruptly scanned inside her car, looking in the backseat and through her mirrors, for possible intruders. The cell phone rang. Startled and nervous, she pushed the answer button after the second ring. She put the device to her ear, wrinkles on her forehead.

"Good evening, Ms. Fanning," said a man's voice even before she could speak. Kate's breathing momentarily ceased. Reflexively, she pushed the button that immediately locked all her doors. She looked around the parking lot trying to spy who might be calling her. No one in sight. There were empty cars and SUVs all around her, but not a soul. The man's voice was strange to her, a hint of a strange accent barely perceptible.

"I am calling you to enlist your services."

"What? Who are you? What do you want from me?" asked Kate apprehensively.

"You are going to help me with a very special project."

"No, I'm not. Who are you?"

"And you will keep your mouth shut."

"I'm calling the police right now." Kate prepared to hang up the phone, but the next few words paralyzed her.

"Do you want to see your sister Amelia alive again?" The mysterious man's voice was somber and dreadful. Devastated by his words, Kate put the phone back to her ear, but remained unable to enunciate a word.

"What?" she finally uttered tremulously. The word was barely audible, because she was overwhelmed by fear and panic.

"You won't see Amelia again, unless you cooperate fully with me. Stay on the line. I'm going to make a third-party call. I'll be listening. You listen and speak, but I will kill your sister if you say anything I don't like. Got it?"

"Yes." Kate's voice was quivery. After a moment, a familiar voice emerged from the cell phone.

"Did you find her? Is she all right?"

"What's going on, Mom?" Kate spoke into the phone, trying to appear as normal as she possibly could.

"Kate," said Barbara Fanning. "I didn't recognize the caller ID. I thought it was the police."

"The police?" Kate knew now that the mysterious caller was serious. The son of a bitch kidnapped her little sister.

"We didn't want to worry you, Kate. We went to the mall to shop for clothes. We were coming to surprise you with dinner. Your sister Amelia disappeared at the mall. She went to look for my cell phone. It's all my fault." Barbara wept, tears flowing down her cheeks. She blew her nose into a tissue provided by Bill. Unable to continue the conversation, Barbara gave the phone to her husband.

"Hi, honey, it's Dad." He tried to sound strong and composed. Inside, he was scared to death.

"We called the police. They're looking for Amelia. They told us to drive home and wait."

"Why didn't you call me?"

"There's nothing you can do, honey. We didn't want to worry you yet." There was a moment of silence.

"Oh, Dad. I'm sorry. I'm so sorry." Kate began to cry. "I love you," she said, fearful to say anything else.

"We love you too, honey. I'll keep you in the loop. You let us know if you hear from her," said Bill.

Deep inside Kate, emotions of fear and disquietude were quickly overtaken by rage and disgust. She could just explode. She wished she could strangle the mysterious man, the monster, the instigator of all this. Her teeth clenched, her jaw muscles tightened. The noise in the background, mostly Barbara crying and sniffling, was suddenly interrupted by dead silence. A few seconds later, the man spoke, his voice engendering a deep horror. Kate hungered for an opportunity to squeeze the life out of him, kick him, stab him, and rip his genitalia. Anything that would cause him physical pain to the degree of emotional discomfort he was causing her and her family.

"Now, will you cooperate?" questioned the man.

"I want to talk to my sister. Now."

"You will soon. Not now."

"When? I want to know she's all right."

"You'll talk to her when I say so," he commanded, demonstrating his controlling position. "Will you cooperate?"

"Yes." Kate's voice was engulfed with fury. "What do you want?"

"I will call you back. If you discuss any of this with anyone, anyone at all, I will kill Amelia first, then Maggie, then your parents. Then Frank and you," he said ruthlessly.

"Tell me what you want from me, then let my sister go and leave me the hell alone."

"Keep the phone. I will call with instructions soon." The phone went dead.

Kate could not move for several minutes. Her fists were tight and she had a taste for blood. The blood of this son of a bitch who would use a child to get what he wanted. *He better not harm her. I will find him and kill him.* A phone ring interrupted her thoughts. This ring was familiar to her. Her hands trembling, she opened her purse and checked the caller ID. It was Frank. She was in no shape to talk to her fiancé. She feared her words would give away her emotional state at this time, and that would be dangerous to Amelia. She needed time to think. With each ring, rivulets of tears flowed down her cheeks and inflamed the fury inside. She sat behind the steering wheel of her Honda, feeling impotent.

Should I go to the police? she mused, her mind racing. *Should I tell Frank? Should I ask Dr. Norris for help? He has experience with this sort of thing and I know I can trust him. He would help me through this.* Her thoughts were crowded in her brain. Images of Amelia tied up, frightened and crying, overwhelmed her reflection. *How do I communicate with Dr. Norris without the beast knowing? He'll kill her if I talk to anyone about this. I have to find a way.* She tried to suspend her painful thoughts but could not. She realized she was too upset to be able to think about this critically. She sat in her car terrified, gripping the steering wheel with white knuckles, her brain bubbling with disgust and rage.

11

Outside her apartment, an ambulance sped by hurriedly, sirens blaring. The hullabaloo woke Kate from deep sleep. She sat up in bed, wild-eyed, a cold sweat all over her body. She had been having a nightmare about Amelia and the monster who now dictated her fate. The reality of her sudden awakening hit her hard, and she began to sob at first, then a loud bawl, the need for vengeance coursing through her veins.

"Why is this happening to me? What did I do to deserve this? What about Amelia? What did she do to be in this predicament? She must be so scared."

Kate looked at the bedside clock. It was 05:33. She got up and went to the bathroom. She walked to the kitchen and started to make coffee. She took a shower and returned to the kitchen.

The cell phone rang, not the ringtone she was accustomed to, but the ringtone that gave her ghastly feelings up her spine. The caller ID indicated, "Caller ID blocked."

"Hello," she answered hesitantly.

"Good morning, Ms. Fanning," answered the familiar vile voice.

"Where's my sister? I want to speak with her," demanded Kate sternly.

"Katie," spoke a tremulous, frightened voice, several moments later.

"Amelia. Are you okay? Did he hurt you?"

"No. I'm okay. Why is he doing this to us?" beseeched the young prisoner, tears flowing down her cheeks. This weakened Kate's determination, and she began crying as well. There was a commotion, several cries by Amelia on the phone, then silence. A door thumped loudly.

"As you can tell, your sister's okay. For now anyway. Now, are you ready for my demands?" probed the man.

"Yes," answered Kate, muscles tightening, teeth grinding, culminating in a trembling rage. She squeezed the cell phone as she would love to squeeze his neck, given the opportunity. "What do you want?" She listened until the man stopped talking, and then, wordlessly, snapped her phone shut. Message received. She sat there. Numb. As the mind haze slowly dissipated, Kate's thoughts shifted to the remote past. She smiled, her anger ever so slightly beginning to melt away.

"It's my turn, Daddy," exclaimed the twelve-year-old girl taking the rifle.

"Be careful, Kate. This is not a toy. Guns are serious business," said Bill Fanning for the umpteenth time. Little Kate was proud. As the oldest daughter, she was given the opportunity to go into the woods with her father and learn about guns. About shooting. The targets had no prayer, and soon one by one would be hit by shrapnel and crumble into smithereens. This was the third time Kate had gone shooting with her dad, and the fear of the first two times was now well behind her.

Three large cans rested on a large rock, each about four feet from each other. The exhibit stood approximately five feet up from the ground, roughly sixty feet away from where they were about to shoot. A loud bang resonated throughout the canyon at about the same time as the first can was hit, disintegrating it as multiple pieces rushed in the direction away from the shooter. The second can suffered the same fate, the hit more on-target, signs of improvement. The third can now stood alone, awaiting the loud bang.

12

It was lunchtime, and a group of nurses and young doctors met at the coffee shop, armed with Dr. Jack Norris' Starbucks card.

"I'll order for Dr. Norris. I know what he wants. I'll go last and pay," said Shalyn Ayer. All complied, and soon they were on their way back to the hospital. It was almost time to start the afternoon office hours.

"Thank you, thank you," said Jack, receiving the hot beverage and his Starbucks card. "I really needed that. Thank you, Shalyn."

"Thank you for buying us coffees," she replied with a smile. "Kate, didn't you want Starbucks? You're usually the first in line."

"I haven't been in the mood for anything. Sorry. Too much stress getting ready for the wedding, I guess," returned Kate shyly, walking away, hoping to avoid demonstrating the turmoil inside her. It was imperative that she appear normal. It was required that she go about her business as usual. Just another day in paradise.

Dr. Gary Lewis emerged from one of the cubicles.

"Kerry is an otherwise very healthy thirty-five-year-old woman with recurrent fainting. If she stands for prolonged periods, like standing in line or at work, she develops a queasy sensation in her belly, breaks out in a cold sweat, gets increasingly dizzy, and then faints. She becomes as white as a ghost during the attacks. She sometimes feels her heart pounding. She was diagnosed with ministrokes, but a CT scan of her head was normal. I think she has neurocardiogenic syncope," said Gary confidently.

"It sure sounds like it," agreed Jack. By then, several med students had surrounded the two. "Go ahead and explain the mechanism of neurocardiogenic syncope and how to treat it," continued Jack. All eyes turned to Gary.

"I don't have a working knowledge of the subject," said Gary diffidently.

"It's okay to say you don't know, Gary," joked Frank, smiling.

"Okay, smart-ass, you tell us the mechanism of neurocardiogenic syncope," challenged Gary.

"I'd tell you, but my dog ate my homework last night," said Frank. "Besides, I haven't had much time to study. I've been given a riddle that has occupied all my free time. You have a wolf, a rabbit, and a carrot on one side of a river and you're trying to get them to the other side. You have to carry them one by one. If left alone, the wolf will eat the rabbit and the rabbit will eat the carrot. Wolves don't eat carrots. How do you do it?" continued Frank. Jack smiled.

"How do you do it?" reiterated Jack.

"I figured out the first step, but I'm stuck after that. First, take the rabbit across," stated Frank.

"Good. That works, since the wolf and carrot are left alone and they're safe together. What's the next step?" asked Jack, looking at the group of trainees. A long pause of silence, wheels churning in their brains. "Well, think about it and let me know when you figure it out. Now, anyone want to take a stab at neurocardiogenic syncope?" asked Jack.

"Refresh our memories, please," asked Gary.

"Gravity. Gravity is the problem," began Jack. "We have a system that pulls blood against gravity from the legs to the abdomen then chest and into the heart. Many folks don't do that well, so blood pools in the lower extremities. Less and less blood reaches the heart. Even a normal heart can't pump enough blood to the brain if it doesn't have enough blood to pump. When insufficient blood is pumped out of the heart, the brain shuts off for a few seconds—a fainting spell. When the patient falls, gravity is no longer a problem and the patient recovers spontaneously, usually quickly. The episodes are typically brief, just a few seconds, a minute at most," proclaimed Jack.

"We can get a head-up tilt table test to make sure. The main treatment is water and salt, to avoid dehydration. That much I know," said Gary proudly.

"Finally, someone knows something around here" joked Jack, winking. "Very good. Let's go see her." Drs. Jack Norris and Gary Lewis entered the patient's cubicle. Jack shook the patient's hand.

"Hi, I'm Dr. Norris. Dr. Lewis told me about your problem. These types of fainting spells are common. Tell me about what you normally drink?"

"I drink five or six Cokes a day, one cup of coffee, and a little milk with cereal in the morning," answered the young lady.

"I bet your urine is pretty concentrated. Dark yellow?" asked Jack.

"I guess. I don't usually look at it, but I've noticed it is sometimes deep yellow. Sometimes it has a strong odor."

"Those are all signs of dehydration. The condition you have that causes you to pass out is called neurocardiogenic syncope. People that have this problem can't afford to be dehydrated. You need to drink water. Juices and milk are okay too. Anything without alcohol or caffeine counts. Drink whatever it takes to make your urine clear, like the color of a weak lemonade. Start with sixty-four ounces a day. If you get dehydrated, you'll pass out again."

"My internist thought you might order an ultrasound of my carotid arteries to see if there are blockages. What are the carotids?" asked the intrigued patient.

"The carotids are the arteries that feed blood to the brain. If these are blocked, a patient can have strokes. You faint suddenly and unexpectedly, then recover by yourself. A blocked artery doesn't fit that bill. If you had a blockage in the carotids, it would be there before, during, and after the pass-out spell. Besides, you're too young to have blocked arteries. I don't think we need to test for that," answered Jack calmly and reassuringly.

"Do I need medicines?" she asked.

"Not for now. Let's try fluid. Have some sport drinks. These have salt, which you also need to build up your fluid levels quickly. We'll see you back here in one month and see how you're doing, okay?" Jack smiled. She reciprocated. They left the room. Gary gave the patient her marching orders and entered the small dictating area.

"I have a patient to discuss with you. This is a fifty-one-year-old woman with recurrent rapid heartbeats," said Shalyn, who emerged from evaluating her patient first. Shalyn was a dark-haired woman with a lot of confidence, the result of years of experience in the cardiology outpatient clinic. She handed Jack an EKG tracing.

"Typical atrial flutter," said Jack, following Shalyn into the patient's room. She was sitting on a chair next to the small desk.

"I'm Dr. Norris," he said to the woman as he entered.

"Hi, Dr. Norris," she greeted. All sat down.

"I told her about medications and ablations. We usually try meds first, but she wants to go ahead with an ablation without trying drugs," commented Shalyn.

"I don't like to take medications." The patient frowned as she murmured the words.

"You have a short circuit in your heart's electrical system. Just like a lightbulb with a short circuit, at times your heartbeat flickers rapidly. We can find the short circuit and destroy it with either a freezer burn or a heat burn. That's what an ablation is. We can almost always find the problem and correct it," explained the doctor.

"If you can do that, I'm cured and don't need medications for the racing heartbeats?" asked the patient in amazement.

"That's right."

"How long am I in the hospital?"

"Same-day procedure, you come in and leave the same day."

"Sign me up."

"Okay. Shalyn will give you more details and get you set up." Jack stood up, smiled, and shook her hand firmly. He exited the small room, leaving the two women behind to finish the necessary paperwork.

"Dr. Norris, I'm ready to talk to you about my patient. This is Mr. Oscar Richards. He was referred to us from his primary care physician for recurrent congestive heart failure. He's pretty short of breath right now. I think he needs to be admitted," said Dr. Adelaide Calvin. Ross Landis, a third-year medical student, hung on every word, taking it all in, starving for knowledge. Cardiology was definitely his favorite topic.

"Tell me more about it," asked Jack, assuring her with his calmness.

"He is a fifty-eight-year-old man who had a heart attack three and a half years ago. He did well until about six months ago, when he developed progressive shortness of breath and decline in performing physical activities. He is on atenolol, 25 mg daily; aspirin, 325 mg daily; digoxin, 0.25 mg daily; and Lasix, 40 mg twice a day." Adelaide paused and looked up from the chart she was consulting.

"What's his ejection fraction?" solicited Jack.

"Don't know. No testing done in three years," answered Adelaide.

"Why is it important to know his ejection fraction, Ross?" asked Jack, his eyes now on the med student.

"He sounds like he's in heart failure, which is to say he has fluid buildup in his lungs. That causes his shortness of breath and fatigue. We need to know how his heart is working. His ejection fraction is one of the best ways to define his heart function." The young man was confident but tense.

"That's right. What about his medication list?" persisted Jack.

"Well, he's on a beta-blocker but on one that is untested. I don't know if it'll do him any good. He's not on an ACE inhibitor or statin. All these meds have been shown to prolong people's life. He's on Lasix, which treats heart failure but doesn't prevent recurrences."

"Excellent! Let's go see him." The three entered the room. When they exited, they had a plan. The patient would be admitted for evaluation and acute management.

"What orders will you write for him, Ross?" asked Jack. The questions were designed to teach the doctors in training to think critically about the situation.

"I'll stop his atenolol and begin carvedilol, start atorvastatin, ramipril, and spironolactone. We'll get an echocardiogram and a sestamibi stress test to assess his heart function."

"Very good." Jack was happy with the answers. He smiled at Adelaide and Ross, acknowledging their accomplishment. A wheelchair was fetched to transfer the patient to the hospital. The patient puffed for air briskly. Even the work of a walk to the car could prove excessive.

In a few more minutes, hospital security arrived. Nai Trepur walked into the area where the doctors were talking, with two others in tow.

"The paperwork is almost finished. The wheelchair is on the way here from upstairs. We're almost ready to transfer the patient," informed Kate pleasantly.

"What's happeening?" asked Nai.

"We have a man in heart failure. We need to tune him up in the hospital for a few days," answered Jack.

"Wrong medications again?" asked Trepur.

"You got it," answered Dr. Frank Hanes.

"Do you ever poot patients on the wrong medeecations?" asked Nai, looking seriously at Jack then Frank.

"Sure," answered Jack with a smile. "When I start a medication that turns out to give the patient side effects. When I make human errors. Not because I don't know the literature." An uncomfortable moment of silence ensued, broken by the commotion of an orderly who arrived with a wheelchair. Mr. Oscar Richards called home to inform his family he was being hospitalized and soon the patient, an orderly, a nurse, and the security team departed. The office buzz returned to its normal activities.

Several hours later, the outpatient clinic wing started to empty out, first of patients, then of secretaries and doctors. Finally, the nurses walked out in small groups discussing this and that. It was Kate's turn to lock up again. She began her routine end-of-day work. She also embarked on her commanded, untraditional labor of espionage.

13

Kate entered her apartment, used the bathroom, then washed her hands. As she reentered the living room, the phone rang, the dreadful familiar ringtone giving Kate a wave of nausea and disgust. She picked up right after the first ring.

"Ms. Fanning, did you gather the charts and information I requested?"

"I want to see my sister," she demanded, circumventing the question.

"You will see her when I—"

"Now! I will see her now!" she snarled. "I have to know she is okay. I have to see she's okay." There was a long pause.

"Okay. I'll let you see her. After dark. Tonight," acquiesced the man hesitantly. "Meet me at Gavin Park at ten o'clock by the soccer fields. Come alone."

"Okay."

"Do I need to remind you of what'll happen to Amelia if you try anything I don't like?"

"No," said Kate bravely.

"What about Frank Hanes? Won't he be suspicious if you leave home?" inquired the rogue voice.

"Frank's on call tonight. He won't have a clue that I've left," she said.

"Now, how's the project going?" asked the man.

"It's going just fine. I've reviewed five charts and I have all the information you requested. I'm ready to go make house calls."

"As long as you cooperate, Amelia will stay healthy and happy." Pleased, the man terminated the call.

Kate felt she accomplished oodles, getting the man to agree to let her visit her sister. This little bit of control gave her a sliver of hope. She needed that.

How does he know what I'm doing? she mused. *The other day, his call came in exactly after I was done in the bathroom. He called right after I was done taking a shower, not during. And how did he know when I got into my car after work when he first called me?* her inquisitive mind wanted to know as she pondered the possibilities. *Does he have others working with him? Is my apartment bugged?*

She picked up a book from the coffee table and sat down on the couch. While pretending to read, her thoughts of the circumstances reemerged. Facing the book, her eyes wandered around the room, scanning for possible hideout spots.

If I was installing a spy camera in this apartment, where would I put it? she considered, visualizing the four corners of the living room in her mind's eye. *A corner that would allow viewing of the whole room,* she pondered. Two corners were unadorned by furnishings and were unlikely possibilities to hide a camera. A third corner faced the entrance door into a guest bedroom. *No, this couldn't be it either. He had known I was done in the bathroom and called the second I entered the kitchen the last time and the living room this time. That leaves only one spot with these vantage point characteristics.* That corner had a large bookcase ornamented with teddy bears and several picture frames. Kate got up and took her book to the area, pretending she was looking for another, all the while perusing furtively for the spy camera. *Here you are,* she smirked, appreciating the stealth device while acting as if looking through a book. The unit was tiny and positioned between two teddy bears. *I see what you're doing. I'll leave your spy equipment alone for now. I bet you've bugged other rooms, even my car,* she deliberated. *Two can play this game.* She walked to her bedroom with the book in hand. As she entered the room, she placed the book on the bed and walked to the closet to get a sweater, all

---

along spying for possibilities for additional hidden cameras. None were found. She then walked to her vehicle outside in the parking lot. Again, pretending to pick up a bag with workout clothes, she discerned both the video transmitter and the GPS bug. She returned home to wait for the right time to go meet the monster.

At nine o'clock, Kate was in the Honda, ready to go. The night was dark given the scarcity of moonlight. It would only take thirty minutes or so to reach the meeting location, but she wanted ample time to think and consider her situation.

"I'm here," she spoke into the mobile phone after the first ring.

"I know. I can see you. Get out of the car, lock it up then put both hands on the hood of the car. Speaking of hoods, when I arrive, I will throw you a hood, which you will immediately place over your head. Got that?" he said callously.

"Yes," she answered. The man abruptly ended the phone call. She took a deep breath and got out of the car. She glanced around the parking lot next to the soccer fields. It was dreadfully dark. No soul in sight. Quiet. Eerie. Spooky. In contrast, her inner turmoil was anything but quiet; it felt like gallons of acid were splashing inside her stomach.

A few seconds later, an eternity to Kate, headlights appeared on the opposite side of the parking area. As the vehicle approached, its beams penetrated through the darkness of the moonless evening and fixated on her car. Kate stood there still, her hands on the car as the mysterious vehicle approached from behind her.

"Put this over your head," said the man, exiting his ride. He threw an object onto the hood of the Honda, hitting her right hand. Kate slowly placed the hood over her own head, immediately changing from being blinded by the light to complete darkness.

"Put your hands back on the car," he said. "Are you carrying any weapons?"

"I'm a nurse, not a thug," she said argumentatively. He frisked her from behind. As his hands rubbed over her breasts and abdomen, all her muscles stiffened in disgust. She was scared to death, her heart pounding deep in her chest. Her fists tightened as his hands entered her pockets.

"I don't have any—"

"Quiet," he interrupted rudely as his hands rubbed down her legs, one at a time, culminating in a thorough feel around her ankles. He stood up behind her and grabbed her right arm forcibly, pulling her away from the Honda. He led her stumblingly to his nearby vehicle and cuffed both her wrists to the armrest on the passenger door behind the driver's seat. So anchored, she was unable to sit up comfortably and chose to lie down on the backseat.

"Where are we going?" she asked shyly.

"No talking," he replied insolently. The trip was approximately thirty minutes, all in silence. Under the darkness and stillness of the hood, Kate appreciated the smoothness of the ride for the first fifteen minutes. The vehicle traveled first at a speed consistent with city driving with several stops, presumably at red lights. A quick spot of rough, bumpy road was traveled slowly, consistent with a railroad track crossing. After a turn to the right, the ride sped up significantly, and Kate deduced they were traveling on a highway. After a few minutes, the vehicle turned left and slowed down considerably. Soon thereafter, they entered a road that became progressively rougher.

We're now in the country, reasoned Kate. The road turned even bumpier. The smell permeating into her hood had turned from polluted smog to clean and pure country scent, accented here and there by odors of distant farm animals. These whiffs, Kate knew well from back home.

"We're here," said the monster as the vehicle came to a complete halt. Kate struggled to sit up, a difficult task given the handcuffs. Her door opened a few seconds later. The fresh country air was unmistakable as the man removed her hood. The moonlight was faint, and given the pitch-darkness of the last half hour, Kate felt totally blind. She blinked her eyes several times and the world progressively began to come into focus. Several feet in front of her was a dark mysterious figure. Her eyes first saw his chest. He was wearing a dark flannel shirt. She slowly looked up to see his face. In total surprise and terror, she gasped. He was wearing a Nixon Halloween mask with the classic long pointy nose, rosy cheeks, and shit-eating grin. She looked into his cold, dark eyes. Those were the windows to the monster's soul. Kate saw diabolical malice, shameful pure evil. Powerfully, he grabbed her arm with his big left hand. Yanking on her, he disconnected her gaze. His right hand held a small shiny pistol. He walked her to a small barn, about twenty feet away. Swiftly, he unlocked the door and pushed her inside.

"You have an hour." The door closed behind her. The lock clicked loudly into place. A bit disoriented, Kate looked around. It was dark but the unmistakable silhouette of Amelia made her rush to her side. Amelia had been lying in a small bed. With the noise of the door unlocking, she sat up then stood by the bed. She was shackled to a weight-bearing post in the middle of the barn by a long chain. Realizing what was happening, the girls ran to each other and embraced, tears flowing down their cheeks. Wordlessly, the sisters stood there hugging for a long moment, projecting much-needed courage and hope onto one another.

"Are you okay, Amelia? Did he hurt you?" asked Kate concernedly, caressing her sister's face.

"No, I'm fine. But I want to go home. Why did he take me? Why me?" sniveled Amelia. "Why is he doing this to me? To us?"

"I'm going to get you out of here. I promise. For now, do what he tells you."

"What about Mom and Dad? Are they okay? I miss them, Kate."

"They're fine. I'll have you home in no time. I promise." Kate managed a slight compulsory smile. "Are you getting enough to eat?"

"Yes. He gives me whatever I ask for," answered Amelia, managing a faint smile.

"Have you seen his face?"

"No. He's been wearing that stupid mask in here. At the mall, he was wearing a moustache, a beard, and sunglasses."

"Believe it or not, that's a good thing. If you can't identify him, he won't feel he has to—," Kate paused in midsentence, realizing her message was unnecessary at this moment. After a short pause, the girls embraced again. More tears emerged. Kate had a tissue in her pocket, which she used to wipe her sister's tears. Then, her own.

Kate studied the place. It was a relatively large typical barn. There were several stalls where, Kate imagined, farm animals must have lived. Horses? Cows? Sheep? There were three large wooden pillars, which seemed to support the roof of the barn. A long chain attached to a handcuff anchored Amelia down and prevented her escape. This allowed the captor to come and go as he wished, with only minimal care for the girl. The long chain allowed Amelia to use a small portable commode in an adjacent stall, use the bed and a small desk in this stall, and reach a small refrigerator and microwave in a nearby booth. She had a small TV, video games, and age-appropriate books. He had thought this through, it seemed to Kate. Having worn a disguise, the mysterious man ascertained that he could, one day, let the girls free without the fear of being identified. That meant his beef was not with either of them. *His beef is with Dr. Norris,* mused Kate. *This monster has to be the man Dr. Norris almost put in jail three years ago.* This man was the mastermind behind the Rat Poison murders, a term the newspaper had coined.

Kate examined Amelia's restraints. Was there any way to release her from the cuffs? Kate walked around the barn. The light was poor, and she struggled to see in the dark. *Given the poor lighting, it's unlikely* Nixon *is watching us,* she surmised. Kate found a large nail hammered partially into a wooden beam. She pulled on it with all her might, but it didn't budge. She kicked it from above, then from below, and the nail moved slightly. She continued this multiple times, but little progress was made in dislodging the nail.

"Ame, there's a large nail in that beam in the corner over there," she whispered to her sister, pointing in the direction where she had struggled to remove the pin. "You might be able to reach it. Try to loosen it up when you're alone. If you can remove it, you might be able to work on getting rid of your shackles. I'm going to try to come back and see you as soon and as often as I can."

"I don't want you to leave," returned Amelia somberly.

"I know you don't. But I have to. He'll be coming for me soon to take me back home. He needs me to do some dirty work for him. But he's not after us. He's just trying to use me. I'm going to do everything he wants me to do, so he'll let us go. Don't you worry! He doesn't want to hurt either of us. You do everything he wants you to do. Don't resist. I'll be back soon. Is there something you need?"

The girls spoke for a few more minutes. Kate spoke calmly and reassuringly.

"Time to go home," said the man inside the Nixon face as the large door into the barn opened noisily. He walked toward the girls and threw the hood in Kate's direction. She put it on and stood up. The man took her arm and guided her.

"I love you, Ame," said Kate, stumbling toward the door.

"I love you, Katie," said Amelia, now sitting on her bed. Weeping. Rivulets of tears flowed down her cheeks.

As the outside door to the barn locked, Kate heard a faint click then the noise of something being dropped somewhere. *Some device was dropped into his pocket. There is no electronic gadget governing the door. This must be arming some sort of device. Perhaps a spying device. Or a device that would go off if someone entered the barn clandestinely. Or left the barn.* These thoughts surfaced in Kate's mind during the car ride back to her Honda at Gavin Park.

I need to contact Dr. Norris. How do I do that without the monster knowing? He has bugs in my car and apartment. Where else is he spying on me? I'm sure he's got a bug at work. He may have spies too. He may have accomplices. What he's doing is probably difficult to do alone, she mused. *I can't trust anyone.*

14

"I'll be right there," voiced the elderly woman loudly after the knock on the front door of her home. She put down her embroidery and walked to the small foyer. She opened the door.

"Hi, Mrs. Atkinson," greeted the young woman. "I'm Kate. We spoke on the phone earlier today."

"Yes, Kate from Dr. Norris' office. I recognize you, dear. Come in, come in," welcomed the older woman. "Call me Teresa. Can I make you some tea or coffee?"

The two women walked deeper inside the house and sat at the kitchen table.

"No, I'm fine, Teresa. Thank you very much." Kate had a bad feeling about this but carried on with the script as instructed, nonetheless. If she didn't, the consequences, Kate feared, would be unspeakably sorrowful.

"What can I do for you?"

"Dr. Norris asked me to come see you. Is your husband home?"

"Yes, he's playing cards on the computer."

"Would you mind getting him? I'd like to speak with both of you." The older woman smiled and complied. The more things were proceeding according to plan, the more nervous Kate became.

Teresa arrived with Charlie, who shook Kate's hand then sat down next to his wife, an inquisitive look on his face.

"Dr. Norris sent me to see you both to explain our new home services. We'll care for you at home. I'll come see you periodically and give you Dr. Norris' instructions. If you have any problems, you call me at this number." Kate pointed to the cell number printed on the business card she had placed on the table in front of the elderly couple. "Dr. Norris would like to make some changes to your medications. Will you go get them for me?" Kate smiled as Charlie got up from the table and disappeared toward the bedroom.

"These are all my medications," he said, reclaiming his chair at his wife's side. Kate looked at the labels and made two groups of pill bottles.

"This group you continue to take," she said, pushing several pill containers to one side. "This group, you're going to stop taking. In addition, we're going to add these other medications." Kate opened her purse and removed three new bottles of drugs. "I also typed up a new list of all the meds Dr. Norris wants you to take from now on." She handed over the piece of paper and remained silent for a spell to allow the Atkinsons to review the information.

"This is pretty easy to follow. I take these at breakfast time, these at bedtime. Okay, I got it," said Charlie.

"Kate, Charlie is doing so well now, thanks to Dr. Norris. But why make changes?" asked Teresa curiously.

"I don't really know, but he feels this is a better course to take." Kate had difficulty looking either of them in the eye, the turmoil inside her increasing by the minute.

"Okay. I trust Dr. Norris. If he wants me to change medications, I will," said Charlie, unperturbed.

Several minutes later, Kate exited the Atkinson home and got in her car. More than ever, Kate realized what she was doing was immoral, unethical, and plain wrong. She was stunned, completely terrorized by the actions she was commanded to perform. Alone in the vehicle, she began weeping, a whimper at first, crescendo to a wail, rage cruising through her every fiber. She tightened her muscles and her fists squeezed tightly around the steering wheel, her wrath oozing from every pore. Feelings of terror and disgust overflowed in her head, with a blanket of revengefulness overwhelming her heart. She would get revenge. She would prevail. Amclia would survive the ordeal and she would not let these innocent bystanders suffer at her hand. She vowed she would stop all this.

Still frozen with terror in her car, Kate's mind suddenly drifted to many years in the past, a faint smile growing across her face. A thirteen-year-old girl struggled to jump over the large fallen tree, its root partially embedded deep in the ground. The root and tree stump were in the path to the outdoor shooting range. Her father carried the rifle over his shoulders. When they arrived at the large rock, the young girl positioned the three large cans as she had done several times before. They walked back to the shooting area.

"I'm very proud of you, Kate," said Bill Fanning. "You have gotten better and better at this. Heck, you're almost as good as I am," he smiled, handing over the gun.

"Thanks, Daddy, but I think I'm better than you. I ain't missed yet at two hundred feet. Watch me." She made herself comfortable lying on the ground, the rifle in front of her, the first can lined up in the front and back sights. The safety latch was released and the trigger squeezed slowly and steadily. A loud bang echoed. The first can was hit squarely in the center, forcibly propelling it backwards. Likewise, the second can was struck with a loud thud. The third can now stood perched alone on the rock. But it was no longer a can. It was—it was—it was a Nixon Halloween mask. The loud bang this time was repeated multiple times, followed by the sudden emergence of numerous holes appearing on the mask, which otherwise remained undisturbed. Undisturbed until a few seconds later, when blood began to ooze from each hole.

A car honked its horn nearby and Kate was yanked back to the here and now. In disgust of herself and the situation, she started up her car and drove on, her mind again dealing with the depraved actions she was forced to commit by the monster. The Honda entered a driveway and Kate got out of the car. *I will make this right! I will make this right!* she repeatedly thought. She walked to the front entrance and knocked. A long moment later, the front door opened.

"Hi, Mr. Carter. I'm Kate Fanning. I called you this morning. I'm a nurse and I work with Dr. Norris. May I come in?"

15

The team was ready and the patient prepped. Dr. Jack Norris had made the necessary review of the available records and medical data and now entered the Electrophysiology Lab to perform the ablation procedure. The patient's intermittent racing heartbeats had become a thorn in her side and had been resistant to medical therapy.

"Good morning, ladies," greeted Jack, entering the lab with a student in tow.

"Hi, Dr. Norris," said Vijay, one of the lab nurses.

"Good morning," repeated Tracy, the other nurse. "Ready to go?"

"Let's do it. What do you know about atrial flutter?" asked Jack of the medical student. Ross Landis was in his midtwenties, short, with dark features. He was curious and intelligent.

"A heartbeat disorder caused by a short circuit in the right atrium," he answered, happy he had reviewed the subject matter the night before.

"Good. Let's see if we can get rid of it for good." Jack scrubbed his hands at the sink outside the lab, prepping for the procedure. He entered the room and soon the catheters were inside the heart and in their proper position.

"So how does an ablation work, exactly?" asked Ross.

"The electrical impulses go around the right atrium and that includes a tight passageway in the bottom of the right atrium called the isthmus. It's right here," explained the mentor, pointing to the monitor screen. "If we create a line of electrical block through this narrowing, the short circuit is interrupted and atrial flutter is cured, never to return."

"When you deliver radio frequency through the catheter, does it hurt the patient?" asked the patient astutely.

"It would, if the patient was awake. Fortunately, we have the best EP nurses in the world and they take care of that." Jack winked at the nurse near the patient's head. "Is the patient sedated?" asked Jack.

"He's ready," answered Tracy, touching the man's eyelids and noticing no significant response. "Oxygen saturation is 93 percent and blood pressure, 110 over 68. Do that thing you do so well," she continued.

"Radio frequency on at 70 watts and set temperature to 80 degrees," commanded Jack.

"On at 70," returned Vijay. The room was suddenly inundated with a loud background buzz, indicating that radio frequency was being delivered. This would continue for two minutes, after which testing would be done to assess the result. Four other applications followed until Dr. Norris was satisfied that the desired effects were achieved. The entire procedure took approximately two hours.

"Everything went well and she should be able to go home later today," stated Jack to the patient's family, who had been anxiously awaiting his arrival. Jack's beeper went off: 7999, read the display.

"The emergency room," murmured Jack to himself as he prepared to dial the number.

"Dr. Norris. We have one of your patients here. He came in with a cardiac arrest."

"I'll be right there," said Jack, hanging up the phone.

"Vij, Tracy, I'll be right back to finish up the paperwork. Have to go to ED stat."

"Okay, no problem. I'll have the paperwork ready for you when you return," said Tracy.

Jack trotted to the Emergency Department, Ross Landis in tow. On their arrival, the secretary pointed to room 3, and the two men pushed through the door.

"This is one of yours, Jack. Collapsed at home. EMS called. They found him in ventricular fibrillation. Shocked twice to sinus rhythm with a systolic blood pressure of 80. He rearrested in the ambulance and has been pulseless since. I'm going to quit unless you want to try anything else," reported the ED physician somberly.

"Thanks, Pete. What's the estimated down time at home?" asked Jack.

"Approximately twenty minutes," answered a paramedic doing CPR.

"Thanks, Bo. We should quit. I agree." Jack nodded at the ED doctor, who nodded back.

"Let's quit here," commanded the ED doctor. The resuscitative team complied and all efforts ceased. The monitor showed a straight line, announcing the absence of any heartbeat.

"What's his name?"

"Joel Peters," answered a nurse despondently.

"What else do we know about the circumstances of what happened? Is the family here?" asked Jack.

"The wife's on the way with a son," said one of the paramedics. "I'll go see if they've arrived yet and put them in the solace room." She exited the room.

"We were told he was feeling pretty bad for a few days. Apparently he called your nurse, but was told to continue as he was. It doesn't make sense," said the other paramedic. Puzzled, Jack left the cubicle in search of the family members. Ross followed right behind.

16

Mr. William Stoops had been feeling poorly for three days now and getting worse by the minute. He had felt increasingly weak and fatigued. Getting up in the morning today had been a colossal chore.

"Call Dr. Norris, Bill," insisted Mildred Stoops repeatedly. "If you won't, I will." She was worried about her husband's recent deterioration. "It all started since your medications were changed. Call him now."

"Okay, okay, Mildred. I'll call Kate, Dr. Norris' nurse." He was pale and decrepit. Listless. Puny. Sweat glistened lustrously on his forehead; his words were frail and his hands had become tremulous.

"Here. It's ringing," said Mildred a few seconds later, handing him the receiver. Realizing he had finally accepted her recommendations, she did not waste any time.

"Hi, Kate," he spoke into the phone. "Not too good," he said after a moment. "I feel weak and dizzy. I have—"

"Tell her about the leg cramps and the fainting spell," interrupted Mildred anxiously.

"I fainted yesterday when I got up from the couch to go to the bathroom." Another pause as he listened. "I peed twice yesterday and the urine was dark. Very dark yellow." Another hush. Mildred got closer to the phone, hoping to listen in on the conversation. "It started two or three days after you came to see us and changed my medications. I was doing so good before." Bill listened intently to the words radiating from the phone receiver, while Mildred persisted with attempts to butt in. He hung up the phone.

"What did she say? I couldn't hear what she said. Should I call 911?"

"Kate's going to call Dr. Norris and call us back. I gotta go lay down. I don't feel good." Mildred helped him to his feet and to the couch a few feet away. He sank into the sofa, hard. As he placed his feet up on a cushion, she rushed to the bedroom to fetch his favorite pillow, which she placed under his head.

"Comfy?" she asked.

"I feel some better," lied Bill, appeasing Mildred. He forced a smile when their eyes connected. She reciprocated.

"Should I call for an ambulance?" she insisted.

"No. Let's wait. She'll call right back."

Several miles away, Kate paced the floor of her apartment waiting for the monster to answer her call.

"I just got a call from William Stoops. He's dehydrated and feeling horrible. The changes in his medications have begun to make him sick. What do you want me to do? He needs to go to the Emergency Department or he'll die. Should I—"

Her words were interrupted by the other party. She listened, her hatred for the man growing with every utterance. She squeezed the phone receiver with a fist of death.

"I can't just do nothing," snarled Kate. "I gotta help him." Another pause, more loathing toward the criminal on the other side of the call. "No, please don't hurt my sister," she supplicated. "I'll do what you say. I'll do it," she said, defeated. "Please don't hurt her." Rivulets of tears made tracks down her cheeks, her eyes swollen. Kate slammed the phone down on her coffee table and collapsed, face-first, into her couch. She shouted obscenities into the pillows. She took several deep breaths, attempting to extinguish the fire inside and quench her swelling desire to strangle the mysterious man for what he had done to her, her family, and all the innocent people about to suffer dearly by her own hand.

You will pay, you son of a bitch. For all this, you will pay, you bastard, she thought.

Once she mustered enough ability to hide her true feelings inside, she withdrew a tissue from a nearby box and blew her nose. She took a few more deep breaths and picked up the phone. The call was answered even before the first ringtone had concluded.

"Good evening, Mrs. Stoops. It's Kate from Dr. Norris' office." Kate swallowed and paused. She looked down at her feet in shame and disgust with her impotence to do what she knew was right. "Dr. Norris says it'll take a little bit more time for him to adjust to the new medications. He wants you to stay the course. Don't change anything. Have him go to bed early and rest. He'll feel better by tomorrow." After a pause, Kate continued. "No, no need to go to the emergency room tonight, unless he gets worse," she ad-libbed. "Let's see how he's doing in the morning." With silent tears flowing down her cheeks, Kate hung up the phone.

Although she tried to watch TV, Kate could not stop thinking about Mr. Stoops. She lay on her couch and felt complete despair over what she was being forced to do. Mr. Stoops trusted and depended on her and she chose her sister over him. She recalled her last encounter with the patient at the office, only a few weeks earlier. He was funny and happy, as always, a dear man that deserved better than this. Her thoughts then flip-flopped to her sister, Amelia. *How lonely and scared she must be right now,* she mused. *She is just an innocent, sweet young girl. Is he watching me right now?* Wide-eyed, she daydreamed of the moment she could take revenge on the nefarious, abominable beast responsible for these events. She envisioned ways of torturing him, horrific techniques unparalleled by any in all the horror movies she had ever seen.

Her bedside alarm clock ticked ever so slowly. It was now 2:17 in the morning. Kate's contemplations of Mr. Stoops, Amelia, and the mysterious man persisted, and she had remained without a moment of sleep. With a determined look in her eye, she got out of bed, dressed, walked to her car, and drove to the Stoop residence.

Even from several blocks away from her destination, Kate realized the horror she was about to witness. A lump chocked her throat. She couldn't breathe. Her lips tingled and she felt dizzy and sick to her stomach. As she approached the home, she saw two police cars parked haphazardly, one partially on the lawn. A third vehicle was an ambulance. Kate stopped her car a block away and walked to the area. Several neighbors stood in small groups here and there, mostly in silence. The anticipation was palpable.

"What happened here?" asked Kate as she approached one of the small groups of people.

"Bill collapsed. Mildred called us. We called 911. My husband's in there with them. They've been working on him for almost thirty minutes," said an elderly woman dressed in a dark blue robe.

"Why aren't they going to the hospital?" asked another older woman.

"They're working on him. They have all the equipment and medications, just like the hospital," said one of the women encouragingly.

"Tony's walking back now. Let's see what he knows," said the first woman. Kate knew exactly what was happening. The only reason the paramedics had not rushed the patient to the hospital was that they arrived too late. As the neighbor slowly shuffled toward the group, all stood in silence, waiting for the verdict. The man's face remained hidden by the darkness of night as he continued to approach them. Now thirty feet away, the flashing red and white lights on top of the emergency vehicles intermittently illuminated the man's features. The other scattered groups of neighbors had converged, they too hungry with anticipation. When he finally arrived, wordlessly the man somberly and reverently shook his head at the group, his head bowed. Immediately, sniffles began. Those that came prepared passed around tissues. The monumental feelings of sorrow blanketed the group of bystanders. In silence, people hugged each other. Slowly, the group gravitated toward the Stoops home, hoping to comfort the widow. With disgust and rage all over her face, Kate imperceptibly walked to her car, unnoticed by the others. When inside, she broke down, her emotions boiling. Erupting. She wept and cried aloud. She hammered the steering wheel with her fists. "You will pay. I will make you pay. You will pay!"

Her cell phone rang. The caller ID announced, *ID blocked.* She knew who it was.

"What do you want?" she answered firmly and angrily, her worst nightmare on the other side of the line.

17

Many miles north, in a dilapidated, long-forgotten barn, Amelia worked diligently to free herself up. Stretching her tethering chain, she could reach the large protruding nail still embedded firmly in the wooden post. Standing on it had allowed the spike to move downward. She then used her shoe as a hammer to force the pin upward. Repeating this motion multiple times had enlarged the attachment point of the nail into the post, loosening it. She worked this action over and over, each time more easily, increasing Amelia's confidence that she could withdraw the nail form the post.

Breathless, she sat back on the hay floor heavily. The air in the barn was stale and sticky, making it easy to sweat with little effort.

"I can't give up. I can't give up," Amelia told herself continually as she worked the metal stake up and down, occasionally pulling on it. "Come on; come on," she murmured yanking on the pin. It would not budge. Not yet. Perhaps never.

Although she had high hopes she could eventually free up the nail from the post, the task had proven formidable. Today was her fifth day working at it, countless hours each day. The nail was loosening up, providing her with the will to continue the mission.

Frustrated, Amelia got on her feet and walked to the refrigerator. She removed a water bottle and twisted the top off. Refreshing liquid soothed her insides, quenching her thirst and lessening her misery. The truth was that the project had been a much-needed distraction from the somberness of her situation. It gave Amelia a sense of purpose and direction. As she worked the nail, she felt some of the hopelessness melt away. Focusing on the job ahead, Amelia had not had a chance to ponder the next step. What would she do once the nail was free from the wooden post? What if she couldn't accomplish the task? What if she would not be rescued? What if—. No, it was definitely more productive to keep her mind on extruding the nail.

Refreshed and rejuvenated, Amelia walked toward the pin and resumed the task of removing it. Up and down. Up and down. Once in a while, a twist and a pull. Up and down. Up and down. *I can't give up. I can't give up.* Pull it up, push it down. Pull it up, push it down. Up and down. A strong pull. Unrelenting, the nail remained embedded in the wood. Irritated, Amelia pounded the post, her fists clenched, her eyes scintillating with tears. *I won't give up, I won't give up,* she thought returning to work on the nail.

Her hands were smarting, aching from holding the metal pin. Looking at her bleeding palms, Amelia walked around looking for a solution to the obstacle. She spied a towel near the microwave unit. She wrapped it around the nail and held it firmly with both hands, her resolve fortified once again.

18

"What's wrong, Kate?" asked her fiancé, concern punctuating his words.

"Nothing, Frank. I'm okay," she answered timidly, with a forced grimace.

"Come on, Kate. I know you better than that. Something is bothering you. You've been avoiding me for the last two weeks. I know something is bothering you. Will you please talk to me. I want to help," said Frank tenderly.

"I can't do this. I can't do it," she retorted, avoiding eye contact with him. Her eyes became wet and sparkly as tears materialized.

"Hey. It's okay. Let's talk about it," said Frank calmly, his index finger under her chin gently padding it, hoping to meet her eyes.

"I can't do this anymore," she repeated, crying. She briskly turned around and ran off into the depths of the clinic.

"Are you breaking off our engagement?" he managed to ask as she departed.

"Yes!" she exclaimed as the door closed behind her. Frank stood there breathless, dumbfounded. *What on earth did I do to upset her so terribly*, he thought. He had never seen Kate like this before. His instinct was to pursue Kate, but he felt it would be best to let the smoke clear and reapproach her after a while. He was assigned to ward rounds and was expected in conference room 3 in five minutes. He couldn't be late. He walked briskly to his assigned post, Kate's words still generating sadness as they ricocheted deep in his brain. *What could be bothering her so much? Is she seriously dumping me?* he contemplated. Everything started shortly after he proposed to her. *Was the engagement too much for her?*

Kate wished she could speak with Frank and explain the whole situation. How she wished she could, but she certainly did not want to drag the love of her life into this ongoing mess. She couldn't bring him down too. Furthermore, she wondered if Frank could love her anymore after knowing what she had done to all those innocent patients. She knew she had to speak with Dr. Jack Norris. This whole process had been designed to hurt him. The son of a bitch who now had her sister in captivity was targeting Dr. Norris' patients by switching them to the wrong medicines. This has to be revenge for Dr. Norris having thwarted the Rat Poison project.

I wish I could speak with Dr. Norris. I know I can trust him, she thought. However, Kate knew the mysterious man had cameras and spyware all over her. Maybe even accomplices. She could not trust anyone. There was nowhere she felt safe from him. She didn't want to compromise Amelia's safety.

"Ms. Fanning? Ms. Kathryn Fanning?" rhetorically asked a well-dressed man who had approached from behind, surprising her. She gasped, her nerves frayed. Kate turned to see a well-built man in his early thirties with dark brown hair. Behind him, a man Kate recognized, Mr. Nai Trepur.

"Yes. That's me," she replied, trying to pretend it was all routine, as usual, despite the great turmoil inside her every fiber.

"I'm Detective Brad Mills from the Evansville Police Department. You already know Mr. Trepur. He's the chief of security here at Newton Memorial. Can we talk for a few minutes?"

"Sure, about what?" she asked.

"About your sister's disappearance." He looked perplexed. "A bit of a strange question, don't you think?"

"What do you mean?"

"If my sister disappeared and a police detective came to talk to me, I think I'd know immediately what it was about." The young woman's question had hit the wrong chord with Detective Mills, which immediately raised a red flag in his mind.

"Yeah, I realize that now. I'm just nervous and upset. I don't know what I'm saying anymore. I don't know anything about Amelia's disappearance, Officer."

"I see. Let's go somewhere private and chat a bit, can we?"

"Sure." Kate led the men to an unoccupied patient exam room, as far from the main office area as was possible. He closed the door and the three sat down.

"Meez Kate," started the head of security. "You must tell us all you know. We want to help get your seester back. You must help us, no?"

"Yes. I want to help. Of course, I will cooperate," she said nervously.

"So what do you know?" began the police detective.

"I know she disappeared from the mall here in town. That's all."

"You seem to be taking it exceptionally well," interjected the cop.

"I'm not. I'm worried sick. I'm trying to not let it interfere with my job here at the clinic."

"Have you been in contact with Amelia?" asked Nai Trepur.

"No," she lied.

"See, I think you have," replied the detective after a long moment of staring into her eyes. "Did she run away? Is she with you?"

"No, sir," she held emphatically. She felt petrified.

"You know, if she did run away to be with you, it isn't a police matter. It's a family thing. It's not a crime. But if you're lying to us now"—he paused for effect—"that would be a crime. So, just tell me everything you know and we'll make all this go away."

"I really don't know where she is. I'd tell you if I did." The men looked intently at her for what seemed to be an eternity. She didn't flinch.

"Okay, Ms. Fanning. Here's my card. If you think of anything, call me right away," said the detective. They stood and slowly exited the small room. When the men were out of sight, Kate walked back to the main area where the patients, doctors, and other nurses were busy with the chores of everyday life at the outpatient clinic.

"What happened? Was that a detective with Nai?" asked the concerned voice of Dr. Jack Norris.

"Yes. My sister Amelia was abducted at the mall a few days ago," said Kate, sniffling then searching for a tissue.

"A few days ago? Don't you know exactly how many?" Jack was intrigued.

"Five. Yes, five days ago," she said firmly, wiping her tears again with a tissue.

"Are they suspecting you? How awful it must be for you, Kate."

"Yes. I think they suspect I know something."

"Do you?"

"No. I don't know anything." Kate appeared increasingly more irritated with the questions. Jack noticed it and retreated.

"Kate, please let me know if I can be of any help. Or if you just want to talk, okay? Do you want to take the day off?"

"Yes. That would help. I'm a big mess today. I'm very upset."

"Okay. I'll take care of everything. You just go and call me if you need anything."

"Thank you. Excuse me." Kate rapidly retreated to the women's locker room still grieving. Soon, she departed the clinic area.

Down the hall, away from where the action was, a man inconspicuously entered a small janitorial closet. He dialed a number on his cell phone.

"It's Cesar. The police were here. They talked to the nurse for a little while," he whispered into the device. "The head of security was also here. She left the clinic and he's back to work." A pause. "Okay." Another pause. "No, the local police didn't talk to Norris." A moment of silence. "All right, I'll do it." He terminated the call and went back to pushing his bucket and mop, overlooked by the other staff members.

19

Kate was beside herself. How would she get out of this predicament? As long as the man held Amelia captive, she was paralyzed and impotent to do anything meaningful to help the situation. She would have to follow every command the monster dished out. She had to either rescue Amelia or find the identity of the mysterious criminal. But how would she accomplish one of these tasks without jeopardizing her younger sister's safety? Her cell phone rang, interrupting her deep thoughts.

"Hi, Mom."

"Hi, sweetheart. How have you been doing, Katie?" asked Barbara with a motherly tone.

"I'm okay. I guess."

"Have you heard from Amelia?"

"No. Nothing."

"The police have a theory that she ran away and is with you. I told Detective Mills that's not possible. You wouldn't lie about that, not when we are all so worried about Amelia's disappearance. You would tell us, right? Even if Amelia made you promise you wouldn't tell, right?" Barbara Fanning could hold her tears no longer. With these words, she broke down, weeping and sniffling. She blew her nose with a tissue from a Kleenex box nearby.

"If Amelia was with me or if I knew anything about her, I would tell you. I would, Mom." The suffering in her mother's heart was unequivocal, plain to see even seventy miles away and paralleled her own anguish. The conversation proceeded for several more minutes. Then, the other cell phone rang. The cell phone she wished she never had to use ever again. Unfortunately, Amelia's safety was in the balance.

"Mom, I have another call. I have to take it. I'll call you later." Kate hung up the phone with her mother, put her phone down, and answered the other call.

"Kate. This is George Curry." His voice was cheerless and heartrending. "My wife, Janice, died in her sleep last night. I found—," a short moment ensued during which Kate could hear the man crying softly and wiping his tears. "I found her this morning. She was cold and gray colored. I just wanted to let Dr. Norris and you know."

"I am so sorry, Mr. Curry. Janice was doing so well." Kate's words were mournful and somber.

"She really was. Dr. Norris had found the right combination of medications. That's why I don't understand why he wanted to change everything so drastically. Are you sure you didn't come see the wrong patient when you came to see Janice?" The question choked Kate. She couldn't speak for several beats.

"No, Mr. Curry. I didn't have the wrong patient," she finally said woefully, her voice grief stricken. "Was she feeling poorly yesterday?"

"No. She didn't complain of anything. She went to bed feeling as usual, then died in her sleep. Dr. Norris told us that almost always means a dangerous arrhythmia."

"Yes, ventricular fibrillation. Again, Mr. Curry, I am very sorry for your loss. I will let Dr. Norris know." A few moments later, she hung up the phone, her heart ached, her eyes sparkled with tears, and her soul anguished in misery. She broke down again sobbing in an inconsolable despair. This situation wasn't going away soon. Kate had been commanded to see thirteen patients thus far over the last week. Several of these patients were already suffering, some paying with their lives. These heart patients were fragile. It had taken several office visits to optimize their medical therapy. What she was now doing was undermining these efforts and offsetting the delicate balance of the right mix of drugs—stop helpful meds and add dangerous ones.

Wait a minute! This is a clue! This bastard has to have enough knowledge of medicine to accomplish these med changes. This narrows the field of possible suspects, she speculated. This realization challenged Kate to continue to think critically through the issues. *What else can I use to identify this monster before more people have to die?* Excitedly, Kate vowed to continue to work through this. *This monster has to be stopped.* Worried that the spyware equipment in her apartment may allow discovery of her efforts, Kate sat on the couch, a pillow over her legs and a laptop computer over the pillow. It would be unlikely that he could actually view her search, but it would be important for her demeanor to appear nonchalant, while her brain churned at the speed of light.

The next day, she went to work. She smiled and carried out her chores as back to normal as she could muster. And it was working out. Now that she had a plan of attack and was working at it, she felt less like a victim and more like a doer.

"Hi, Kate. Does Dr. Norris like the patients to have their blood pressures taken on both arms?" asked Shelley.

"Yes, and he wants the BMI recorded," answered Kate with a grin.

"Thanks. There's so much to learn here."

"You're doing great. You're catching on fast," reassured Kate.

"Thanks." Shelley took a patient's chart and headed to the waiting room.

At the end of the workday, when everybody left the clinic area, Kate grabbed a few patient charts and made the necessary clandestine documentation entries, as dictated by the monster. From the corner of her eye, Kate spied the janitor, who seemed to be standing by the janitorial closet watching her. When he realized she turned toward him, he scurried away, pushing a large broom. He entered the men's bathroom. Intrigued, Kate tiptoed to just outside the door. She heard the janitor speaking softly into what she assumed was a cell phone.

"She's definitely up to something." A short pause ensued. "I don't know what." Another break in the dialogue. "Okay. I will. Goodbye."

She heard the mobile device click shut. She scampered away just in time and hid in the employee lunchroom pretending she was cleaning up. After several minutes, she returned to her clandestine mission. The janitor was nowhere in sight. *I definitely can't trust Cesar. He must be involved in this whole thing. He may even be the monster. He was about the right stature. It could be him*, she mused. *If I look into his eyes, I might be able to tell.*

When finished, Kate walked to her car and drove to the supermarket. This store was not the one she typically frequented but it had the advantage of being near a RadioShack. She was interested in making a quick stop there, hoping to remain undiscovered by the monster's spyware senses.

"I want to see my sister. This evening," she said boldly and presumptuously as the man answered her phone call. Tonight, when she would be taken to see Amelia, would be the first of many steps to fight the monster and put a stop to this massacre.

Kate arrived at the soccer fields at 11:42 p.m. She was to be taken by the monster wearing Nixon's Halloween mask to see her sister. Just like before, she received instructions to get out of her car, put her hands on the hood, and face away from the approaching vehicle. Aided by the dark of night, he would exit his car and throw a hood in Kate's direction. She was to put it on her own head and would be frisked thoroughly before being guided to the man's car. Just like before, this process would unfold wordlessly. Like before, her mouth would not be inspected. After all, it was under the hood. He would cuff her to the back passenger seat and drive her to a farm. He would help her out of his vehicle and guide her to the barn where Amelia was hidden from the world. The two girls would be locked inside for an hour or so, at which point the monster would return to take Kate back to her car at Garvin Park in Evansville. Unlike the first trip to the farm, this time Kate had a bug of her own to plant. She would spit out the small transponder device, which would allow her to return to it by GPS, much like the gadget the monster stuck on her car to be able to track her movements. Yes, this would be the first step in the fight-back process. Kate grinned under the hood. *The game's afoot*, she reflected.

20

"Dr. Norris, there's a reporter named Jeff Leones here to see you. Do you have some time to talk to him?" asked Shelley. At the time, Jack was reading a medical journal, waiting for one of his trainee doctors to be done with their patient.

"Sure, I'll see him in my office. Will you bring him in there?" Jack put the medical journal down and walked to his office. A few moments later, Shelley arrived with the journalist. He was a thick man with dark hair dressed in a dark blue suit and a red tie. He carried a small notebook.

"Good morning, Dr. Norris. Thanks for meeting with me," said the reporter politely. The two shook hands and sat down.

"No problem, what can I do for you?"

"My name is Jeff Leones and I work for the *Evansville Courier*," he started, presenting Jack with a business card. "A man called me yesterday evening with some disturbing news. The man wouldn't give his name, but stated that he had inside information that a lot of your patients are dying." The reporter paused momentarily while retrieving a pen from the inside pocket of his jacket. He also produced his glasses from a small case inside his coat pocket. "He urged me to investigate it," he continued, adjusting his glasses and placing the case back in his pocket. "I thought I'd start with you. Are you, in fact, noticing a lot of your patients dying inexplicably?" The reporter paused, pen and paper at the ready.

"I take care of extremely sick heart patients. Some have died. But I don't know if a lot of them are dying." Jack was taken aback with the question, not sure what to say or think. "I'll need to research it."

"Okay. Fair enough. Would it surprise you to know that my research has shown that four of your patients died unexpectedly over the past nine days? Before that, for the last three years, you had lost five patients a year, on average."

"I don't know what to think." Jack was in shock. "I need to check into it." He felt like his blood had drained from his body, a slight sensation of nausea emerging. The sudden assault delivered by the reporter's news had left him too spent to think clearly. He knew of one of his patients who arrived in the Emergency Department two days earlier in cardiac arrest who could not be saved. Four patients seemed disastrous.

"I wish you would," said the journalist. "This may turn out to be staggering. Something certainly worth your attention."

"Let me ask you a question. How do you know all this?" asked Jack.

"It's a matter of public records. All deaths are recorded and considered public knowledge. All I had to do was investigate as to who the patients' doctors were." Jeff Leones was a proud reporter and, at this time, his demeanor was that of a cat who just swallowed a mouse. "If this pattern continues, I would think this is a matter of public interest and worthy of print."

"Can I get you to please hold off on disseminating this information until I can investigate it a little bit on my end?" asked Jack.

"Sure. I'll give you seventy-two hours. Check it out and give me a call." Both men stood, shook hands, and walked out of the small office. Jack guided the reporter to the main exit and walked back toward his office.

"Shelley. Please page Shalyn for me. She's over in the hospital making rounds. Ask her to meet me in her office as soon as she can," he said, passing by the petite medical assistant.

"Sure, no problem," she replied, a worried look on her face. Dr. Norris was rattled and flustered. That was apparent to her, despite her youth and inexperience. Although she knew not why, Shelley was sympathetically disconcerted. She hurried to the nearest phone and paged the nurse practitioner, as instructed.

Jack wrung his hands as he waited in the head nurse's office. He was jumpy and tense. His brain raced a thousand miles a minute. Jack sat down and tried to collect his thoughts.

A few minutes later, Shalyn arrived.

"Hi. What's on your mind?" she asked, entering the small room. Jack was deep in thought, but her words brought him back to reality.

"Shalyn, what have you heard about my patients dying at an alarming rate? Is it really true?" he inquired, consternation in his voice.

"I know of two patients of yours who died recently. I was going to tell you when I saw you. I know one of them was stable and doing well. The other patient I didn't remember," she answered, noticing the turmoil oozing out of Jack. She sat down and faced him. "Want me to look into it?" she offered.

"Yes, please. I think we need to get our hands around the facts and, if it's true, figure out what's happening, and do something about it, quickly."

"I think we'll find out it's a statistical aberrancy—more deaths now, fewer later on. It'll all even out in the long run," offered Shalyn soothingly. "From a medical point of view, no other possibility makes sense. We give people the right meds for their heart problems and advise them on healthier lifestyles. Some get better and thrive, others don't. We're not here giving out poisons or untested therapies." She paused pensively. "But I'll get the facts for you. How did you find out about all this anyhow? Doctors are typically the last to know when patients die."

"I was just visited by a newspaper reporter who received a tip from an anonymous informant that he should look into this matter. That my patients are dying," said Jack.

"An informant? Anonymous informant? What's that all about?" Shalyn looked puzzled.

"Of course, the implication is that I'm not a good doctor and I'm somehow causing these deaths. That I don't have my patients on the right meds." Jack paused. He was in a trancelike state, the weight of this information still weighing heavily on his mind and heart.

"Now, wait just a minute. Who's saying that? That's ridiculous," interjected the nurse. "Who is this anonymous character? Someone after you?" she whispered.

"Yeah." His voice became even more subdued. Concerned. "What if he's back, Shalyn."

"Who?" she solicited. "The Rat Poison guy? Lagrange?" she murmured after a short moment.

"Maybe. It may be. Who else would want to discredit me in the community? In my world?"

"Do you think he wants revenge?"

"I thought he'd come back to poison and kill me. If this is him, he's just out to ruin me. Lucky me, huh?"

"Oh my," she said. "If that is all true, a string of deaths among our stable cardiac patients, the whole thing does have a flavor of sabotage. Nothing else would make a lot of sense. I'll start on it right away. What do you want me to look for?" she voiced. "We'll fight it. Together." She stood up, ready for action.

"Find out who has died in the last six months for all our doctors. Then, go back and get the facts for the last three years for comparison. Bring me the charts for those who have died. Let's start there."

"I'll start right now. I'll have the info by tomorrow." She prepared to exit the office.

"Shalyn. Thank you. Let's keep this hush-hush until we know more." She turned back, their eyes locking for a split moment. All was understood between them. Shalyn would be a great ally in this time of difficulty, as she had always been throughout the years they'd worked together. Alone again, Jack rubbed his right temple and contemplated the recent events. After a long moment, he grabbed the phone and prepared to call Claire. He needed her to help him think through all this. As he picked up the receiver, a voice interrupted him.

"This gentleman is here to see you, Dr. Norris." It was Shelley. An older overweight man accompanied her into the office.

"You've been served," he said emotionlessly, handing him an official-looking letter. "Have a nice day." The man exited the office and disappeared. Uncomfortably, Shelley followed suit. Alone, Jack looked at the envelope for a few seconds then opened it up.

"Shit. I'm being sued."

21

Kate was having lunch alone, sitting on an outside bench under a large oak tree. A few yards away, five ducklings followed mamma duck into the pond. The serenity expressed by the picture-perfect scene was medicinal to the young nurse. She needed time alone. Time to reflect. Time to make tough decisions about her next move.

"Hi, Kate. May I join you?" asked a familiar voice.

"Not now, Lance. I need to be alone," she said, her eyes sparkling from tears about to be shed. She sniffled.

"I don't want to bother you, but I have something very important to tell you. Please, may I have a few minutes of your time?" he insisted. She nodded. "I have some pictures to show you." Lance removed three five-by-eight photographs from an envelope he was carrying and placed them on the bench facing Kate. "Do you know this man?"

The nurse put her sandwich down on a napkin and studied the pictures. She picked one up and brought it closer. She focused on the man's face.

"This is Cesar, the new office janitor," she said after a moment of silence. "When—why did you take this picture?"

"I was just playing around with my new camera, taking pictures of this and that, when I saw you. I was sitting up there." He pointed to a branch about ten feet up the oak tree right besides them. First,

I saw you talking to Dr. Norris. Then I saw this guy several feet from the two of you. I coulda swear he was spying on the two of you. It seemed to me he was trying to listen in on your conversation while hiding from you." He paused. "So I took his picture to show you. To warn you about him." He paused again. Kate looked on, a serious look on her face.

"Wow! Thank you, Lance," she finally broke the silence. "Do you know anything about this man?"

"No. Never saw him before."

"Okay, Lance. May I keep these pictures?"

"Yes, they're yours to keep."

"I'd like for you to keep all this between us. Don't tell anybody. Don't show these pictures to anyone else. Okay? Please?"

"Sure. No problem," he said. "Are you in trouble, Kate? Because if you are, I'd like to help. You can count on me."

"You're a sweet guy, Lance." She forced a smile. "Remember, keep this hush-hush. Now, would you mind if I finish my lunch alone? I really need to think and I do that best when I'm outdoors and alone."

"I don't mind, Kate. I'll leave you be," he said, departing the area.

"See you later, Lance," she said, picking up her sandwich, her gaze back on the pictures of the janitor.

As he walked away, Lance waved goodbye. *I can't believe I got the guts to approach her. She's so sad. She must be thinking about her fiancé. They must have had a fight. No wonder she's so sad*, he thought. *Maybe they'll break the engagement. If they do, I'll be there to pick up the pieces. There's still hope for us, Nurse Kate. There's some hope.*

Lance walked to his car and used the keyless remote to unlock it. He opened up the trunk and removed from it his Canon Rebel camera already mounted with its enormous lens for close-up shots. Close-up shots of Kate. He would sneak around and click off a few, highlighting her beautiful, mesmerizing features. He had never taken her picture while she was sad, so the prospect of so doing today caused him some excitement. He grabbed his equipment and closed the trunk. In the near distance, and from behind, he heard the noise of screeching tires. He turned to see what was happening. What occurred next surprised and shocked Lance. A dark-colored van had come to a sudden halt a few feet from him. One man exited the vehicle and snatched his camera equipment. Two others clutched his arms forcibly and yanked him into the back of the van. The doors shut with a loud thud, as Cesar, behind the wheel, accelerated away. The whole operation took four seconds and remained inconspicuous. Several yards away in all directions, hospital personnel went about their business, none aware of the horror now inscribed all over Lance's face. The van continued nonstop out of the parking lot and soon it was off the hospital's campus and off sight.

22

Kate had begun to feel a glimmer of hope, now that she had a plan of action. Despite the risk it would undoubtedly carry to Amelia and her, she felt that enlisting Dr. Jack Norris was an absolute necessity. This had to be done clandestinely. The monster could not even remotely suspect it. Kate worried about who else he had in his corner, providing damning testimony of her moves. She wondered if there were spy devices in the office, and if so, where they were hidden. Her anger was slowly being overcome by angst. She experienced headaches and stints of nausea. Her palms were sweaty and her heart palpitated. Kate vowed not to allow any of these physical ailments to detract her from what she had to do next. Her baby sister, Amelia, was counting on her. Kate had arrived at the outpatient clinic early and had begun to execute her plan. She was busy at work at her desk, away from prying eyes.

When Jack entered the break room at the clinic, the murmur of the ongoing conversation was suddenly replaced by uncomfortable silence, all eyes on the newly arrived doctor.

"What?" asked Jack of the lunching group, looking at the front of his pants. "Is my fly undone?" Jack approached the table where several employees were eating.

"No. It's not your zipper," answered Gloria, one of the office nurses, worry lines all over her face. "We're concerned about you. How you must be feeling about what is going on with your patients."

"What about my patients?" The comment intrigued Jack.

"There's a rumor that a lot of your patients are dying all of a sudden," said Shelley. "People that had been doing well. That were stable, then die. Like Mrs. Tenaski."

"Roberta Tenaski died? Oh no! I hadn't heard about her. She was so sweet. And, yeah. She was rock stable and doing so well. I just saw her a couple of weeks ago," said Jack, teary eyed. "I can't believe it." The blow of hearing Mrs. Tenaski had died softened Jack's frustration with people talking about him, about his work.

"Dr. Norris, I need you to look through these as soon as you can. Right now, if possible. There are important messages and labs that need your immediate attention," said Kate, entering the room holding a stack of patient charts and breaking Jack's concentration and thoughts.

"Okay. Put them in my office, please. I'll get to them later."

"I'd appreciate it if you worked on them immediately. I need to call some of the patients *today*." Kate put emphasis on the last word. She turned around and exited the room. Confused, Jack followed her out.

"Wait, Kate. What's wrong? This is just not you. I know there's something wrong. What is it? Let me help. Please!" Jack was disconcerted. Disregarding his words, Kate continued to walk away briskly, almost galloping, and disappeared around the corner. She entered a small room, dropped the stack of charts on the desk, and exited. She closed the door behind her. A sign on the door proclaimed *Jack Norris, MD*.

Perplexed, Jack walked slowly into his office, mystified. *What the hell is going on around here? My patients are dying, my staff is looking at me differently and acting so bizarrely. And*—after standing in front of his desk for a long moment, pensively, he sat down—*Kate is behaving so unusually. There is definitely something going on. But what?* Intrigue rising, Jack picked up the first chart from the pile. In it, a yellow tab indicated the document of interest. He opened the chart to that page. It was a slip with the results of blood drawn earlier that morning. All values were normal. He scribbled his initials on the page, indicating that he had noted and reviewed the document. The second chart had a similar yellow tab calling attention to a normal EKG done earlier. Irritably, he signed the tracing. "What is the rush in doing this now, Kate?" he murmured, signing the X-ray report on the third chart. Like all the others, this had been a routine test showing no pathology, which could have been signed anytime later. Infuriated, Jack dumped the chart loudly on the *Done* pile with the others, but the next record piqued his attention. A short letter from a referring doctor captured his attention:

> *Dear Jack, I saw our mutual patient, Robert Armstrong, today. I had a meeting with him and his family, where we discussed his desire to proceed with . . .*

The letter went on and on but what stood out for Jack was the word *meeting*. It was highlighted with a yellow marker. After reading the rest of the message and signing it, as was customary, Jack hurriedly opened the next chart. Nothing there other than routine gobbledygook. No special markings. The next chart had two yellow tabs. The first was on a lab slip with the number *2* yellowed out. It was a magnesium level of 2.1, which is normal. Having this yellowed out would make no clinical sense. It had to be a message from Kate. The next chart had nothing special, but the next had a report on bacterial susceptibility to different bactericidal agents. The letters *AM* of the antibiotic AMPICILLIN were yellowed out.

"Okay, what do we have so far, Kate?" he mumbled to himself enthusiastically. It was now clear she was sending him and only him a message. "Meeting at 2 AM. Okay. Tell me where. Two in the morning is awfully early, Kate. This had better be important. Very important!" Jack smirked but hurriedly opened the next patient record. The next two charts had nothing yellowed out. The one after that had the *Metro* portion of the word Metropolitan yellowed out. A few charts later, the word *soccer* was yellowed out in a letter asking for Jack's opinion about a patient playing soccer given a history of heart arrhythmias. Having reviewed all charts, Jack concluded he had deciphered Kate's message: *Meet at Metro Soccer Complex at 2 AM*. Since there was a request from the young nurse for Jack to rush reviewing the paperwork, he understood the meeting was to take place that very night. The entire pile reviewed and documents signed, Jack calmly took the charts to Kate, who nervously sat at her desk.

"All done. I got them all," said Jack, his eyes fixated on hers. With an almost-imperceptible nod, Jack handed the stack to Kate, who immediately appeared to become calmer, a deep sigh of relief audible as she exhaled.

Not far from the place where this exchange took place, the janitor paused. He was pushing a large cart, dumping the contents of small garbage pails into his large container. Blending in with the office décor and overlooked by all, he unhurriedly walked away from the medical personnel. When he reached his janitorial closet, he removed his cell phone from his shirt pocket and dialed.

"Something's happening. I don't know what yet, but there is definitely something going on."

23

On the way home, Jack reflected on the afternoon's events. After putting their son to bed, Jack and Claire would have a long powwow. She had always been instrumental in helping him think through difficult situations.

And so it was. Sitting at the dinner table with a cup of Starbucks, the Norrises conversed. Jack filled her in on the multiple patients that had died suddenly, most of whom had been seen in the office recently and had been stable and doing well. Shalyn had collected the office charts of those who had died unexpectedly, and Jack had reviewed the information critically. These deaths had been truly unanticipated and statistically improbable, given their known stability. If any one of these patients had a cardiac arrest, any doctor would have chalked it up to the fact that sick heart patients die. Medications and standard medical care can only go so far. Jack was worried due to the coincidence of multiple rare events having occurred.

"No way this is coincidence. There's something going on," he declared confidently.

"But what? Do you think Lagrange is back? To get revenge on us?" she supposed, but not quite sure yet if she was ready to take that leap of logic. She sensed that her husband was apprehensive, even frightened, atypical feelings for Jack. This, more than anything else, alarmed her. Jack told Claire about the clever way Kate had arranged

118

a covert meeting with him. Jack could tell Kate was frightened and angry, but determined. His patients dying unexpectedly and whatever was going on with Kate had to be related, although neither Jack nor Claire had the faintest idea how.

It was ten minutes after one in the morning. In the garage of his home, Jack passed by his Lexus LS430, the car he drove regularly, on the way to the four-wheel Chevrolet Tracker. He used this vehicle when the snow piled up too high for his luxury sedan to navigate. Having come close to a crash on the way to the hospital one wintery morn, Jack realized that the Lexus was not a good car to drive in the snow. Furthermore, the luxury automobile was light silver, not a good color if you want to remain unnoticed in the dark of night. On the other hand, the Tracker was black. Since this vehicle was used infrequently, Jack kept it covered with a protective tarp, which was anchored on the garage floor with four small bricks, one at each corner. The distance between the corner edge of the tarp and each brick was exactly nine fingerbreadths. Jack used this method to ascertain that the Chevy would remain undisturbed without his knowledge. About one year ago, a teenager the Norrises had hired to watch their home while they vacationed out of town had denied moving the Tracker from the garage. Jack had the distinct impression the vehicle's position in the stall had changed and that the boy had probably taken the Chevy out for a spin. He could not be sure of his impression and the vehicle had suffered no harm, so he let the matter go. The cover and bricks would remain unsuspected and trustworthy informers of a repeat offense forevermore. Tonight, this policing tactic proved invaluable, thought Jack. He used his hand to measure the distance between the bricks and the corners. They were all exactly nine fingerbreadths. Assured the Chevy Tracker had remained untouched by evil hands, he removed the tarpaulin, opened the garage door, and drove on, as the garage door slowly closed.

The moonlight was dim due to the sky's overcast ceilings. Jack drove to three blocks away from Metro Sports Center and parked in a bar parking lot. He was sure no one had followed him. Several other vehicles in the lot would help camouflage his intentions. His would blend in with the other vehicles and, Jack hoped, would remain unnoticed to the world. Jack wore black pants and a dark blue shirt. On his head, he placed a black cap. He now had twenty minutes to walk three short blocks, which he could do easily in less than five. He would approach from the rear and hunch down by some bushes in the dark. Metro Sports Complex was the place he frequented to play indoor soccer once a week for several years. He was familiar with the building, parking lot, and surrounding area.

"Dr. Norris. It's me. Did anybody follow you?" came a familiar young lady's voice.

"No. Nobody followed me. What's going on, Kate?"

"Thank you so much for coming. I really need your help." Both her voice and her hands were visibly shaking.

"Okay. Calm down. Tell me everything." Jack's voice was soothing and reassuring.

"A man, no, a monster, abducted my sister, Amelia." She paused and removed a small picture from her shirt pocket and handed it to Jack. "He's got her in a barn on a farm about thirty minutes north of town. I don't know exactly where, but I've been there."

"Why did he take your sister? What does he want with her?" He handed the picture back to Kate, who placed it back in her breast pocket. "She's very pretty."

"I keep her picture here next to my heart. He's blackmailing me. He's had me change several of your patients' medications and some of them have died of cardiac arrests." Her pupils dilated; then her eyes began to sparkle, followed by rivulets of tears. Kate dabbed her watery eyes with the heel of her hand. Jack produced a tissue from one of his pockets.

"You're doing fine. Take your time. When you can, keep going. Tell me everything."

"He's had her for several weeks. The police think I have her. They've threatened to put me in jail. And they will soon. If I go to jail, the monster will kill my sister. He'll kill her if I go to the police. Then me. If he knew I was here with you, he'd kill her in a heartbeat. I know he can." She paused to sniffle. Jack looked around the parking lot. He noticed no one.

"You're doing great. Keep going," Jack reassured.

"He's got bugs in my apartment and in my car. I exited through a bathroom window and walked here, so he wouldn't see me leave the apartment. I only live ten blocks away. I think he's got people working with him at work. I can't trust anybody." A pause. "Except you, Dr. Norris." Kate's words were constricted by fear. No, terror!

"You did the right thing meeting with me. And it was clever how you arranged the meeting."

"I put a GPS bug by the barn. We need to get Amelia. Will you help me, please? She's so frightened. And my parents are beside themselves. My mom can't sleep or eat." More sniffles.

"We'll figure out a way to get Amelia back. I want you to take me to her in a few minutes. Can you track to her position by GPS?"

"Yes. I have the GPS receiver in my pocket." She forced a grin.

"Continue. Tell me everything. Don't leave anything out."

"The monster had me go visit several of your patients at home. I have a list of the patients. But I think he's done some visits himself. The patients are dying and they think you've recommended the medication changes. So they do it faithfully. Your patients love you, Dr. Norris." She paused for a moment and forced another smile, her blood boiling inside. She handed a list to Jack, who looked at it briefly and placed it inside his back pant pocket.

Kate then explained she had demanded to go see Amelia and how the monster had her meet him at Garvin Park when it got dark, put a hood on her head, and handcuffed her to the backseat of his car then drove her to the farm. She'd been there five times to spend an hour or two each time with her sister.

"Do you know who he is? The monster? His voice? Or his smells? Mannerisms? Anything even vaguely familiar to you?"

"No. He wears a Nixon Halloween mask. I've not seen his face. I suspect the new janitor, Cesar. He's always spying around. I think he's either him or working with him. But I can't be sure. I've racked my brain trying to figure it out. I don't know who he is. Sorry." She began weeping again. Jack held her for a long moment. "I've looked deep into his eyes. I know I can recognize him if I look deep into his eyes again. I haven't been able to connect my eyes with Cesar. He's always hiding away, like a cockroach."

"We'll find him. Don't worry," said Jack comfortingly. "When you go to the patient's home, do you go alone from your apartment?" asked Jack, intrigued.

"Yes. I get a call on a special phone he gave me and he tells me where to go and what to do."

"So there are no bugs on you or your clothes, right?"

"No, only at home and my car."

"Okay. Good. I want you to go about your normal business. Do everything he tells you to do, except don't tell the patients to change their meds. Go to the patient's home but just spend some time with them talking. See how they're doing. Since he doesn't hear your conversation, he won't realize it. Tell the monster you changed the meds, but don't. It'll be a long while until he realizes the meds weren't changed, and by then we'll nab him. And save Amelia. You have to become a good actress. Can you do it?"

"Yes," she said convincingly. "Will you call all the patients I've seen and change everything back? Please tell them I'm so sorry." Her eyes moistened again and new tears flooded her eyes.

"I will. I promise. As soon as it's safe. We need to make sure Amelia is going to be okay. What about the patients he's seeing himself? Do you know who they are?"

"He's got a huge list of your patients and he's drawing from there, but I don't know which patients he's seeing."

"Where did he get the list?"

"I printed it out from our computer at work." Kate went on to explain how she obtained the list with the inclusion and exclusion criteria commanded by the monster. "There must have been three hundred names or more," she finally said, angry with herself, her jaws contracting and her fists tightening. They hugged again for a long moment, contact much needed by Kate. She so desperately needed Jack's forgiveness. If he couldn't forgive her, she doubted she could ever look at herself in the mirror again.

"I want you to give me your permission for me to talk to Claire and to my friend Susan Quentin." Kate nodded. "Susan's a police detective, although she's on leave. She's having a baby." Both forced a quick smile. "What's the name of the detective you've been dealing with for Amelia's disappearance?"

"Brad Mills," she answered.

"Let me see what I can do about that. If you're ready, let's go see where the creep keeps Amelia."

"Dr. Norris," said Kate softly, "is this the man you stopped three years ago. The Rat Poison guy? Is he trying to get at you for revenge?"

"I think so. I'm so sorry you got involved in all this. We'll work it through. I promise, we'll do all that can be done to get back to our normal boring lives, okay?"

"Boring's good." Both smiled, hugged, and prepared to leave.

"Dr. Norris," said Kate pensively, "do you think he's bugged your car and home too?"

"I'm sure my car is bugged, but I'm driving a different vehicle tonight. I'm sure he's not touched this one. As far as my home, I have the best alarm system in the world. A hunting dog named Trinity. I'm pretty sure he's not been in the house itself. But I'll watch out for bugs around the property. I'll ask Claire not to talk about any incriminating stuff in the house or car, just in case. Now, show me where Amelia is. I'll drive us to a point nearby. Don't worry, we'll stay far enough away that he won't realize we were there."

Beneath the cloak of nightfall, both stood up from their previous crouching position behind a large shrub and inconspicuously walked back to the Chevy Tracker.

As their exodus unfolded, approximately thirty yards away from their meeting point, a low-lying bush twitched almost imperceptibly. Like an unrelenting sleuthhound, a man with dark clothes spied in the dark. It was Cesar Madera, the janitor at the office.

"He met with her," he said softly into the cell phone with a Hispanic accent when the other two were out of sight. "Just now." He listened. "Kate Fanning." Another pause. "I heard almost everything. They left together," he stated, his words nearly inaudible. "OK, will do. I'll call you later when I know more."

24

Very pregnant, Susan waddled over to the front entrance when the doorbell rang.

"Come in. Great to see you," she welcomed the couple. "I didn't know you drove a Tracker. What happened to the Lexus?"

"It's a long story," said Jack, entering the home. "I'll explain later. We brought you a caffeine-free Starbucks. We didn't want to drink alone," he added, showing Susan his cup. They walked to the kitchen table and sat down.

"He's back, Susan," started Claire. "Lagrange is back for revenge," her eyes gleaming from tears yet unshed. She sniffled. Jack hugged her for a long moment.

"I've had a weird unexplained feeling in my chest that something was wrong for a little while now. Recently, several of my patients who had been clinically rock stable suddenly had problems. Some have died. One of my nurses, Kate Fanning, met with me late last night. Some unidentified man kidnapped her sister, Amelia, and has her hidden away. This man made Kate copy patient charts from my office, then made her go visit some of the patients at home and change the medications on my behalf. I've lost five of them so far, that I know of. There may be more, and who knows how many are in trouble and about to die." Jack paused.

"So this man knows something about medicine. Lagrange sure fits the bill. Does Kate have any feeling as to who the man might be?" asked Susan, increasingly intrigued by the information.

"No, she has no clue. She suspects one of the janitors at the office. We're both sure it's Lagrange," offered Claire, poorly hidden anxiety in her voice. "When will all this be over?"

"Susan," resumed Jack after a short moment of silence, "we know you're on leave of absence. We don't want you to do anything at all, but would appreciate your thoughts in working through this."

"Of course. I'll do what I can. We'll get through this," she said, this time holding Claire's hand and looking her in the eye reassuringly.

"Thanks, Susan," said Claire.

"The first step is to get Amelia back. I know where she is. I feel awful that Kate and her sister are involved. Do you have any thoughts?" asked Jack.

"Hmm." Susan paused pensively. "I think our best bet is with the police. I don't see what else we could do without including them."

"Kate is absolutely opposed to getting the police involved. This guy has a lot of monitoring equipment all over the place," said Jack. "But I agree with you. How else can we get the girl out of there?"

"I could see about arranging a covert operation involving a small rescue team and go in during the night," suggested Susan. "We've had some success in the past with similar operations," said Susan, pausing for a beat.

"Let me talk to Kate first. I'll propose that to her. I'm meeting her again tonight," said Jack. Claire's eyes filled with trepidation and horror.

"Jack, you're not trained to engage Lagrange. Please don't try to do it yourself." The words barely escaped, obvious unrest in Claire's voice, her throat choked with emotion.

"I won't, sweetheart. I know this is way over my head," reassured Jack.

"If Kate agrees, I'll talk to my contacts at the police department and I'll try to assemble a small team of trained cops I trust that can go in and get the girl alive." Though Susan tried to disguise it, her face glowed with concern, her words distressed. "Of course, there are risks in this type of operation. Be sure Kate understands that. But there are risks in doing nothing too."

"Thanks, Susan. We appreciate your help," said Claire. Jack nodded in complete agreement.

"The next step after the rescue operation is to find out where Lagrange is. Do you have any ideas?" inquired Susan.

"I'm sure he's disguised. He probably works at Newton Memorial. I'm going to try to get a list of all people hired at the hospital and clinic over the last three years. I don't know if that'll help, but it's a start," said Jack.

"Okay. Keep me in the loop," asked Susan.

25

At two in the morning, Jack and Kate met again behind the same shrub in the parking lot at Metro Sports Center.

"How are you managing?" asked Jack, obvious unease in his demeanor.

"I can't wait till this is all over. How about you and Claire?"

"This is a tough time for all of us. Claire and I met with Susan. She thinks the best way to get your sister out of there is to go in with a small police team. People trained in this type of rescue. She'll assemble the group of officers herself. There are risks, of course. We all wanted you to be part of this decision before anything is done. The cops don't know anything yet except, of course, for Susan. Nothing will be done without your approval," Jack spoke, looking the young nurse right in the eye. He paused.

"I'm so worried about Amelia," said Kate after a long moment. "I worry if we intervene, but I worry more if we do nothing. I can't stand by and do nothing any longer."

"I understand. If you agree, Susan can get a team together within twenty-four hours."

"But I want to be nearby. I want to be the first person to comfort Amelia after she is rescued."

"Okay. I'll go with you. I'll be with you the whole way. Susan is expecting my call." Jack pulled out his cell phone. Kate nodded silently. She bit her lower lip as her eyes moistened up again. Her jaw muscles tensed. Her fists tightened.

"Susan, it's me. I'm here with Kate. She's being so brave. She agrees we need to do something. How soon can you get a team together?" Jack spoke firmly into the receiver while looking reassuringly into Kate's watering eyes. "Tomorrow at two in the morning. Let's all meet here at Metro Sports Center." A pause ensued as Jack listened. "Kate and I want to be nearby. We'll guide the team there and watch from a safe place, okay?" Jack listened intently, his ear glued to the receiver. "She won't have it any other way. And neither will I." After a short moment, Jack hung up the phone and gave an encouraging nod to Kate. Invigorated, she nodded back. Revitalized, the two hugged for a long moment, then retraced their steps back home with plans to meet in about twenty-four hours in the same place.

"It's going down tomorrow night," said the janitor into his mobile device, again ensconced in a dark spot, this time closer to the action, allowing him to eavesdrop on the previous dialogue. "The local police is forming a small assault team and they're going in tomorrow to rescue the girl's sister." The janitor smirked and listened. "I knew this would happen." Another pause. "They couldn't leave well enough alone."

By 02:50 the next morning, Jack, Claire, and Kate were in position. From approximately a quarter mile up the road, the three looked on as the small group of policemen covertly traversed the cornfield that stood between them and the small barn. Armed with machine guns, the cops hunched down as they slowly walked toward the cabin that had provided little Amelia shelter for the last few weeks. Inside, the girl slept peacefully, unaware of the circumstances lurking about. The moonlight and cloud cover added to the mystique of the occasion and aided in providing cover for the law enforcers. A cloud pergola over most of the area impeded, for the most part, unwanted illumination by the small moon overhead. The three observers from afar squinted in hopes of witnessing every move, as the small cadre pushed on. Jack gave a reassuring nod and wink toward the two women, hoping, in vain, to disguise his apprehension.

On the opposite side of the barn, there was a tall, large bale of hay stacked on a terrain elevation. Perched on top of it, a man with night binoculars watched the law enforcement agents' methodic, slow, stealthy progress toward the building. From his elevated vantage point, Cesar Madera could see both the advancing bluecoats as well as Amelia, who slept soundly on the cot inside the structure. In her wildest dreams, the young girl could not fathom the ongoing efforts to liberate her, now about seventy-five yards outside her door.

"I can't believe this, but they're really coming," he spoke softly but tensely into his cell phone. "Yes, a rescue operation." A pause. "Okay." He closed his phone and stuck it in his pocket. He shook his head slowly, still reflecting on the goings-on. In the background, katydids and bullfrogs harmonized with each other, providing nighttime hums.

As well-trained guerrillas armed to the teeth, the cops unhurriedly and soundlessly continued to approach the outbuilding, now approximately fifty yards from the structure.

The intensity of the moment was unbearable for Jack, Claire, and Kate. They felt powerless, immobilized by intense emotions of fear and horror coupled with colossal anticipation.

"I am so nervous," exclaimed Kate, stating the obvious. "I can't stand this much longer."

"I know. These guys are supposed to be great at this type of rescue. They've been assembled from all over the state. They'll get Amelia out safely," said Jack reassuringly.

"I wish we could do more. More than watch from way out here," returned Kate.

"It's all in their hands," said Claire, trying to put on a brave face.

"I'm hopeful. I am very hopeful that—," Jack started to say. What happened next smothered his words and choked his throat.

At that moment, a loud explosion and a massive flash lit up the nightfall and echoed deafeningly in their ears. Taken totally by surprise, the beholders held their breaths, their eyes fixated on the barn ablaze. In bewilderment, hands clasped mouths, hearts froze, and color drained from their faces.

"No! No! No!" yelled Kate, her words increasingly loud and panic-stricken as the unspeakable emerged into reality before her eyes. She stood up and prepared to run toward the burning structure down the hill. Jack caught up to her after only a few steps. He held her tightly, irate tears flooding his eyes, adrenaline saturating his veins.

"I'll kill that bastard. Lagrange, you're a dead man!" yelled Jack angrily. His agony and loud exclamations caused several of the police officers to turn toward Jack and the small group.

Claire joined them, and the three wept inconsolably for several long moments, floods of tears making tracks on their cheeks. The heartbreak and devastation was overwhelming to the three, paralleled only by unquenchable feelings of guilt.

"We'll get through this. We need to stay strong," supplicated Claire when she was able to speak again, hoping to impart a sense of calm to the disaster and turmoil of the situation.

In the background, Amelia's most recent abode gleamed brightly in an expanding fiery ball. Burning, the brilliant structure collapsed. Insatiable sorrow swathed Kate, Jack, and Claire.

Soon, more cops descended onto the scene. Then fire trucks and ambulances. Several minutes later, police dogs and their handlers abounded in the area, initiating a massive search, hoping to apprehend the executioner.

While Claire and Kate sat in the car, Jack made his way to the control area.

When he returned to his vehicle, he informed the women that the explosion occurred as the cadre of police officers approached the barn. None of the cops were hurt, but the structure, and everything inside it, was totally destroyed. Although a thorough search could not be accomplished until morning light, it would be improbable anyone inside the building would have survived. The search for the assassin would persist all night, but so far, no one had been taken into custody.

"I am soo sorry thees happened," the group heard as a familiar man approached them.

"This is horrible, Mr. Trepur," agreed Claire, tightening her grip on Kate's hand.

"I came as soon as I heard of eet, to offer my assistunce. I am soo sorry?" he said.

"Thanks, Nai," replied Jack. The sadness and sorrow was overwhelming and Nai Trepur's presence added some tranquility and strength. Nai slowly advanced nearer the small assembly and simply placed his hands on the shoulders of the huddled group, feeling their pain, seemingly frustrated that he could do nothing to ease their agony.

26

"How's Kate doing?" asked Susan when they arrived at her home.

"Not well. She blames herself for her sister," answered Claire. She and Jack sat down. "She's staying with her folks."

"By the way, your office and home are both free of spyware. I had the police check them thoroughly and they are both clear," said Susan. "Kate's car and apartment had several bugs but they've been cleared."

"Great. Our cars checked out okay too. Thanks for ordering those checks for us, Susan. We appreciate it," said Claire.

"The Rat Poison incident occurred three years ago," started Jack, summarizing the known facts. "Simon Lagrange escaped and presumably left the country and changed his appearance. He is now back in town to get revenge."

"Could it be a patient? Someone pretending to have heart symptoms?" interrupted Claire.

"It could be, but I don't think so. This guy knows too much about my life and me to be able to get that information as a patient who sees me once every few months. My theory is that he's been working close to me." Jack paused, noticing Susan's face, an obvious question sprouting.

"Why doesn't he just kill you? Maybe using Rat Poison again?" inquired Susan pensively.

"I don't know, but he didn't. It seems he'd rather destroy me professionally by ruining my reputation. He changed my patients' medications to make them sick. Some died, as you know," replied Jack.

"He may be out of Rat Poison to use on you. He doesn't have a way to manufacture it, since the FBI confiscated the manufacturing facility," added Claire. "Jack, you ruined his career. He wants to reciprocate. Destroying your reputation would last forever. If he were successful at it, he would simply watch as you suffer. He would find that more fulfilling."

"I think you're right on, Claire," concurred Jack. Susan nodded in agreement.

"Also, he used to have endless financial resources. He doesn't seem to have that any longer. This is to our advantage," offered Susan.

"So, he infiltrates my scene and finds out how I do things. He researches how to hurt patients by changing their medications. I think he's working with me. Around me." Jack paused.

"Makes sense," agreed Susan.

"With that in mind, I obtained a list of all employees hired over the last three years." Jack removed a computer printout with several pages from his pocket and placed it on the table for all to see. "Removing all the females, that leaves us with seventy-four men on the list. We can also remove from the list people who are less than thirty. Lagrange has to be in his late fifties, or even sixties. I find it hard to believe that any plastic surgery would make him look less than thirty. So we can get rid of the medical students and residents who are in their twenties. Of all the men left on the list, most of them work in areas of the system that I don't typically have much to do with, like the laboratory, kitchen, laundry, garage, and grounds. That leaves nine people that work with me or I see frequently. We should start there. They are highlighted on this list with yellow marker. Of these, the one that Kate and I suspect the most is Cesar Madera. He's a new janitor who was assigned to the outpatient clinic. I've noticed he hangs around the area. Sometimes I think he's listening in on our conversations. What's our next move?" Jack looked at both women, who sat pensively throughout the dissertation.

"Good job, Jack. I always knew you'd make a great detective," said Susan, hoping to inject some humor into the somber proceeding. "I'll talk to Brad and recommend he bring him in for questioning. Any other suspects?"

"There are four doctors I know and see once in a while. They're not in cardiology, but I imagine they should be looked into also, at some point. The others are security personnel and male nurses, one in the Emergency Department and another in the operating room.

"Okay, we'll start with the janitor. Meanwhile, I want you, Claire, and Nick to leave town until the situation clears up. I'll arrange for police protection round the clock until you are able to depart," demanded Susan.

"Okay," said Claire, looking at Jack, who nodded in agreement.

"I'll keep you in the loop," said Susan as she prepared to make a phone call to the Evansville Police Department.

The couple left the detective's home and walked to the Lexus parked outside. Before reaching the vehicle, Jack spoke, "Tomorrow morning, we both need to call the hospital and make arrangements at work. We'll drive to the airport and decide where to fly when we're in the air. In case anyone is listening, let's not discuss where we'll fly until then." Jack and Claire drove home in silence, both finding it hard to believe their worst nightmare was becoming reality. Again. It was dark out. By the time they arrived, a police car and two police officers already loitered about their driveway.

They greeted the officers and went inside the house. They paid and dismissed the babysitter and put Nick to bed. With Trinity, the dog, by his side, Jack walked around making sure all doors and windows were locked. From time to time, he would look outside the window to see the police car and officers in the driveway.

"Are you scared, Claire?" asked Jack.

"I'm petrified," she answered. "I'm worried about you and me, but most especially about Nick's safety."

"Me too," said Jack. "We'll be as careful as we can and think rationally through this. We'll get through this. We'll be all right, I promise." Jack petted Trinity. The dog seemed to smile appreciatively, then curled up in a ball at Jack's feet.

"Trinity really makes me feel safer," said Claire. "She's so good at warning us if anyone comes close to the house."

"Yes, she is," said Jack, scratching behind the dog's ears. "It's funny how she doesn't bark at the cops. She knows we're okay with them being out there. But I just know she'll bark if anyone else tries to come in. You're amazing, aren't you, girl? You're amazing," said Jack, massaging Trinity's head.

The couple read for about two hours, barely speaking throughout the entire time. They got ready for bed, kissed, got between the sheets, and turned off the lights, Trinity curled up next to Jack's slippers.

Outside the house, on the driveway, one of the officers returned from a walk around the home. He entered the police car. A light illuminated his sleepy but awake partner, who nodded. Silent words elucidated that all was clear and quiet and both cops sat back comfortably, their eyes scanning the surroundings.

A mysterious figure loomed outside in the dark, his back to a windowless wall. The man had approached the structure unnoticed, under the cloak of nightfall. He glanced in all directions, careful not to allow his footsteps or even his breathing to give away his position. Confident that being discovered would lead to indubitable tragedy, the perpetrator moved painstakingly, unhurriedly, cautiously. This side of the building was in total darkness, aiding his progress, to some extent soothing his frayed nerves. He reached the corner, where the moonlight provided for slight illumination. Before turning the corner, the man froze, spying in all directions, ensuring that he not be surprised by a patrolling sentinel or nocturnal passerby. He stood, unmoving, quiet, holding his breath. Certain that he would not be detected, he inched forward again, crouching. Right above his head, he touched a cold object—a metal plate. What was that? Something hanging on the wall? He looked up hoping to glance at what it was.

Jack awoke, a low-grade dog growl percolating at his bedside. It was 02:10 in the morning.

"What is it, girl?" he asked rhetorically. Claire stirred, then slowly sat up in bed, the cobwebs in her mind unraveling.

"Did you hear something?" she asked, her concern rising.

"No. Trinity growled. I'm going to check it out," he said, inserting his feet into his slippers. Their hearts hammered intensely inside their chests.

"I'll come with you. Are the cops still out there?" she asked.

"Yes," he answered, looking out the window. The dog was calm now and wagged its tail. A cold wet tongue lapped Jack's hand once then ceased. The couple exited the master bedroom, followed by the dog. They walked slowly toward the baby's room. Peeking in, they saw little Nick sleeping peacefully. They trudged downstairs toward the kitchen.

A sudden scratching sound caused the couple to stop in their tracks, aghast, and hold their breaths, their eyes keenly moving toward the clamor. The obscure noise hit them like a thousand gallons of icy water, freezing their every muscle fiber. They reflexively tensed and prepared for a fight, their fists clenched. The scraping sound they had heard was duplicated once, then again. The noise was reproduced as a tree branch brushed gently on the kitchen window near them, buffeted by small gusts of wind. With a nervous smile, Claire gave a loud quivering sigh of relief. The two relaxed, the weight of the world suddenly sliding off their shoulders. Convinced they were not in imminent danger, Jack and Claire returned to their bed and soon were deep asleep.

Approximately twelve miles due southwest from their bedroom, the mysterious man looked up to see what the metal plate he touched was all about. It was a sign. A placard. It read *Hangar M-11*. Above it, another: *Evansville Airport*. Assured he was at the right place, the man continued his slow procession toward the front entrance. Making sure no one was watching, he used a lock pick to open one of the doors. The door closed after he entered. He carried a medium-sized bag with him containing his instruments. His equipment. Once inside the hangar, the man used a flashlight to visualize Jack Norris' airplane. On its tail, the Beechcraft Bonanza proudly displayed the aircraft's identifier: *98GK*. Alone in the dark, the man climbed on the right wing and opened the door into the cockpit. As he entered the plane, he looked behind him yet again, ascertaining that he remained alone. The world was clueless to his intentions. The large hangar door budged in and out ever so faintly, yielding to the gentle pushes and pulls of the howling wind outside. The man took his handbag and flashlight and disappeared into the aircraft's cockpit.

27

It was 05:37 a.m. Kate awoke for no reason, her mind in a fog. Dazed, she staggered toward the kitchen. Being back home on the farm with her parents had given her much-needed relief. Finally, she was able to settle down and, eventually, even fall asleep for a couple of hours.

Is this the same night? she thought, perplexed, her mind slowly creeping back to reality. She walked downstairs, looked inside the refrigerator and poured a glass of milk. She sat at the kitchen table, feeling happy to be home. She scratched her head and massaged her temples, while drinking slowly. Outside the kitchen window, Kate spied the moon, competing with the waking sun for provider of illumination of the backyard and the farm beyond. She walked toward the kitchen window over the sink to observe the beauty and serenity of the developing morning. Looking outside, Kate's face reflected on the glass. Suddenly, her heart dropped into her stomach. She let go of the glass of milk, causing it to shatter at her feet. Kate gasped, and her hands, now covering her mouth, began to tremble uncontrollably. Right outside the window, she beheld a man's face staring back at her. At first, she could not place the image. Her heart pounded even harder and faster and her breathing rate quickened. After a split second of absolute panic, Kate realized she had seen this face before, but where? This man was—he was the—he was the new janitor at the office.

The man was Cesar Madera. Kate picked up a cordless phone lying on a nearby table. She tried to dial 911 but her hands shook with pulsing adrenaline, making the task impossible. Outside the window, Cesar was still and appeared especially calm, providing her no reassurance. Fumbling with the phone but with an eye on the prowler, Kate now realized there was a child standing next to the man. A young girl of about ten. Maybe twelve. No, older. They were holding hands. The child's face remained hidden by darkness. The child moved slowly toward the window, gently persuaded by Cesar. Why would he have a young girl with him? Who was she? Her skin, she could now appreciate, was much lighter than his, making it unlikely she was his daughter. Kate's mind raced, quickly trying to make some sense out of this senseless situation. She stood aghast, paralyzed by fear, unsure of what to do next. As the child's face became illuminated, Kate's demeanor changed and a big grin replaced the previous worry lines on her face. Kate realized the girl was Amelia. She hadn't perished in the blaze of fire after all. Amelia was alive.

"Amelia, you're okay," exclaimed Kate, putting the cordless back down on the table. Tears of joy began flowing down her face, a flood of pinned-up emotions released.

"Please let us in. I'll explain everything," begged the man with a slight Hispanic accent, his words hushed. He produced a badge. An FBI badge now held at Kate's eye level, just outside the kitchen window.

"Come to the back door," said Kate, pointing the way enthusiastically. She opened the kitchen door and the two entered. Kate and Amelia embraced for a long moment, both sisters weeping, tears of joy. Tears of happiness and relief.

"Sit down. I'll get you something to eat," she told Cesar, "but first I have to go get my parents. You're alive!" exclaimed Kate, again hugging her little sister. "Let's go upstairs and wake up Mom and Dad." Cesar sat down while the two girls disappeared into the rooms beyond. Soon they returned with their parents.

"Hello, my name is Cesar Madera. I'm an FBI agent. I was assigned to protect Dr. Jack Norris. I—"

"You saved our little girl! Thank you, thank you," interrupted Barbara, embracing Amelia tightly. More tears of joy.

"Yes, thank you," said Bill, shaking the FBI agent's hand. "You must be starved. Both of you. We'll make you breakfast. How about some coffee?"

"Yes, please. We've been hiding all day and have not been able to eat anything. We didn't know who to trust. We're both starving, aren't we, Amelia?" said Cesar.

"Yes. I'm very hungry. May I have hot chocolate?" asked Amelia.

"Of course, anything you want." Barbara began with food preparation, while Amelia and Kate sat at the table with Cesar. Bill was making coffee.

"Start from the beginning. Amelia, how did that man get you?" asked Kate, starved for information.

"That man found me at the mall. I was looking for Mom's cell phone. He told me he turned the phone in to mall security and guided me to their office. Except he took me to a deserted back room. He put me to sleep with a rag over my face. I woke up in the barn, where you later came to see me." Amelia looked at Kate, who nodded. "I removed that nail from the post in the barn, remember?" She paused. Kate nodded. "With the nail, I freed myself from the handcuffs. I was waiting for you so we could plan an escape. Together. Last night Cesar came and rescued me. He saved me from that fire," added the young girl nervously. Her hands trembled. Kate took her in her arms and hugged her. Barbara joined the two sisters.

"You're okay now, Amelia. It's all over now, baby," said Barbara reassuringly.

"How did you get to be in the vicinity of the barn when it exploded?" asked Kate, now facing Cesar.

"I've been following Dr. Norris. We know there's a man in town trying to hurt him. We don't know who the man is yet," began the agent. "I have been following him for weeks trying to gather intelligence. I arranged to have a janitorial job at the clinic as a cover. I followed Dr. Norris when he met you at the sports complex and later when you went to show him where Amelia was. Realizing the potential for danger when the police team approached the cabin, I went ahead, infiltrated the barn, and removed Amelia. Fortunately, just before the explosion."

The aroma of breakfast food soon permeated the kitchen, and in no time, a feast would be ready for consumption: warmed muffins, eggs, bacon, and toast with orange juice followed by Barbara's apple pie, the best pie in the world.

"Do you think you accidentally set off the explosion?" asked Kate pointedly.

"I don't think so, but I can't be sure. It is possible I tripped something. We were already outside the cabin several feet. I thought we were in the clear, so the explosion came by surprise." Cesar stopped momentarily. Thinking. "I guess I could have set something up that took several minutes to detonate. I don't know for sure."

The food was served. Breakfast commenced. Any words exchanged between them had to do with how delicious the food was, and to ask for seconds. And thirds. Kate ate slowly. Pensively. Wistfully thoughtful, still puzzled by it all.

"If you didn't trip something that detonated the explosion, that means the monster was there and caused the fire. If that's the case, then he was there late. Later than he would want to be," surmised Kate.

"I'd like to arrange for you and your family to be relocated for some time, Bill," said Cesar. "Until this whole thing clears. I'd like to put a couple of agents in here in case the bad guys return. They obviously—"

"They? Is there more than one?" asked Kate nervously.

"I don't really know for sure. Given the complexity of the situation, it is likely, but not necessarily." Kate nodded in agreement and Cesar continued, "Whoever is behind all this knows where you live and has been spying on you."

"I know he bugged my apartment and car," interrupted Kate. "The police was over my place and debugged me," she said, smiling.

"We'll check your home and car too, Bill." Bill looked at Barbara. They both nodded simultaneously.

"Sure, whatever you need to do. We appreciate all you've done already. And we are thankful for any help going forward," said Barbara, rubbing Bill's back in a loving gesture.

"Will that bad man come back again for us, Cesar?" asked Amelia diffidently.

"He might. That's why we're going to take you and your family away until we put him behind bars. Think of it as a vacation. A vacation away from home."

"What about school? School will start in another month or so. Will we have school where we're going?"

"Hopefully, you'll be back home by then." The FBI agent smiled at the girl, providing her some much-needed reassurance.

When stomachs were full, Cesar gave the Fannings his business card. Written on it was his cell phone number. The agent called the local FBI headquarters, and soon a motorcade of several unmarked vehicles arrived on the farm.

Agent Cesar Madera called Detective Brad Mills and set up a meeting with him. Back at the Evansville Police headquarters, the FBI agent confessed his previous concealed efforts on behalf of the bureau and apprised the police detective of the recent happenings. The two law enforcers compared notes and vowed to work together to bring the present situation to a swift resolution.

28

Present time

"I'm going to fly my family out of town today, but I'll return and join you and the police in figuring this out," said Jack to Susan on the phone as the car pulled out of the driveway, airport-bound. Nick was securely fastened into his car seat in the back. Trinity would stay home and guard the place from within. The dog wagged her tail as the garage door slowly descended then locked in the shut position. The couple thanked the police officer for watching over them through the night and departed.

As Jack and Susan conversed on the phone, Claire made a face. A face of resentment. She did not want Jack to return to Evansville until it was all over and Lagrange was behind bars, better yet, six feet under. But she knew there was no way to convince her husband otherwise. He was stubborn, and truthfully, if he stayed with her and away from the action, he would go berserk and drive her crazy. She was starting to accept the idea, although she knew being away from him would be nerve-racking.

"So what are you going to do when you come back home?" asked Claire.

"First, I want to spend some time consoling Kate and her family. I feel their involvement is all my fault. I feel awful about it. I promise to call you several times every day to give you briefings and get your opinion on things. Remember to use the disposable cell phones so there's no chance of Lagrange finding us somehow by triangulating our mobile signals. He may or may not be able to do that, but I don't want to take any chances. He's pretty cunning," said Jack.

"Don't worry. I won't forget. My own cell phone is off and will remain off for the duration," said Claire. "Do you have your disposable cell?"

"Yes. I'll keep it on all the time, and all communications with you or Susan will be through that phone. I'll keep my own cell phone on. I don't want Lagrange to think there's anything different going on."

The ride to the airport would be approximately twenty minutes, and soon they would fly to safety somewhere out of town. The exact destination was yet to be determined.

On arrival at the airport, the group entered the airplane after the airport crew helped Jack pull the aircraft out of private hangar M-11. After the pretaxi check of the plane, Jack obtained permission from the Evansville Tower controller to taxi to the appropriate runway.

"Nine-eight-gulf-kilo, cleared for takeoff runway 18. Fly runway heading until further instructions," commanded the air traffic controller matter-of-factly.

"Cleared for takeoff, 18, runway heading, 98-gulf-kilo," acknowledged Jack cryptically, gunning the engine. The aircraft first crawled forward but rapidly accelerated to seventy knots per hour, at which point Jack rotated the yoke and the plane became airborne.

"So, where to, miss?" he asked, looking in Claire's direction.

"St. Louis. I hear the shopping there is marvelous this time of year," she replied.

"St. Louis it is. Never been there before. This is as good a time to fly there as ever," Jack replied as he inputted crucial data into the onboard GPS. Soon the Beechcraft Bonanza was heading west on autopilot.

The trip was uneventful. The landing at Spirit of Saint Louis Airport was impeccable. Claire's cousin Jill had been contacted from the airplane and was waiting with Lauren, her four-year-old daughter.

Claire and Nick would be staying with them for the duration. Goodbyes were said and Jack took off again, this time to the east.

As his aircraft gained altitude, Jack activated the autopilot, allowing him to marvel at the breathtaking monuments that characterize St. Louis. In awe, he admired the majestic Gateway Arch adorning the magnificent, yet quaint, meandering Mississippi River, as the Bonanza progressively distanced herself from the beautiful metropolis. The cloud cover he encountered at three thousand feet prohibited further view of the city. Jack returned all his attention to the cockpit. He scrutinized the onboard instruments. All was well. His cruising altitude was nine thousand feet, which he reached a few moments later.

The first three quarters of the trip gave Jack time to think, the flight providing ample serenity to reflect. But then it all changed, as Jack was suddenly faced with Simon Lagrange, who, flying a faster airplane, was now mere seconds from revenge. Threatening to create a midair collision, Lagrange put Jack on the defensive, culminating with a cockpit explosion that filled the air around Jack with heavy smoke, and probably Rat Poison, or so Jack thought. Fortunately, he was ready for this mishap. Hidden in the cockpit was a mask, which Jack immediately placed over his face. Although Jack could not see much of his immediate surroundings, the airplane's autopilot continued to fly smoothly and straight ahead. Jack groped blindly for the small window of his cockpit and opened it. Despite the blanket of thick smoke, Jack managed to turn on all the fans. Still sightless, he stretched over and fumbled with the latch on the passenger-side door, which, with a small struggle, he managed to push open. This allowed the smoke to escape from the airplane as the poisonous gas quickly dissipated into the atmosphere. The airplane continued to fly straight and leveled. Once he could see the instrument panel, Jack removed his protective mask and took over the controls of the airplane and caused the aircraft to stall. This he accomplished by creating a set of conditions whereby the airplane could no longer sustain adequate lift. Without appropriate interventions to correct the problem, the aircraft would spiral downwards and fall out of the sky.

During flight training, stall maneuvers are practiced multiple times to teach the student pilot how to avoid the situation and, if it was ever to occur, how to recover from them. This time, though, Jack's intention was to create a full stall and give the impression that he was a dead duck and that a crash was imminent. He would spiral earthbound in a full stall, dive into the thick cloud cover, then quickly recover from the stall and land safely. That was the plan. If it worked, hopefully Lagrange would buy this as a plane crash and leave him alone, at least for a while. The problem was that Jack had never entered a full stall before. He theoretically knew what to do, but was yet to be put to the test.

The Beechcraft Bonanza plummeted three thousand feet, punching through the cloud cover, spiraling out of control. The throttle had been pulled back to minimum, but the aircraft hurled toward the ground at over 250 knots per hour, far exceeding prescribed safety limits. Jack pushed hard on the rudder pedal and pulled on the yoke, compelling the airplane to fly straight again. He was successful. Once fully recovered from the stall, Jack took a deep sigh of relief. When he had regained control of the aircraft, Jack headed to Evansville Airport. Air Traffic Control had been attempting to contact Jack, but he had disregarded their hails, hoping to give Lagrange the impression that he would crash. Despite the cold rage inside him, Jack was able to make a feathery approach, landing using a different tail number. Though illegal to do so, he would later contact the tower personnel and explain the incident.

As he sat in the airplane now on the tarmac, Jack looked at his hands. They quivered uncontrollably, the tremors resulting from the adrenaline rush still in his system. His heart pounded hard and fast and he was breathing like a racehorse. He was diaphoretic and had an empty feeling in the pit of the stomach. The color had drained from his face. He reassured himself by appreciating that he was on the ground and it was all over now. It was all over, at least for now. The process of identifying and apprehending Simon Lagrange was still afoot.

If, in fact, Lagrange bought into the crash scenario, this would give Jack a slight edge, but not for long. It would be difficult, perhaps impossible, to have the local news agencies report on a plane crash that never occurred. He would entertain this possibility and enlist Susan's assistance, if she felt this was advantageous.

Once the Bonanza was in the hangar, Jack exited the structure, but first he pulled out one of his hairs and trapped it on the hangar door approximately two feet from the ground. A small portion of the dark brown hair hung there partially visible at knee level. Visible only if one knew to look for it. The door was locked, although this hadn't stopped the perpetrator before.

Jack first called the Airport Tower. He would have a lot to report, explain, and debrief. There would be forms to fill out, statements to provide, and papers to sign.

"Honey, I'm on the ground. Do I have a story to tell you!" said Jack into his cell phone once he was done with the air traffic controllers. "I'm going over to Susan's. I'll call you from there and explain the whole thing to both of you. I want to call her first and ask her if I can come over right now," he exclaimed, speeding off the airport parking lot, but not before he inspected the vehicle top to bottom, back to front, and every nook and cranny.

29

Jack explained the airplane incident and how he barely got out alive. Susan listened intently to every word, stopping his rhythm infrequently to ask for clarification of a poorly understood point. On the speakerphone, Claire listened, giving a gasp of terror here and there, as the story unfolded.

Susan, by then aware, enlightened the others about the janitor and how he had rescued Amelia.

"He's obviously off the list of possibilities," said Jack.

"What if he is Lagrange but rescued Amelia to get us off his scent?" interjected Susan, unconvinced, the detective fibers in her body vibrating. "Remember, his objective isn't to kill Amelia. It is to ruin, maybe kill you, Jack. He may have infiltrated the FBI somehow."

"How can we further rule him in or out?" inquired the phone line carrying Claire's voice.

"I'll check with the FBI and snoop around. Let's not rule him out just yet. Nonetheless, he is lower on the list now than he had been," coached Susan.

Jack pulled out the infamous list from his pocket, the record showing the names of people who had begun employment at Newton Memorial Hospital over the last three years.

"There are still several possibilities," reflected Jack aloud. On the list there were eight names yellowed out with a magic marker.

He placed the paper on the table and turned it so that Susan could see it. She picked it up and examined it.

"The question is how we dissect this and start ruling people in and out. We'll have to go one by—"

"No way!" proclaimed Jack exultantly, interrupting Susan's thoughts. "No freaking way."

"What is it, Jack?" asked Claire.

"What are you thinking, Jack?" asked Susan.

"It can't be that easy, can it?" responded Jack. He took the list from Susan's hands and circled a name on it. He placed the paper up against a nearby window to allow the outside light to illuminate the document. This facilitated reading the marked letters backwards. "Susan, what do you see?"

"No freaking way!" exclaimed Susan enthusiastically as she read the circled name's mirror image. She shook her head slowly. "It can't be that easy. It never is."

"The two of you are driving me crazy. What are you seeing?" begged Claire, unsure of what to think.

"Nai Trepur is Ian Rupert backwards," said Jack, smiling. "Could it be a coincidence?"

"Nothing's this easy," said Susan.

"Ian Rupert, as in the doctor that invented Rat Poison, who was killed three years ago? Who used to be Lagrange's boss?" asked Claire excitedly.

"Yes. He's the one Simon Lagrange is revenging. It has to be Nai Trepur. He fits the bill. He's new since the Rat Poison incident. He joined the security forces at Newton Memorial. He's always hanging around the clinic and hospital. It has to be him," offered Jack confidently.

"Why would he use that name and take the chance of being discovered from that alone?" asked Susan.

"I can answer that one," Claire piped in. "This man has a definite sense of superiority. He thinks he's above the law. Above the police. Above Jack. This is part of the syndrome. He's a narcissist."

"You know, Kate called me earlier today. She was intrigued by the fact that the calls from the monster had stopped after the barn explosion. Now I realize why. It all makes sense. Nai Trepur, or whatever his real name is, was at the explosion with us. So he knew all about it. No reason to keep calling Kate. He no longer has the advantage. Do we have enough to bring him in for questioning?" asked Jack, looking at Susan.

"I think so. I'll call Detective Brad Mills right now and explain everything to him. I'm sure he'll agree it is time to have a chat with Monsieur Nai Trepur."

"If it's him, he really did a good job disguising himself," commented Claire.

"Amazing what bariatric and plastic surgery can do for you," agreed Jack. "That also explains the tiny scars on his face and abdomen."

"Even his voice sounds different," said Susan.

"I'm sure he had surgery there too. He's been working out. He's done a lot of work. He had a lot of money to use for this, but it does look like the money supply is probably shrinking," said Jack.

"Let's hope so." Claire's voice was softer and much more relaxed. Jack and Susan looked at one another and smiled. Jack let out a deep breath.

"We'll put out an APB on Lagrange. Every police agent will be looking for him. We'll get him," stated Susan, contentment in her voice. "You leave this to the cops, Jack. Don't go looking for him yourself, okay?"

"Of course. I understand," declared Jack.

30

Although Claire had begged him to lay low for a while, there was urgency to what Jack felt had to be done next.

The outpatient clinic nursing staff, except for Kate Fanning, assembled in the large lunchroom, at Jack's request. Kate had been given time off to be with her family and recuperate from the horror she had recently endured.

"The office is closed today and until further notice. We need as many people as we can get to call patients and go through charts. I'll get as many residents and fellows as I can to help us with this task. The situation is this: A man by the name of Simon Lagrange coerced Kate Fanning to go to several patients' homes and change their medications. He abducted her younger sister and told Kate to do this or he'd kill Amelia. We think that Simon himself has made some of these house calls as well. These med changes have caused several of my patients to die. We need to identify the patients, call them, and get them back on the right medication schedule. I need to see them in the office or Emergency Department today or tomorrow, no later. I have a list of people, but it may be a partial list." He handed the list to Shalyn Ayer, the office manager. "We need to work fast and identify those at risk. I am going to go see the news media and ask them to report on this. This should be front-page news to them. I hope that we'll get to the bottom of this really soon. Shalyn will be in charge. Any questions?" Jack continued to stand, surveying the room for inquisitive looks. He exited the break room and headed for his office. Behind him, a swarm of nurses prepared for the task ahead.

"Mr. Leones? This is Dr. Jack Norris. Do I have a story to tell you! I need you to print a story on the front page of your newspaper. May I meet with you right away?" A meeting place was arranged. Jack prepared to contact the television newsrooms to engage them in the process as well.

By that evening, the nurses and young doctors had contacted multiple patients. Kate or Lagrange had visited twenty and had their prescriptions changed drastically. Of these, eight had already had some disturbing symptoms and were advised to meet Dr. Norris in the Emergency Department at Newton Memorial. The ED personnel had been informed of the situation and were expecting the onrush. Dr. Norris would visit them in the hospital as he oversaw the process. He would explain the whole affair to the patients and their families. The patients would be observed in the hospital for a day or so, as they were returned to their previous stable medical regimen. The patients that as yet exhibited no symptoms were told to resume the medications as before and were given outpatient appointments with Dr. Norris for the next day. All would be explained then.

"Good work, everybody," thanked Dr. Norris that evening as he again stood in front of the office personnel. "Between your efforts here and the TV and newspaper, hopefully we'll have everybody back on track in no time. Thank you all for your hard work."

31

The cell phone rang while Jack was reviewing a stack of charts on his desk. He had just talked to Claire and right before that, Susan. The call intrigued him. Who could it be? Jack stopped leafing through the documents and fished the cell phone from his pocket. It was a number he did not recognize.

"Bonjour, Dr. Jack Norris," proclaimed a voice with a thick French accent. "So you survived the plane crash, huh?" continued the man, now with a hint of a southern drawl. "I knew you would."

"Where are you, Lagrange?" growled Jack.

"Have I ruined your life sufficiently yet?" inquired the man.

"Not at all. Keep trying. Come on, face me like a man, you son of a—"

"I'm going to disappear for a while, let you wonder what I'm doing, where I'm going," interrupted the man.

"You coward. Have something to say, say it to my face," barked Jack.

"When will I be back? I may be back as a Texan," he said with a heavy southern intonation, "or an Arab," he continued changing his accent to a Middle Eastern pronunciation, "a Brit?" altering it yet again.

"I will kill you, Lagrange. You fuck with the bull, you get the horns. You're a dead man," roared Jack loudly into the mobile device, attracting multiple office personnel to the entrance to his office.

Among them was Shelley, who directed Detective Brad Mills to the young doctor's office. All others scampered. Trying to get Jack's attention, Shelley meekly cleared her throat.

"Lagrange just hung up. I was talking to him," announced Jack, noticing his visitors.

"Rosie, I want you to trace a call for me. From this cell phone," exclaimed the detective after confiscating Jack's phone and dialing a number. "It's Dr. Jack Norris' cell phone," he continued. "Just happened, a few seconds ago. I want to know who called and where he called from." A moment later, he ended the call and handed the mobile device back to Jack. Both sat down. Shelley excused herself.

"Sounds like you know the whole story," said Jack.

"I do. Susan Quinton filled me in on everything," stated the detective.

"What's the plan?" asked Jack.

"The plan is we, the police, find and arrest Lagrange. You leave this whole thing alone. Don't interfere with—"

"I want to help—"

"No. Absolutely not," barked Detective Mills. His face was stern. "Look, I know you have a history with the Evansville Police Department. You helped Susan and the others find the bad guys. You were very helpful. I get that. I really do." A pause for effect. "But, not on my shift. I don't want to tell you this again. Do not interfere, Dr. Norris. I will put you in jail, if you do. Do I make myself clear, Doctor?"

"Yes, crystal clear," answered Jack gravely.

"Good. I'm as serious as a heart attack." Somberly, the detective exited the office and disappeared from sight. Jack took in a deep breath.

I know I can kill this son of a bitch, thought Jack as the detective exited his office. *I can squeeze the life out of him, after all the harm he's done to me and my family and friends. I better not find you before the police do, because I will take you down.* Jack felt the hatred bubbling inside his being, an uncharacteristic feeling, but one he could not deny. He noticed he was sweating profusely and panting ferociously, like a wild animal waiting to taste the blood of his prey. Jack detested this feeling, but he detested more that he was made to feel this way. Attempting to shake it all off, he inhaled deeply once, then again. Slowly. Deeply. Feeling the air fill his lungs, Jack began to sense his revulsion melt away, little by little. His left hand squeezed his right fist hard. His teeth still clenched. *I'll kill you, Lagrange. I'll hunt you down like the dog you are and I'll destroy you*, he mused, rancor still ruling his mood. Jack inhaled deeply again, oxygen flooding his lungs. In then out. Slowly. In and out. Slowly.

32

Detective Mills was already in the interview room when the prison guards escorted in the prisoner. The detective remained sitting for a moment, then stood, signaled the guards to wait outside and the man in the orange jail attire to sit down. The man took his seat and extended his wrists forward, showing the handcuffs. One of the guards used a small key to release the cuff from the prisoner's left wrist and attached the cuff securely around a small ring soldered to the side of the table. The prisoner sat down. The table itself was firmly attached to the floor. No words were exchanged. The two guards exited the room and the door closed behind them.

"What can I do for you, Officer?" inquired the prisoner.

"Mr. Ganz, tell me about Simon Lagrange," asked the cop, spreading pictures of the criminal all over the table.

"Simon who?" remarked the prisoner, ignoring the photographs.

"Nai Trepur, Joshua McCarthy—"

"I don't know anything about him. I'm in prison. I've been here for three long years."

"And you have many more to go. I may be able to make your stay here a little bit more comfortable. What do you need? A computer? Your own TV? Dope? What?"

"Thank you for your concern, Officer"—he paused, searching for the name tag hanging from the detective's breast pocket—"Brad Mills. But I'm really quite comfortable already."

"Okay, how about helping me as a gesture of your desire to do your civil duty?"

"Civil duty? Me? I have no civil duty."

"Then help me as a fellow detective. An ex-cop. Help me find Lagrange."

There was a short pause, followed by intense laughter from Mike Ganz. This boisterous hilarity continued for an uncomfortably long moment. "I should help you because I'm an ex-cop?" Another chuckle. "That's your argument? I'm a bad guy now. I'm on the other side of the fence, Detective Mills, of the Evansville Police Department," said Ganz, now with a serious tone of voice. "I have nothing to tell you. I'm missing *Wheel of Fortune* for this? Guards! Take me back to my cell." The prisoner stood up and banged his left arm on the metal table loudly. "This bozo is wasting my time."

The two prison guards arrived and, without a word, released the handcuff attaching Ganz to the interrogation table and escorted the prisoner out of the small room, leaving Detective Mills alone. He gathered his belongings and walked toward the main entrance. He passed by many groups of people—guards, prisoners, visitors, and lawyers—all coming and going. The Terre Haute High Security Federal Correction Complex was certainly a busy place, housing the worst of the worst Hoosier criminals. The place gave Mills the creeps, and he couldn't wait to get in his car and hit Route 41 South on the way back home. The sooner he exited the large building, the better. His disgust with the place was probably the main reason why Detective Mills, usually an exceedingly observant man, failed to recognize one of the prison guards that passed a few inches from him. The man was dressed in the typical blue uniform, his name tag proclaiming his name to be *Jimmy Nutley*. As the two passed each other, Lagrange looked away to avoid detection when he himself noted the Evansville detective. At that precise moment, Officer Jimmy Nutley, a.k.a. Simon Lagrange, felt his heart fall to his stomach and the color drained from his face. The feeling faded away quickly, as he noticed that the detective did not recognize him. He stopped for a second then looked back at the retreating police officer, who he knew was on the hunt for him. Simon Lagrange smirked and kept on walking.

"That was a close one," he whispered to no one.

33

Jack Norris was in his office working fast to continue to identify all the patients who may have been contacted by Kate or Lagrange.

"Hey, Jack," said a familiar voice entering the small room.

"Hi, Cesar. What's going on? Got some news for me? Have a seat."

"Yes, I came by to give you some news, as promised. The FBI lab analysis determined that the bomb in your airplane was the same material used in the killings of three years ago. What was it called? Rat Poison?"

"Yes. We called it that. That's very interesting. Does that mean he is able to manufacture more material?" asked Jack.

"The stuff was weakened and old. We think this is the last of the material he's had for the last three years. It is our feeling that he is no longer able to manufacture the materials, which is great news for us," said the FBI man. "None of the bombs in the barn were of this material."

"Did you find anything interesting in the barn? Any clues?"

"No. It was burned to the ground. Nothing there of interest."

"Any clues as to where Lagrange might be hiding?"

"No. Everybody's looking for him. But so far, no luck."

There was a moment of silence between the two men.

"Wanna go get a cup of coffee? I'm buying," said Jack, getting up from his chair with a forced smile.

"By the way, do you know a Lance Lantz? He works here in the lab," asked Cesar.

"I know of him, why?" answered Jack.

"He came close to breaking my cover when all of this was going down. We had to take him into custody for a little while, but he's back to work. Poor guy peed all over his pants in my van. Can't get rid of the stench."

"That's what happens when you go around snagging innocent people," said Jack.

"Innocent? He's been stalking and taking pictures of your nurse, Kate. I still don't think she knows anything about it. But, I'm not sure she'd approve of it. It's all harmless, but I don't think he'll do it again."

"Let me guess, you scared the *piss* out of him, right? Now you're complaining about it."

"Let's go get some coffee. What do you say, Jack?"

"Let's."

34

The sun peeked over the horizon, illuminating the east part of the compound. Outside the scattered buildings, all was quiet, except for the slight noise created by the wind from the southwest. Inside the large federal penitentiary, the morning buzz was beginning. The morning bell rang, signaling that it was time to get up, clean up, and prepare for chow. At breakfast, the food would be obtained while in an orderly line and little talking would be permitted. Once the inmates were seated at the long table, the guards would gesture that conversation could resume. The decibels in the air would rise appreciably.

The Terre Haute High Security Federal Correction Complex was a huge place full of bureaucracy. Contriving a plan to become part of the staff, however, was actually easier than to infiltrate the Newton Memorial Hospital security force, in part because at the latter, a directorship was necessary. At the correctional facility, a grunt position was desirable to accomplish the project.

"Hey, you. Ganz. Over here, in a double," spat the guard authoritatively, getting the prisoner's attention. Mike Ganz was tossing laundry in the oversized washing machine. The large room was steamy and noisy, but otherwise deserted. Before speaking, Officer Jimmy Nutley, a.k.a. Simon Lagrange, had ascertained that the two were in fact alone.

"Papa. It is you," grinned the inmate poignantly, quickly curtailing his emotional display. "You came. As you promised," he continued, now in a quiet monotone. Mike's first instinct had been to smile and run over to the newly arrived man for a long hug, but the effort was quickly arrested. He knew there were cameras everywhere. It would be important for it to appear to a potential viewer that the guard was speaking of chores to be done or chastising him from a previous action or inaction. That the father and son longed for each other's company and had much catching up to do was to remain concealed.

"I don't have much time. Listen carefully. Memorize my instructions precisely," instructed the guard sternly and expressionlessly. The two conversed for several minutes. Every few seconds, shifty eyes would wander side to side, indiscernibly looking for potential hidden ears. He nonchalantly walked around the room as he continued to speak. Mike Ganz soaked it all in, like a sponge, the information etched deeply into his brain.

"Merci, Papa," said Mike, continuing to perform his daily chores.

"Remember all my lessons, Ganzo. Know your prey. Know your enemy. Know all about them. What time they get out of bed. What they have for breakfast. The route to work. The favorite food and drink. Everything. This takes time and patience. Lots of patience. Drive by their home many times until you know all about them. Work with them, side by side. Watch them. See how they interact with their habitat, their companions and coworkers. Observe. Take notes. All this may become useful as you carry out your missions."

"We'll be together soon, Papa."

"Don't write anything down, Ganzo. Remember the numbers: 9142300. Exactly! Got it?"

"Yes, Papa. I got it." Mike Ganz strived to remain emotionless outwardly, but inwardly, he was dying to show his devotion and admiration for his father. But he mustn't.

"Au revoir, Michel," said the guard in French. "See you soon," he reiterated, now in perfect English, as he exited the room. He would finish his shift on the opposite side of the prison, ensuring that the two would not meet again. He would later drive home and put his letter of resignation in the mail, invoking health reasons to relinquish his newly appointed position as a prison guard.

Simon Lagrange was pleased. This portion of the mission was executed without a hitch. All was well.

35

The two lovebirds sat opposite each other at their favorite table in their favorite restaurant.

"Are you sure you understand why I had to break up with you?" asked Kate, looking the young doctor squarely in the eye.

"I do. I do. I wish you had trusted me, but I also see that you didn't want to involve me and jeopardize Amelia."

"It's not a matter of trust at all, Frank. It was a matter of putting you in danger and, yes, jeopardizing Amelia's safety. I didn't know who was on his side at the office. I knew he had bugs all over my car and apartment. I didn't want you in there. I didn't want to put you in danger," she said tenderly.

"I know, Kate. It's all over now. We have Amelia back and—"

"It won't be over until Simon Lagrange is behind bars or dead," she spat. It was obvious the wounds were still fresh and unhealed. Kate took a deep breath. Then smiled. "I'm sorry, Frank. This is so upsetting to me. I need to let it go."

"And you will. With my help, this *time*," said Frank. "Do you know anything about Simon Lagrange? What's happening to him?"

"No one has heard from him in many weeks. He is on the FBI's Most Wanted List."

"I've seen him on TV many times. He's been in the news. Do you think he'll return to Evansville?"

"I hope not, for his own good. I'll strangle his neck. I'll shoot him dead, if he shows up around here." Kate's demeanor changed again from Nurse Jekyll to Ms. Hyde as the terror inside began to percolate once again. She took a deep breath and smiled at Frank. "So the wedding's still on, right?" she asked, putting on a happy face and changing the subject.

"Are you kidding? I can't wait to wear your ring, sweetheart. Of course it's still on."

"Are you ready to order?" inquired the server politely, approaching the table.

The couple had a scrumptious meal then drove to his apartment. The time they spent apart and the excitement of the last several days had made them yearn for each other. Finally alone, Frank locked the front door, isolating themselves from the world. He took off his jacket and threw it on a nearby couch. Her desire expanding by each tick of the clock, she grabbed his tie and pulled him toward her. Hurriedly, he unbuttoned her sweater. He searched then swiftly unfastened her zipper. Her dress fell at her feet and she stood facing him, wearing only her bra and panties. She unbuttoned his shirt, then his trousers. Soon, the couple stood naked, kissing, touching, caressing each other ever so softly. They embraced lovingly. Frank carried Kate to the bedroom and placed her gently on the bed. Tender kisses exchanged accentuated by erotic gentle massages and embraces. All undergarments were gently and slowly removed, and soon he was on top of her.

Several miles away from Frank's apartment, another couple rejoiced in one another's company. Dr. Jack Norris and his lovely wife Claire were together again. All was quiet. The police would keep a close eye on their home and all was, little by little, returning to normal.

"I'm so happy you two are back home," said Jack, sipping from his wine glass.

"We're happy to be home too. Although Nick had a great time with his cousin. They played constantly. Lauren is a great little girl. They got along famously." Claire paused to sip her wine. "I missed the hospital and my patients too."

"Are you nervous about Simon Lagrange?" he asked.

"I will be until he is apprehended. You?"

"Me too."

"But life goes on, and we must continue with our lives. We trust in the police. I know everything is being done to put him behind bars." Another sip.

"We can't think too much about it."

"Do you think he changed appearances again? Moved away? Maybe out of the country? Where would he go?" she pondered.

"I don't know. He's got connections in France, so if he leaves the country, he would probably end up there. But, I can't help but think this is not over yet. He'll want to finish the job and get his pound of flesh. His revenge."

"Why wait, though? Is he letting things cool off to catch us off guard again?"

"Yes. I'm sure he is. But I'll be ready for that son of a bitch. This time, I know I would kill him." Jack's muscles tensed. His breathing deepened.

"Do you really think you could kill someone, Jack?"

"I know I could kill him. In a heartbeat," he replied, taking slow deep breaths, calming himself down. The wounds of late had penetrated the scars of years back. And the healing would not begin until the ordeal was over.

36

Simon Lagrange closed the door behind him as he exited the small room. Over the door, a label read *Men's Dressing Room*. He was wearing green scrubs. A tag over his left breast displayed a hospital's logo *Clarian Health System* and stated *Chad Kingston, RN*. Also displayed was a young man's picture, which clearly did not resemble the bearer. With some bodily discomfort, Simon Lagrange moseyed down the hall, slowly. He walked by a window and paused. Outside in the distance, large spotlights overhead dumped illumination on a group of young boys playing soccer: moms, dads, and grandparents rooting them on with spectacular fanfare. Mesmerized by the hullabaloo, he allowed his mind to wander and mix with the brilliant lights. The past came to being.

"Kick the ball, Ganzo. Kick it now," shouted the Simon Lagrange of years past. He was in his thirties and portly. At his side, another man in his twenties sat on the bleachers.

"You're such a dad, Simon. Let the boy play in peace," said Ian Rupert. Ian was thin with thick dark brown hair. He was wearing a suit, distinguishing him from all the others.

"I know. I get so excited. I can't help myself," said Simon. "When do you go back to school?"

"Mid-August. I can't wait. I love med school. I love to discover. I love to learn."

"What kind of doctor do you want to be when you grow up?"

"A good one. I don't know yet. I don't want to work primarily with people. I don't like people. They can be disgusting. And demanding. Maybe radiology. Or pathology. Something where I don't have to take care of people."

"Get there, Michel. Run faster," barked Simon excitedly, now on his feet yelling toward the soccer field. "Sorry," he said when the play was over. He sat back down. "How about research?"

"What?" asked the young man.

"Research. What about doing research when you finish medical school?"

A group of residents walked by the contemplative older Simon, bringing him temporarily back to the here and now. Clueless, the bunch walked rapidly and conversed thunderously. There was occasional loud laughter. The cluster passed by and Simon resumed his slow walk, holding on to the walls. The corridor was again deserted and silent. Simon's mind drifted back in time once again.

"Do you promise to uphold the laws of the United States of America and its Constitution to the best of your ability?"

"I do," solemnly stated the whole group in unison, each person's right hand up in the air. The answer essentially ended the ceremony whereby the new FBI agents were now sworn in. Applauses abounded from the audience.

"Are you proud of him?" asked Dr. Ian Rupert, now older. He wore a suit, his hair impeccably combed.

"I am so proud of my little Ganzo. I'm proud of you too, Ian. When do you start your new job?" asked Simon Lagrange, still clapping and looking at his son, standing on stage with the group of new FBI recruits. Simon was now in his forties. He had gained more weight, causing him to move slower.

"I start this July."

"What will you be doing, exactly? And where?" asked Simon.

"It's a research position in Indianapolis. Indiana University. I'll be the head of cardiovascular research. You should move there with me. It's a nice city."

"You'll be the head of the whole department in no time. I know you, Ian. Mark my words." Simon looked at the young doctor. "My Michel too. He'll go up the ladder of ranks in the FBI quickly. Just like I did when I first started in the French Secret Police."

"You haven't told me much about your previous life in France," asked Ian, intrigued. "Tell me more."

"I started when I was Michel's age. Within five years, I was a captain. That's when I was handpicked to come to the United States to become the head of security at the French Consulate here in Washington. It was a big step up from being a demolition man. I went from being a bomb expert to babysitter to a whole bunch of diplomats. But I took to the new job like I had been at it all my life. Now, I'm tired. I'm thinking about retirement. I've been doing this for far too long. Maybe I'll go into research. Cardiovascular research. With you, huh?" The two men smiled. Michael Ganz approached the two, interrupting the conversation. Long hugs between the three men ensued.

A smile still on his face, Simon Lagrange continued to walk slowly down the hall. He reached an elevator and pushed the *down* button. While waiting, Simon's mind wandered back in time, again.

"I am working on a drug to help patients with heart failure," stated Dr. Ian Rupert, the sign on his desk proudly proclaiming he was now the head of research at Newton Memorial Hospital.

"What's the drug called, Ian?" asked Simon Lagrange, sitting comfortably and sipping from a coffee mug. Simon was now in his late fifties. He looked to be older, given his significant weight gain.

"It doesn't have a name yet. We refer to it as LFJ659," answered the director. "I've done all the bench work on cell preps, and it looks great. I'm about to begin research on rats. Once that's done, we'll go on to the human phase."

"I am very proud of you, Ian. You have done great work. I have read all the papers you have written. I am so proud of you. Your dad would be proud of you too." Simon wiped a tear from his eye. "Your dad was my best friend. The best partner I ever had."

"You are not responsible for his death, Simon. Don't blame yourself," said Ian.

"I was the one that told him to enter the building from the back while I entered from the front. The explosion was—," the words choked Simon's throat.

"It wasn't your fault. And you have become a great dad to me. You have done more for me than he ever did. He was always so busy. You have always had time for me. And for Michael. I am forever grateful to you." After a pause, Ian continued, "I have a job for you. Here in Evansville. My research lab director just retired and I want you to take over that position. I'll teach you everything you need to do. You can help me with the new drug. I have high hopes for it. I think it'll help many patients feel better and live longer. What do you say?" finished Ian enthusiastically.

"I retired from the police force. I will think about your offer," said the rotund older man.

"Put it there, Simon," said Ian, smiling, extending his right hand.

"I've changed my name; I don't want my previous identity to linger on. There are a lot of bad guys still looking for me."

"Is one of them the man who killed my father?" asked the director.

"I wish I knew," said the older man after a long pause. "Simon Lagrange is dead. My new name is William James." The two shook hands.

The elevator descended slowly to the basement, and the door opened. The older man in green scrubs shuffled out of the car and proceeded down the hall.

Because of Jack Norris, my son's in jail and Ian Rupert is dead, he mused. His eyes welled up with tears. *Ian was a son to me. For that, you will pay, Dr. Norris. I will ruin you forever. I will get my revenge.*

He reached his destination. A sign on a door read *Pathology Laboratory.* He stood up straight and walked in. The door closed behind him.

37

The day had been long with very sick hospitalized patients to manage. Now, it was time to go home and recharge. Jack longed to see Nick and Claire, but he would have to settle for a phone call, his loved ones out of town for the day. He planned on a long jog with his evening canine companion, Trinity. The outdoors would do him a lot of good. Jack walked out of the main building with two of the medical students, discussing details of their required homework assignments for the next day.

"Hey, Dr. Norris. Is it Miller time for you?" asked the security guard.

"Hi, Dillon. How're you doing in your new position?" asked Jack, waving goodbye to the students, who walked back into the hospital.

"It's a piece of cake. It still blows my mind that Trepur—huh, Lagrange, was able to fool us all. If I could get my hands on that bastard—" The guard stopped in midsentence, his gaze far deep into the parking lot.

"What is it?" asked Jack.

"I just thought I saw him. Probably not him." Dillon looked intently into a group of visitors deep in the parking area.

"Where? Where did you—? Yeah, I see him too. Come on, Dillon. Let's go get him." Jack darted off toward the man they

---

171

thought might be Lagrange. From their vantage point, the two observed a man walking away from them who was getting into a small light blue vehicle. Maybe a Honda. Maybe a Ford or Chevy. The person had similar hair characteristics and body build to Lagrange's. At this time of day, many people were coming and going, in and out of the area, so the progress of the two men was slow.

"Hey, you! Stop!" yelled the security officer as they made their way into the lot.

"Is it really him?" asked Jack.

"I'm not sure." They continued to weave in and out of groups of people, hurriedly hoping to stop the man who was now starting up his car.

"It may not be him," said Jack. The car drove off its parking space and slowly proceeded toward the exit. The two men continued their foot pursuit.

"Pete to Dillon, come in, Dillon," yelled the walkie-talkie hanging from the guard's belt. The two stopped, Jack's eye still on the moving auto.

"This is Dillon, what's up, Pete?" said the officer into the device.

"We have a dispute here in the office. Can you come by right now?"

"Sure, I'll be right there. Over and out." The security guard locked eyes with Jack. "It's probably not Lagrange, and by now the car's probably out of the hospital grounds. Sorry, but I gotta go." The guard walked briskly back toward the hospital, leaving Jack alone, amongst busy strangers who walked by in all directions. Jack turned toward the position where the suspect vehicle was lasted spotted. *There he is. He's behind some stopped cars.* Jack ran to the doctor's parking garage, which was only a short walk away. He entered the Lexus and drove rapidly to the exit. He stopped at a red light on St. John's Drive and Washington Street. The light blue car had already exited the hospital campus at another street up the road and was now going by the intersection where Jack waited. *It's a light blue Nissan.* As the vehicle drove by, Jack was able to get a better glimpse of the driver. Though he still couldn't be sure it was Lagrange, the resemblance was great. Jack took a right turn and accelerated. The van behind him hit his brakes then honked his horn loudly, having been cut off. Jack raised his right hand apologetically and looked in the rearview. The Nissan was about five cars ahead of him as he stopped at a red light. Jack opened his door and planned on dashing toward the other vehicle, when, after only one and a half steps, he noticed that the SUV in front of the Nissan turned right at the red light, and so did the light blue car.

"Huh, don't do this to me," said Jack to himself as he ran back into the Lexus. The light turned green, and the van behind him honked loudly once more. Jack raised his hand contritely and rushed to reenter his vehicle. Soon the traffic was moving forward again, but slowly. Jack turned right as soon as he could. He drove on, all the while spying for the compact car. *There you are!* he thought when he saw the vehicle again up ahead. The Nissan was now about ten cars in front of him. After a few more blocks, the light blue car turned left. Jack imitated the move as soon as he could.

"Where are you, Lagrange?" whispered Jack as he slowly inched Green River Avenue, his neck craned hoping to spot the Nissan. The light of day had been mostly replaced by dusk as the diving sun little by little disappeared into the horizon.

"Hey, you jerk. Watch where you're going!" yelled a man in his twenties, who was crossing the intersection. The light had turned red, but Jack hadn't noticed. The man thumped the hood of the Lexus forcibly, yanking Jack's attention into reality.

"Sorry, man. My fault," said Jack, his right hand in the air. As soon as the pedestrian crossed the road, Jack's mind was back on the mysterious man's car. The light turned green and Jack gunned the accelerator once more. *There he is*, thought Jack, spying the vehicle. The eight cylinders kicked in as the Lexus sped on. The compact car turned left and so did Jack, now only three cars behind. The Nissan turned right into a driveway. Although there were wall-to-wall houses on both sides of the street, there was nobody around. A garage door started its sluggish upward motion, as the man sat in the small vehicle. Jack turned onto the driveway and parked inches from the Nissan.

"Hey, sir. Can I talk to you for a minute?" yelled Jack, exiting the Lexus. "Is that you, Lagrange?" Startled, the man slowly and nervously turned to see who was causing all the ruckus.

38

The three people that made up the cleaning crew were hard at it. Raul, Maria, and Sabrina were two hours into their chores, which would typically take three to three and a half hours every day. The outpatient clinic was otherwise deserted at this early time of the morning. Soon, the nurses, patients, and doctors would arrive, and they would all expect the place to be presentable. Still left to clean were the back bathrooms and the five small offices. Mexican music blared loudly from a portable cassette player, accompanied at times by Raul. He took the men's bathroom, while Sabrina entered the women's, each propping the door open. Maria went into one of the offices. It was pretty well organized and little effort would be required today. A sizeable pile of charts in a wooden box labeled *To Do* was positioned in one corner of the desk. Otherwise, the clutter was minimal and could be left alone. Maria emptied the trash from the small metal can under the doctor's desk onto her larger garbage container, which she wheeled around the office. As she placed the emptied canister under the desk, she pushed the chair over, causing it to fall with a thunderous racket. Disgusted with her clumsiness, Maria walked over to pick up the fallen furniture. As she did so, she noticed a fresh, small, round-shaped crimson stain on the carpet.

"Sangre?" she mused. "Blood?" The drop grabbed her attention and piqued her curiosity. A few feet away, two more drops, then another, all leading toward the closet. As usual, the closet door was closed, but the doors were unlocked. Maria opted to take a look-see inside. She opened the closet doors. A light automatically turned on, illuminating the inside of the small space.

"Ay, Dios mio!" she exclaimed loudly.

"Que paso?" said Raul as he rushed in. "What happened?" Maria was frozen in place, her hands cupping her mouth and face. Raul stepped in the direction of her gaze. Sabrina ran in as well. Her inquisitiveness took the best of her and soon she was at Raul's side investigating that which so frightened Maria.

"Que es?" she asked, approaching Raul.

"Call 911. Rapido," he shouted. Sabrina, who spoke the best English, picked up the phone and dialed.

Within minutes, sirens were heard just outside Newton Memorial Hospital, and soon thereafter, two officers arrived in the outpatient clinic area. One of them spoke Spanish to the excited cleaning crew, who directed him immediately to the closet. The door was ajar. On the floor, in the corner, barely out of sight, the cops beheld the unmistakable evidence of a crime.

"Call the Crime Lab, Matt," commanded Sergeant Pedro Sanchez to his subordinate. "I'll work on getting us a search warrant. Don't touch anything. They'll want to dust for fingerprints."

"What is it? What's in the closet?" asked the younger cop, vying for position to see the mysterious contents.

"It's a bloody T-shirt."

"This is a cardiology office, right? Maybe they study blood in here, Sarge."

"You may be right. But there are also fresh blood drops," said Officer Sanchez, pointing at the stains right outside the closet and behind Jack's chair.

"What's under the T-shirt?" asked the younger cop, using a pen to lift up the jersey. "Wow. Now, I'm convinced." Partially hidden by the shirt was a large, serrated hunting knife, its blade measuring approximately seven inches. It was stained with blood.

"Yikes, this is the real McCoy," said the older officer.

The call to headquarters was placed, and soon the room was crawling with criminologists. A court order had been verbally obtained. The closet and its content were photographed copiously from multiple angles. The bags containing the bloody garment and the bloodied knife were confiscated and processed to be examined in detail macroscopically and microscopically in the lab. The plastic evidence bags were labeled *"Obtained from a closet in the office of Dr. Jack Norris."*

An hour later, a search warrant was obtained and a Lexus sedan in the doctor's parking lot was searched. One of the officers jimmied opened the driver's door, and eventually, the trunk lid was popped. In the trunk, a bloodied machete was uncovered. Also, there was a small Styrofoam cooler.

"Looky here! Look what I found," said Detective Brad Mills, uncovering the lid of the cooler, visually inspecting its contents. Three cops approached the trunk of the car.

"What the hell is that?" one of them asked.

"It's a heart. I think it's a human heart," said the detective, his eyes fixated on the fleshy organ mostly submerged in ice. "Call the Crime Lab people. We need this processed as soon as possible."

"How do you know it's a human heart, Brad?" asked one of the uniformed cops.

"I actually pay attention when I attend the autopsies at the medical examiner's office. I'm fascinated by how the body works," he answered proudly.

"Well, we'll soon see if you're right. I'll be impressed if you are." One of the cops made a call to headquarters using his radio while the others returned to their assigned posts and duties.

The items were photographed, processed, then transported to the Crime Lab, to join the previously gathered material evidence. The organ and tissue, as well as blood on the machete and knife, would soon be analyzed and identified.

In an hour's time, some of the answers were in. This was definitely a human heart. It was relatively fresh and did not contain formaldehyde or any preservative as would normally be used in teaching specimens. Genetic material testing was pending, but the preliminary results were known.

"Hello," said Detective Brad Mills, answering his mobile phone.

"You're not gonna believe this, Brad. It's Simon Lagrange, the guy you've been after for months. It's his heart," said the criminologist assigned to the recently discovered lifeless organ. "I've also determined that Simon Lagrange, Nai Trepur, and James Miller are all one and the same person. Exact DNAs."

"No shit. It's his? Are you sure?" asked the detective.

"Genetics don't lie, my friend. One hundred percent match. It's him."

"Can you say anything about mode or time of death?"

"Can't say much. I can tell you that the murder occurred more than four or five days ago, but less than two weeks."

"Okay. Thanks for the call. Let me know as soon as you find out more." Brad disconnected and paused for a moment, scratching his head. "He went ahead and did it. I can't believe he really did it."

An arrest warrant was sought and obtained. The hunt for the obvious killer was afoot.

39

Jack Norris and his medical students, interns, and residents had started rounds about two hours before. His beeper alerted him that someone in the outpatient cardiology clinic needed his help. He dialed the number.

"This is Dr. Norris. Shalyn paged me."

"One sec. I'll get her." A pause.

"Good morning. Have you been to the clinic this morning?" said the nurse practitioner a few moments later.

"No, I started at the hospital today. We're making rounds now. What's going on?" he asked, intrigued.

"The cops are all over the place. They roped off your office." With these words from Shalyn, Jack felt like someone sucker punched him in the stomach, forcing the air out of his lungs. He felt drained, as memories of the massacres of years ago resounded loudly in his head. A feeling of doom grew in intensity as he spied three cops in uniform come around the corner. The police officers walked briskly toward him.

"Dr. Jack Norris, you are under arrest for the murder of Simon Lagrange. You have the right to—," proclaimed one of the officers monotonously, a memorized string of words.

"Woah, woah, woah! Hang on," interrupted an excited and flabbergasted Jack. The recent events were unfolding way too rapidly for his mind to comprehend. "I killed who? When? How?"

Jack did not know what to say. His brain was racing too fast for him to catch up.

"Remain silent," continued the cop. "Anything you say can and will be held against you in a court of law." The officers forced Jack's hands behind his back, and within seconds, he was in handcuffs.

"You're making a mistake. I didn't kill anybody," protested Jack as the cops escorted him down the hall. "This is a mistake," said Jack, addressing the medical students as he was being shoved away. "Find another attending physician and finish rounds."

The medical personnel stood there, dumbfounded. Perturbed. Jack and the cops turned the corner and were out of sight. The young doctors looked at each other, none knowing what to say.

The cops were nice enough to enter and exit the hospital via a back entrance, so most of the routine at Newton Memorial remained undisturbed.

When the group reached the parking lot, Jack was guided into the back of one of the squad cars. A patrolman sat behind the wheel and the journey to the police headquarters began. Detective Brad Mills arrived from the outpatient clinic and sat in the front passenger seat.

"So, why did you keep the heart?" asked Mills nonchalantly.

"I kept the what?" asked Jack.

"The heart. When you killed Lagrange, why keep the heart? You like souvenirs?"

"Wait a minute, I didn't kill anybody," interrupted Jack.

"Look, I understand why you did it. I mean, you told me you were going to do it, last time I saw you. Of course, I told you to leave it alone. I must tell you, though. We've been looking for him all this time. How did you find him before we did? Did he come to you? Did he threaten you and your family again? I don't blame you, really. I probably would have killed him myself. But, I wouldn't keep the heart as a souvenir."

"No. Nothing like that. I did what you told me. I left it all up to you. I haven't seen or heard from Lagrange in weeks."

"So, what's his heart doing in your trunk? And his bloodstains in your car? And the machete?" Mills persisted.

"I don't know. I didn't put them there. I'm being framed. Can't you see?" beseeched Jack in agony. "I'm being framed!"

40

Jack was taken through the arrest process, fingerprinted, and photographed from the front and side. He was given the opportunity to make a phone call. Jack called Claire. After what seemed to be an eternity of waiting inside a filthy cell, Jack was escorted to the interrogation room. After a long while, Detective Mills came in with a cup of coffee and a cardboard box labeled *Simon Lagrange—Evidence.*

"Sorry, we don't have Starbucks," said the interrogator, placing the burnt coffee in front of Jack. "Do you take sugar or cream?"

"No, thanks. This is fine," lied Jack, the stench of bad java hitting his nostrils.

"Are these your clothes?" asked the detective, throwing a bag on the table in front of the prisoner, containing workout garb visibly stained with blood.

"I don't know, maybe," said Jack hesitantly as he picked up the sack.

"Here, let me make it easier for you. He grabbed the plastic bag and turned it so Jack could read the words on the backside of the shirt: *Norris* on top, *The Heartbeats* under that, and a large number 7 underneath it all. "This is your soccer team jersey, isn't it?"

"Yes."

"We found it in your office. These bloodstains on your jersey were tested," said the detective, pointing at the crimson blotches.

"The blood belongs to one Simon Lagrange. How do you explain all this?"

"I'm being framed. Someone wants you to think I killed Lagrange, but I didn't."

"Do you know Dillon Pierson?" asked Mills.

"Sure, he's a security guard at Newton. He's in charge now. Why?"

"Did he see Lagrange on hospital grounds about a week ago?" A pause. Jack appeared mystified. "Were you with him that day?" continued the detective.

"I see where this is going? Yes. I was talking to him just outside the hospital when we both thought we saw Lagrange. As it turned out—"

"Did you pursue that man?" interrupted Mills. "He turned out to be Lagrange and you killed him!" declared the detective, now placing several black-and-white photographs on display on the table right in front of Jack.

"These are pictures of me driving off Newton's parking lot. So what?"

"These are pictures of you, speeding out of the hospital chasing Lagrange, the day officer Dillon Pierson and you spotted Lagrange. These pictures don't do it justice. You should see the videos." By now, Mills had slowly walked around and was now right behind Jack. "Here are the time and date stamps of when and where the pictures were taken." A pause for effect. "See this light blue Nissan? This is Lagrange in there, isn't it?" stated Mills. Jack shook his head vigorously in disagreement. No! "As it turned out, we believe the murder occurred about one to two weeks ago. These pictures were taken ten days ago." Mills again pointed at the date on the pictures. "What a coincidence, huh? You would have had plenty of opportunity, and we all know you have plenty of motive." After a short pause, Mills' demeanor changed. He appeared more understanding and calm now. "Look, this guy came back to settle the score with you. For revenge. Jack, you're a good guy. You helped put him out of business years ago. We all appreciate your help then and now. Hell, we should be giving you a medal. But we must go through this rigamarole to get the paperwork in order. That's all."

"I didn't do it, Detective Mills. I did think I saw Lagrange in the parking lot that day. I followed that man to his home only to find out it wasn't him," explained Jack. "I apologized profusely and drove home."

"Did anybody see you? Can anybody corroborate your testimony?" asked Mills.

"Yes. The guy I scared shitless that day, but didn't kill."

"Where does he live? I'll go find him and clear this whole mess."

"I don't remember. I just followed him. I didn't pay any attention where we were going. I don't go to that part of town, usually. I'm not that familiar with the streets and—" Jack paused. "Hey, check my GPS. Check the GPS in my Lexus. You might be able to find out where that took place. The man's home. I remember I used my GPS to navigate to my home afterwards. Will you please check it?" asked Jack.

"I'll do that." Mills paused. "You better be telling me the truth," said the detective.

"Look, if I killed him, why would I keep the evidence? To incriminate myself? And the bloody clothes? Why wouldn't I burn it all? Get rid of all evidence against me. I wouldn't keep it," prevailed Jack.

"You would be surprised what some people do. I've seen it all. Keeping souvenirs is actually quite common, especially in your situation. This guy really tormented you and your family. I think keeping a memento of the struggle he put you through would be understandable. Hell, maybe I'd do it too." The cop appeared to understand.

"I didn't do it. I'm innocent. I'm being framed."

The conversation went on and on for some time, but never did Jack admit to any wrongdoing. Detective Mills was called away from the room, leaving Jack once again alone.

Several minutes later, Susan and Claire entered the interrogation room, bearing name tags.

"Oh, Jack. Are you okay? Did they hurt you?" asked Claire, running to his side and hugging him.

"No, I'm fine. I can't believe this is happening to me. To us." Susan hugged Jack after Claire. All sat down.

"You know I'm innocent, right?" Jack looked intently at both women.

"Oh yes. We both know that beyond the shadow of any doubt," started Susan. Claire nodded, agreeing.

"We need to prove it. How do we do that? Where do we begin?" asked Jack apprehensively.

"Just tell the truth. Now and always. The worst thing you can do is not to be forthright. When cops realize that, it throws the whole balance off," said Susan.

"I have nothing to lie about." Jack was scared. Never had he been in this precarious situation.

"We'll find a way to prove you didn't kill Lagrange, honey." Claire could feel Jack was terrified by the whole situation. And so was she.

"I know I can count on both of you. Thank you."

"You bet. Do you need anything?" asked Susan with a forced smile.

"No, I'm fine. I know I'll be out of here in no time," lied Jack, tossing a fake smile at the ladies.

"Have you called a lawyer? There's an attorney I would strongly recommend by the name of Lee Chappell. I've seen him in action, and he's pretty impressive," said Susan.

"Will you call him? I don't know if I will be allowed any more phone calls. They took my cell phone away when they searched me at the hospital."

"I'll take care of it. Don't worry. We'll be back tomorrow." The group stood and hugged.

The two women were escorted out of the jail area and out the front door.

Alone again, Jack felt his temples throbbing. "Why is this happening to me?"

—

41

"Dr. Norris, I'm Lee Chappell," said the attorney as he entered the interrogation room. He handed Jack a business card. He was dressed in a dark blue suit, a white shirt, and a red tie. He was in his midforties with carrot-colored hair and pale features. "How was your night?" The lawyer sat in front of Jack and removed a large legal pad and pen from his briefcase.

"As you can imagine, Mr. Chappell, I couldn't sleep at all. The bed was okay, but I couldn't rest my mind."

"I understand. Well, I read through your file," began the attorney. All business. "I have some questions to go over with you. Your arraignment is at four o'clock this afternoon. I'm hoping to have the judge release you, but that's not a slam dunk." Chappell paused.

"I'm innocent, you know. I'm being framed," interjected Jack.

"I believe you, but we'll have to see if we can convince the judge and a jury of that."

"As you reviewed my situation, is there any good news?" asked Jack.

"One good thing is that they don't have a body, although a heart is a good start for them. Who would want to kill Lagrange and blame you for the murder? Any ideas?" Chappell paused. Noticing that Jack remained pensive, he continued after a long, uncomfortable moment, "We need to create reasonable doubt, and if we could

186

point the finger at somebody else, that would help our case. Any thoughts?"

"None whatsoever. I can't think of anyone. Other than Lagrange himself."

"Well, he's not in a position to be blamed any longer. Anyone else? Take your time and think this through carefully."

"No. Sorry. No one comes to mind," said Jack forlornly after a long pause.

"I need to go and file some documents with the court. Why don't I come back in a few hours and we'll continue our conversation. I need to prep you for the arraignment, okay?" The attorney stood up, followed by Jack. They shook hands and Jack found himself alone in the small room once more.

I guess I'd better get used to being alone, he murmured to himself. Jack walked around the table inside the small room for several minutes. Thinking. Pondering. Two guards entered the interrogation room. It was time to return to his prison cell. While Jack was being escorted, his mind continued to churn. Something was bothering him. *Who would be trying to frame me? I have no enemies. Not to that extent. What would it take to hate someone so much that you'd kill a man, cut out his heart, only to frame that person?* They arrived at the cell. He entered, and the door behind him clicked shut loudly. Jack walked to the small window and looked into the outside world through the bars. His thoughts returned to the revenge and the intricate plan somebody had conceptualized to frame him of Lagrange's murder. Jack could not even begin to compute in that realm. This domain was incomprehensible to him. The only person he could think of that would want to frame him would be the man whose heart now lay motionless somewhere in the pathology laboratory. *Could Lagrange possibly commit suicide and ask someone else to cut out his own heart? Could he? Could anyone? He'd done some pretty awful things, but that would be inconceivable. What if he was dying? Maybe he had cancer and knew he only had a few days to live. As a final act of defiance, he could have paid somebody to cut out his heart after he died and deliver it to my car. Just to ruin my life?* Jack shook his head side to side. *Is this possible?*

Jack's thoughts returned to the barbeque party. *We were all playing volleyball and basketball and soccer. Having fun. Trepur, or Lagrange, whatever his name was or is, mostly sat and watched. The bit of physical effort he did, he became a little short of breath.* Jack had noted the man's air hunger had worsened over the last several months, as Lagrange would visit the clinic or arrive with the security team when patients had to be transferred to the hospital for inpatient care. Invigorated, he knocked on the cell door.

"Guard. Officer. May I make a phone call? Please."

After over half an hour, Jack received notice that he would be permitted one phone call. A cordless phone was provided. He dialed Claire's number.

"Honey, will you get a hold of Kate Fanning? I have an idea, and I need her help," he said when she answered.

Finding Kate proved to be an exceedingly difficult task. Claire checked at work but the nurse had not been there since the barn explosion. Exasperated, she called Susan. The detective on maternity leave performed her investigative magic and soon was on the phone with Cesar, who put the two in touch. Kate agreed to visit Jack in prison and would be at his side in no time.

The most difficult part was convincing her parents that she should leave their secluded hideout to return to the devil's den. Kate discussed Dr. Norris' willingness to help her at a time when she really needed help.

"If it wasn't for him, Amelia would still be a prisoner. Or worse, dead," she offered calmly. "Mom, Dad, I must go. I feel I need to do this." Silently, the parents acquiesced.

"Call us as soon and as often as you can. We love you so much, Kate." Barbara and Bill hugged and kissed their daughter.

Kate got in her car and departed, en route to Evansville.

42

"Thanks for coming, Kate."

"Yes, I did notice he was getting more short of breath with less effort," said Kate after hearing Jack's thoughts and observations about Nai Trepur.

"That goes along with my theory. I need to prove it," said Jack.

"I want to help you, Dr. Norris. You helped me when I needed you. Please let me help."

Having received marching orders, and armed with enchantment and charm, Kate arrived in the laboratory at Newton Memorial. She searched for Lance Lantz.

"Lance. I need your help," she exclaimed. "Is there a private place where we can go talk for a minute?"

"Sure. Yes. Sure," fumbled the young technician. "Anything. What can I do?" He led her to an empty supply room. In it, there were several shelves of medical supplies needed to run the laboratory at Newton Memorial. They stood next to a shelf of needles of different sizes and specimen collection vials.

"I want you to measure a natriuretic peptide level on an old blood sample."

"Why? On who?" he inquired nervously.

"Remember how all the hospital employees had to have blood work to measure hepatitis B titers? You still have those samples, don't you?"

"Yes. I think so. Do you want me to measure your levels of natriuretic peptide?"

"No, not mine. Somebody else's," she said, batting her eyes irresistibly.

"You know I can't say no to you, Kate. I'll do it. I'll do it, even if I get fired."

"Nobody is getting fired. But nobody needs to know, right?"

"Who is it on?"

"Nai Trepur."

"The guy Dr. Norris just killed?"

"He's innocent. But yes. That patient. Will you? Please?"

"I'll have the result in about half an hour."

"Thank you, Lance." Kate kissed him lightly on his right cheek and departed the room. The door closed behind her. He stood for a long moment, mesmerized and enchanted by her kiss. By her words. By her essence. All these things played vividly in his mind. He smiled big. Then went to work.

Within an hour, Kate was at Jack's side again. When she arrived, Claire and Susan were already there. Jack had been given visiting privileges much more freely than customarily, due to Susan's influence on the police force assigned to the local prison.

"Two thousand, seven hundred and ten," said Kate with a mission accomplished tone and demeanor as she entered the interrogation room, joining the others.

"Yes, that is very high," said Jack. "That goes along with my theory."

"What's high? What theory?" asked Claire. Susan looked on.

"Natriuretic peptide should be less than one hundred. Lagrange's was over two thousand," Jack explained.

"What does that mean?" interrupted Susan.

"He was fluid overloaded. He was in congestive heart failure. Nai Trepur had a cardiomyopathy," said Jack, smiling.

"So you think he died and had somebody cut out his heart to incriminate you?" asked Claire.

"I guess you can get someone to do anything for enough cash," affirmed Susan. "But that's pretty bizarre."

"Dr. Norris thinks Lagrange is still alive," announced Kate, beaming. "I think he may well be right."

"Come again," said Susan, taken aback. "I'm no doctor, but I know you can't live without a heart. And his heart is on a slab in the lab. I've seen it myself."

"Cardiac transplantation," said Jack triumphantly.

"What?" exclaimed Claire, mouth agape. "How did you come up with that?"

"How can you be sure, Jack?" asked Susan.

"I can't be sure. But knowing this guy, I'll bet you I'm right. I think he had a heart transplant and stole his own heart just to incriminate me. When his previous plan didn't work, he thought he'd get me with this scheme. And he still might." There was a pause. "We have to prove this is correct. We need to find Lagrange. This is where you all come in. I doubt he'll waltz right in here to visit me." A door knock was heard, leading all to perk up. There was a moment of incredulity. Could it be him? Another knock.

"Come in," said Jack finally.

The door opened, and in came the attorney. All shoulders fell, expelling air from breaths previously held. Smiles all around, except for the newly arrived, who now wore an expression of surprise.

"This is my lawyer, Mr. Lee Chappell," introduced Jack. "Claire, my wife, and Kate, one of my nurses and a great friend," continued Jack, smiling. "You already know Susan." They all shook hands and sat down again.

"Not sure how to interpret your expressions when I first came in," started Lee, getting out his notes.

"We think we have it all figured out," said Kate.

"Really? That's great news," said Lee, not sure how to take the statement.

"I have good reason to believe that Lagrange is not dead. That he had a heart transplant and stole his own heart," said Jack.

"Hmmm. That's a good one," joked Lee for a moment. His smile faded as he noticed the group was not laughing. "Wait. Are you serious?"

"I really believe that. We need to prove it. We need to find the body. We need to find Lagrange. He's probably still pretty sick. Heart transplant surgery has a way of stealing your breath away for a while. Can you get me out of here so I can help with my own investigation?" said Jack.

"We'll know in a little while. The arraignment is coming up soon. We need to prepare for it."

"Before we do that," said Jack, "there are no centers in Evansville doing cardiac transplantation. If I'm right about all this, Lagrange would have to have gone to Indianapolis, St. Louis, or Louisville. I'm betting on Indy, since he resides in Indiana. He may have had a cardiologist here in town. Since it wasn't us, will you check with the other cardiology group in town? The Evansville Heart Associates? If and when he's back, he'll need antirejection medications. There are very few patients requiring these prescriptions, so it should be relatively easy to check with the pharmacies here in town. We have to find him."

43

"He is a private pilot and owns an airplane. Your Honor, he is a flight risk. He stands accused of murder and cutting out his victim's heart as a souvenir. We believe there is mental defect, given the heinous nature of the crime," proclaimed Assistant District Attorney Goldstein, an elegant man in his late thirties, wearing a dapper dark blue suit.

"Your Honor, may I remind the court that we have not yet found a body to go with this supposed crime and—," began Jack's attorney at the ongoing arraignment.

"Wait a minute, Counselor. Are you disputing that there has been a crime? For Pete's sake, the heart is in the morgue," interrupted the judge wearing his traditional black robe.

"It is our theory that Simon Lagrange had a cardiac transplant and—"

"And stole his own heart to implicate your client?" chortled the lawyer across the aisle.

"We believe that my client is being framed. Dr. Norris is a respected cardiologist who is the director of the Cardiology Department at Newton Memorial Hospital. His services are of paramount importance to the community, Your Honor. Until the people produce a dead body to go with the heart in the morgue, there is no way to be sure that a crime has indeed been committed."

"Though your theory is intriguing, it is but a far-fetched theory at this time. What I have in front of me is the strong possibility that Dr. Norris did in fact break down in the face of tremendous adversity and murder his tormenter. That he in fact cut out the heart as a souvenir. It is my ruling that Dr. Norris be remanded to the custody of the State of Indiana and that he be examined by a court psychiatrist regarding his state of mind during the incident as well as to assess him for his ability to help with his own defense." The gavel struck the pad announcing the decision.

"I'm sorry, Jack. You have to stay in prison. I'll appeal the decision and continue to do all I can to get you out of jail. I'm really sorry," said Lee. Jack looked back. Claire was sitting next to Susan. Claire was crying. Susan had her arm around Claire, comforting her. They all locked eyes for a few seconds as two guards escorted Jack beyond the doors of the courtroom. Jack mouthed the words, *I love you.*

The courtroom emptied out little by little. Several feet outside the main door, Claire, Susan, and Kate met at a bench. They all sat down, feeling wiped out. Dismayed. Defeated. Claire dabbed her eyes with a tissue.

"Wait here one minute," said Susan, standing up and waddling over by the elevator where she spied Detective Mills. "Brad. Wait a second," she yelled, holding her pregnant belly as she continued to wobble. The two conversed for several long moments; then Susan returned to the bench where the other two women lingered.

"He doesn't buy the possibility that Lagrange had a heart transplant. He says there isn't enough evidence to accept that theory," she said as she approached the others.

"Is he willing to help us look for evidence to prove it?" asked Claire.

"No. For now he's convinced that Jack killed Lagrange."

"What do we do now?" commenced Kate after a moment of silence, eager to get on with the investigation. "The cops won't help us. We have to do it ourselves."

"Can we count on Cesar Madera?" asked Kate.

"I don't know," said Susan. "I'll talk to him. He may help us unofficially and behind the scenes."

"Okay. Kate, find out if Lagrange was a patient with the Evansville Heart Associates. If he is, get an address, phone number, car plates, the day of his next visit. Anything you can think of that might be useful," said Claire. "I will go around to all the pharmacies here in town with Lagrange's picture and see if they have any patients on antirejection medications for heart transplantation.

"Sure. I'm on it," said Kate.

"Susan. Your job is to go have a beautiful healthy baby." Claire flung a smile at the pregnant woman and gently touched her gravid belly. "I know you want to help us and you can. Continue to open doors for us with your police and FBI contacts. Go home and stay by the phone. You will be the point person for all of us. We'll report our findings to you, and you contact Jack. Call Detective Mills and see if you can get him to agree to help us and let us contact Jack as often as necessary. They're pretty stingy about letting us talk or see him."

"Consider it done. I'll also get them to delay Jack's departure from the local jail. I think I can avoid having Jack transferred to the state prison. I'll help for as long as I can," said Susan, invigorated.

"When are you due?" asked Kate.

"Last week," said Susan and Claire, almost in unison. They laughed, got up, and walked out the courthouse building.

—
195

44

Claire's task was to visit all the pharmacies in town, armed with Simon Lagrange's picture. She researched first where the pharmacies were located. She would begin with those closest to Newton Memorial Hospital and branch out from there. Thank goodness for the Internet. She produced a printed list of pharmacies.

Next, her attention was turned to antirejection medications. Patients undergoing cardiac transplantation would require treatment for some time with drugs that suppress the immune system to avoid rejecting the donor's heart. Prograf, or tacrolimus, Claire discovered, would be the most common agent used for this application. Since the number of patients undergoing heart transplantation in a relatively small city like Evansville was limited, or so she hoped, the plan was to use this information to narrow the field of search for the assassin.

Claire first called the pharmacies and asked if they had the immunosuppressant Prograf in stock. That question, she soon realized, was the most efficient to get the pharmacist on the line. The phone-answering employee, typically not the pharmacist, would have no idea, but would get a pharmacist on the line. Sometimes Claire had to actually request to speak with the pharmacist. In all but two establishments, she was able to communicate directly with a PharmD. She would first explain that she had a heart transplant and was looking to purchase Prograf. She had a prescription from her doctor, but before coming out, she wanted to know if she could get it there. She heard repeatedly that this agent was exceptionally rarely used, and that it would take several days to obtain it. She would ask if they were presently supplying any patients with this drug. From a list of over fifty pharmacies, she narrowed the directory down to twelve. These would be the most likely stores to be providing Lagrange with the immunosuppressant.

She purchased a map of the city and painstakingly placed a red mark corresponding to each of these pharmacies. She would start at the ones closest to the hospital.

"Hello there. My name is Dr. Claire Norris. I'm a doctor at Newton Memorial Hospital. I'm looking for this man. He's a patient of mine. Have you ever seen him?" she would inquire, placing the large photograph of Lagrange at eye level, facing the pharmacy employee. She repeated this process again and again. For this round, she tried to avoid the actual pharmacist whom, she reasoned, might hit her with the HIPAA violation thing. She rationalized that the hourly employees behind the counter would be less likely to be aware of the strict patient privacy regulation imposed nowadays. Was this really against the HIPAA regulations? She wasn't sure, but better not to find out. She pressed on, asking as many people as she could find to look at the picture.

No takers. After several hours of canvassing, no one had admitted to ever having seen the man in the picture. Claire was exhausted, having been at this for over four hours. She took a break and called her parents, who were babysitting Nick and Trinity. All was well on the home front.

She entered another pharmacy.

45

"Joy, how are you? It's Kate. Kate Fanning," she said into the phone.

"Kate Fanning who?" joked the young nurse on the other side of the call. "How are you, Kate? Long time no see. Or hear."

"I know, I know. Listen, I need a huge favor. Can I buy you lunch?"

"Always game for a free lunch. When and where?"

"Today. I want to bring lunch for the entire staff. I'll be there at noon."

"Wow, you're very generous, Kate. What's going on?"

"I'll explain everything later. How about pizza?"

"Pizza's fine."

They hung up. Kate got busy with the necessary arrangements. After ordering the food, she drove to the parking lot of the office where her friend worked. Scheming, Kate sat in her car. What would be the best tactic? Should she be sneaky? Should she come up with a story to try to get results? *I could say he's a psych heart patient that disappeared and we need to find him. I could say he's a drug seeker and I want to tell them to be aware of it in case he comes to see them at this office. Or should I be direct and honest?* she mused.

"If it's me in their position, how would I like it done?" said Kate out loud to no one else in the Honda. "Direct and honest is always the best way!" finally adjudicated Kate.

At noon, a van from a local pizzeria pulled up to the front of the Evansville Heart Associates office and delivered several pizzas and soft drinks to the lunchroom. Kate was already in the waiting room. The receptionist promised she would alert Joy of Kate's arrival and returned with a message that she should wait a few minutes. A long moment later, Joy peeked through the window looking out to the waiting room. She smiled ear to ear and pointed to the entrance door. The door opened and the girls hugged. Joy escorted Kate to the lunchroom, where the stacked boxes liberated an appetizing aroma, making stomachs churn in anticipation.

"This is Kate. I must warn you, she's our competition. But she is one of my best friends ever," introduced Joy, looking at several employees entering the break area.

"I brought you all lunch, so please go ahead and eat. Don't let this get cold. I need your help. All of you."

With smiles on hand, the nursing staff got their food and drink and sat down. As this ritual was unfolding, Joy and Kate talked.

"So how are things at the Newton Memorial Outpatient Cardiology Office?"

"Not so good," said Kate. Noticing that everybody had their food and were now sitting, she continued, "A terrible thing has happened over there. Do you guys remember the Rat Poison incident three years ago? Well, the one bad guy that escaped is back for revenge. And he's winning. He has my doctor, Dr. Jack Norris, in prison. It's a long story, but we think that the bad guy may be a patient here. I have his picture. Will you all please look at it and see if you recognize him?" She passed the picture around. Several of the nurses put their pizza down and got up to gather around the one holding the photograph.

"I don't know him," said one of the nurses.

"I've never seen him before," said another.

"He's a master of disguise. He may have had a moustache or beard. Notice his eyes are a little yellowish," continued Kate, becoming increasingly discouraged that maybe she would not get any leads, as time went on.

"Yes. I do notice a little bit of jaundice here on the picture. Ever so slightly," said a nurse, another nodding in agreement, then another. "But I've never seen this man in here." She gave the picture to someone else.

"Will you keep the picture and show it around? Maybe your doctors would take a look?" Kate asked Joy.

"Sure. I'll let you know if anybody says they have seen this guy."

Business out of the way, Kate got some food and a glass of water and sat down with her old nursing school roommate. They talked and remembered good and bad times spent together in years past. The nurses thanked Kate for lunch and returned to work. Kate left the office feeling empty and deflated. She had been optimistic that this trip would have given her a momentous push into the resolution of this mess. Disappointed, she fished out her mobile phone from her purse and dialed.

"Susan, no luck from the Evansville Heart Associates office," she said.

"I just heard from Claire, Kate. She had no luck with the Evansville pharmacies either. Next step is Indy. Come on over, and we'll plan it all."

46

"Thank you for setting up this interview so quickly, Patti," said Dr. Frank Hanes, shaking the recruiter's hand and tossing her a toothy smile. "This is my fiancée, Kate."

"You are welcome. We have become very busy here over the last year or so and are interviewing both cardiologists and nurses. When you told me your fiancée is a cardiac nurse and is looking for a position as well, it was the answer to my prayers. It is our pleasure to have you both here. I'll have you meet several of our key cardiologists and tell you both about our group and the positions." She smiled as she helped prop open a door leading into the back office. The couple followed her. The group walked toward a woman sitting at a desk. "This is Gretchen. She's the head of the nurses that work in the file room. I'm going to leave you with her, Kate. She'll show you what we do back here. Dr. Hanes, I'm going to take you to meet some of our cardiologists and let you chat for a while. I'll come back for both of you at noon to go to lunch with our chief executive officer and some of the medical directors."

The plan was working beautifully. Once left alone with the nurses, Kate would do her magic, hopefully resulting in identifying the monster. As these thoughts went through her head, Kate lightly patted her purse containing Simon Lagrange's picture. She was hoping she would be able to show it around and get a name to go with the face. When and how to do it was still up in the air.

As was typical for nurses dealing with other nurses, Gretchen made Kate feel especially welcomed. She explained her procedures in the back office and often asked Kate how they did similar tasks in Evansville.

"Having a nurse that is already trained in this type of position is a huge bonus. I hope you and your fiancé decide to come work with us," said Gretchen, feeling a particular connection with the interviewee despite the short time they'd been together. "I know you'd be great here."

The nurses spoke for about an hour as Kate followed Gretchen around observing her routine. Kate watched the old pro at her post. She worked the different computer stations with ease, moving from program to program, dealing with problem after problem. She described how each program helped solve the different issues at hand.

"This patient needs a prescription refilled," said Gretchen. "This program allows me to search for the patient's name and ID number. It also gives me their pharmacy phone number." She paused. "Ah, here he is. This embedded program allows me to verify his prescriptions and dosages. He is on Coreg CR at 80 mg daily. No annotations about any problems or changes. So it's a go." She pointed to a phone number as she dialed the pharmacy.

Her computer ID, Kate noticed, was always the same, *Gretchen*, as was her password, *gretchenrn123*. This information would surely become valuable. She committed it to memory.

Kate remained unsure as to what to do and how to approach the situation. How should she ask the question she drove to Indianapolis to ask? Would a wall of HIPAA concerns be immediately raised and stop her progress? *I am not allowed to divulge patient information to you*, she was sure her host would declare. Her options ricocheted wildly in her head. Should she be upfront and honest or beat around the bush? Unlike in Evansville with her nursing school roommate and close friend, Kate knew here in Indy with a group of nurses she just met, the candid methodology would probably fail. It may even get her in trouble. How would she herself feel and act if she was in

Gretchen's place? She would invoke HIPPA. As time progressed, Kate mentally opted for the underhanded approach.

"I'm particularly interested in cardiac transplantation nursing. I know you have a transplant department here, don't you?"

"Yes. A very active one. I'll introduce you to Serena, later. She's rooming office patients right now."

"Great. I'd love that." Kate eyed the big clock on the wall. It was approaching lunchtime.

"Gretchen, now tell me the really important stuff. What's the routine about lunchtime around here? I hold my stomach in very high regard," said Kate with a sly smile, rubbing her tummy.

"Do you know any nurse that doesn't hold lunch as a sacred time of day?" Gretchen tossed the smile back at her. "Between noon and one, we just about close back here. There are several places to get food but the pharmaceutical companies bring the doctors lunch most days. The nurses and office personnel are invited. I'll show you to the break room downstairs in a few minutes. It's almost that time, isn't it? My stomach says yes."

"I'm having lunch with my fiancé and some of the medical directors, as part of his interview. But believe me, I'd rather hang out with you guys." A pause. "Maybe soon, if things work out."

About fifteen minutes later, Patti, the interview coordinator, appeared. Kate thanked Gretchen and the other nurses, and the two women departed the large back office with the exchange of chitchat. The two met up with Frank, who was conversing with one of the cardiologists. More chitchat. Kate was introduced. The couple was led to a beautifully decorated meeting room. In the middle of the room, as its showpiece, a flamboyant table surrounded by a dozen chairs, each just as ornate. To one side, a long counter displayed several trays of food, which delighted the senses with the many aromas, a candle warmer underneath most of them. On another counter, there were various types of breads, cheeses, fruits, and dessert. Next to this, the beverage area contained just about every type of nonalcoholic drink there was.

Introductions were made, and the group headed to the buffet. As soon as all sat down, Kate excused herself, claiming she needed to use the facilities.

"I know exactly where to go," she exclaimed to the group, a twinkle in her eye appreciated only by Frank.

Good luck, Kate, thought the young doctor, looking back at the others sitting around the table, ready for conversation.

Kate tracked back to her previous location. The secret, she recognized, was to appear as if she knew exactly where she was going. If she did, she would not appear out of place. New faces must walk these halls every day. If you look like you belong, everybody leaves you alone. True to Gretchen's word, the enormous file room was just about empty. Above a few of the many cubicles, she could see the tops of two nurses' heads. Soft voices explained medical data to inquisitive or nervous patients on the other side of the line. She walked into a moderate-sized out-of-the-way room with a computer. She used the knowledge she acquired from observing her host earlier in the day to enter a Web site that allowed inquiries about patients. Under diagnosis, she entered, *cardiomyopathy*. A list of a gazillion names popped up in seconds. She then prespecified, *Caucasian, male*, and *age: 40-60*. Several hundred patients popped up. "Need more specifics," she told herself, raking her fingers through her hair. She typed, *Evansville*. The return was blank. *Okay. No Evansville addresses. You must have an Indy address. You wouldn't live far from this office when you come up here.* Kate searched her brain for specific metrics that would point to the monster.

"Susan. I need a huge favor," she said softly into her cell phone. "Will you find out from the police lab Lagrange's blood type? I need to know right away. I'm up in Indy."

"Sure, I'll text you that information in a few minutes." The phone connection was severed. Kate stood up, nervously looking around, side to side. Footsteps coming closer to her location caused Kate to hold her breath. *It's the police. Security. I've been found out.* Her blood ran cold through her veins. Her heart hammered thunderously inside her chest.

"Hello," said a young man. He looked to be in his early twenties. He had pepper hair and dark brown eyes. "I'm looking for Fay. Have you seen her around?" he asked.

"No. She's probably at lunch. Try the break room downstairs," said Kate, faking it.

"Okay, thanks. Later," said the young man as he disappeared out of sight, leaving her alone again. Kate let out a loud sigh of relief, the butterflies exiting her stomach.

"AB negative," vibrated her cell phone. She entered the blood type into the search engine and twenty-three names appeared. A more manageable list. But how to make it even smaller? Kate pondered. She smiled after a long pause. She typed, *transplant date* and entered a period starting three months earlier. Eight names. She searched for the print icon and clicked on it. The printer spat out the names with their ID numbers, addresses, birth dates, phone numbers, and so forth. She clicked off the program and brought up another labeled *Appointments*. She looked up each of the names, then wrote the last and next appointments for each of the people on the list. Satisfied, she returned to the meeting room. When she arrived, she winked at Frank. With that, he smiled. Mission accomplished.

47

"She had her baby!" exclaimed Claire as soon as she saw Jack. "Susan had her baby! A boy. At three this morning." Jack hugged her and both sat down as the escorts, two large prison guards, exited the visitation room.

"That's great news. What did she name him?"

"Sean Michael." Claire's face was illuminated, displaying a gregarious, infectious smile. "I, uh, we bought a little outfit. Look, it has a soccer ball in the front. I thought you'd appreciate it. Here, sign the card. I'll go visit her at the hospital when I leave here." Jack took the pen, wrote *Congratulations*, and signed his name, legibly. Jack's mood was somber. Staying locked up for days, especially for a crime you didn't commit, does that to a man. Claire understood. She could also see that her attempts to improve his mood were hopeless. Silence reigned for a long moment.

"Where's Kate? Last I heard, a few days ago, she and Frank came back from Indy with a short list of possible names. Have you heard from her lately?" asked Jack, trying hard to get his head back in the game.

"No. I've called her cell phone numerous times. I've called Cesar Madera. He hadn't heard from her, so he called her parents. They haven't heard anything either."

"That can't be good. She may be in trouble. Or getting in trouble." Jack shook his head gently. "I can't forgive myself if she gets hurt on my account."

"Sweetheart, you have to stop blaming yourself for what Lagrange is doing to you. And all of us."

"I know. It's not easy."

"What should we do now?" asked Claire.

"Go visit Susan. Give her my best wishes. Maybe she can call Detective Mills and see if he's found out anything about Kate. I think she's in Indy looking for Lagrange. But I'm worried about what she might do if she finds him. If indeed he is in Indianapolis. The cops should know what we know. And Kate needs help in Indy."

"Okay," agreed Claire.

"How are Nick and Trinity? How are you doing? I'm so sorry to put you in this predicament, Claire."

"We're all doing well. My parents are really helping out a lot. Nick's having a blast. Trinity, I can tell, misses you. I'll see if I can bring her with me next time I come to see you." Claire gave a sympathetic smile.

"I miss her too. And Nick, I miss him terribly. I can't wait until this is all behind us. And I know it will be soon." He squeezed Claire's hand. She reciprocated.

They spoke for a little while longer but soon the guards returned. Claire had overstayed her welcome, and it was time to leave. Jack was escorted into his cell.

48

One hundred and fifty miles to the north, Kate reviewed her list once again. She would search one by one, until she found the monster. She had purchased a blond wig, one she hoped would disguise her sufficiently when she came face-to-face with the fiend.

The first two names were crossed out. Nathaniel Byrnes, she discovered, had died from posttransplantation complications six weeks earlier. He succumbed to fungal infections, which had overwhelmed his body. Fortunately for Kate, he had become an easy rule-out. The second patient on her list, Frederick Hook, took a couple of days to locate. When Kate drove past his home, she had seen no activity during the day or later, in the early part of the evening. She came to find out that he had been hospitalized with postoperative complications due to early rejection of his new heart. Posing as a florist delivery service worker turned out to be fruitless. A nurse stopped Kate in her tracks before she could see the patient's face. *Who knew he was allergic to flowers?* she contemplated.

Finally, Kate was able to gaze deep into his eyes. She had disguised herself as a phlebotomist and had entered the room at four in the morning. She gently shook the man's arm. He woke up. Accustomed to the blood drawing routine, the patient acquiesced. As she faked the preparations to draw blood, Kate spoke to Fred, obvious concern deep in his soul.

These eyes are not the eyes of the monster, she thought. *Those I will never forget. Never.* Then she spoke soothingly. "Don't worry about this blood test. It won't hurt and—"

"I'm not worried about the blood test," he interrupted. "My body is rejecting my new heart. I may need a new one. It took me forever to get this one."

"I'll pray for you. I'll pray that you'll be okay," she said sympathetically. Assured she was not facing Lagrange, the killer monster, Kate exited the room before puncturing his skin. "I'm sorry, I came into the wrong room. I'm looking for Mr. Peterson, one floor down."

With the hunt afoot, she was now on patient number three. After two days of stealthy searching, she discovered he was recuperating from his surgery out of town—Michigan or Wisconsin. According to his neighbors, his surgery was approximately two month ago. He's been out of town for the last four weeks, staying with his daughter. There was a slight chance he was Lagrange, but unlikely. On to number four.

Preliminary information indicated Mr. Christopher Weidner was fifty-two and had his heart transplanted six weeks ago. His home was in Indianapolis, approximately twelve miles from the hospital. Kate had located the house and had driven by twice; both times, she had seen no signs of life. She was now parked up the street a few houses, listening to soft music on the radio.

What will I do when I find the monster? These thoughts rematerialized in her head. *Will I shoot him dead on the spot? I'll have to. He'll probably recognize me first, despite my bleach-blond wig.* Musing, she opened up the glove compartment of her car and eyed the revolver. She extended her arm toward the gun to touch it, hoping to derive comfort from the experience. Abruptly and unexpectedly, a loud, piercing shrill originating from within the small storage area created a sense of dread deep inside her chest. The racket emanated from a place adjacent to the gun. For a split second, her bravado unraveled as overwhelming panic overtook her. She began to sweat bullets. The clamor ceased. Then returned. Next to the weapon, she found her cell phone, which again shuddered loudly, pulsating as it rattled against the floor of the glove compartment. Realizing what the sound was pacified her fire. She exhaled forcibly. It was Claire, calling for the umpteenth time. Kate wasn't ready to speak to her. She wasn't yet ready to speak to anyone. Her feelings of repugnance and repulsion for the monster resurfaced, leading to deep ridges on her forehead. *He doesn't deserve to live. I will shoot him dead.* She reclined back into her car seat, trying to let the soft background music soften her agitation.

Kate sat up straight when a car slowly drove into the driveway of the house she was observing. A young man got out of the driver's side and walked around to the passenger seat. He opened up the door. An older woman exited the vehicle from the door behind the driver. The two helped a man get out of the passenger's side.

"Well, hello, Mr. Christopher Weidner," murmured Kate, her curiosity piqued. "Are you Lagrange?" She looked on intently. From approximately forty feet away, it was difficult to be sure. The older man was built approximately like Lagrange. Approximate height and weight, give or take. That there apparently was a wife and son was unexpected, but not impossible. If this was the man, was the whole family involved? Should they all pay? Pay dearly with their lives? What should she do to rule him in or out? With these thoughts reverberating in her head, Kate waited, trying to let the music soothe her nerves.

After about twenty minutes, she was ready. She removed the gun from the glove compartment and stuck it in her purse. Under the cover of nightfall, Kate approached the Weidner residence. She spied in all directions, making sure she remained undiscovered. All was quiet. She advanced toward a window and looked inside the home. The older man was sitting comfortably on a leather easy chair with his feet up. The older lady was giving him a mug of something warm, steam rising from the beverage. He accepted it with a smile. Kate would use the same technique she utilized on the previous patient. She was happy with the intelligence gathered. She walked toward the front door and rang the bell.

"My name is Joan Wall. I work for the transplant center. I know it's a little late, but I was wondering if I could talk to Mr.

Weidner for a few minutes. Check him over and see how he's doing." Ironically, the idea came from the monster himself. *Go out to the homes and pretend you're there to see how the patient is doing*, he would command.

"Sure. Come right in," welcomed the younger man jovially, indicating the way. "I'm Jon. Come right in." The two walked into the domicile and reached the family room. The younger man took the remote control in his hand and pushed a button. Suddenly, the TV muted. "Dad, this is a nurse from the hospital. She's here to check up on you."

"Hi, Mr. Weidner. I'm Joan. How are you coming along with your new ticker?" She smiled and kneeled right in front of the older man. His wife had collected the hot chocolate mug and sat on a couch nearby, a pleasant grin on her face.

"I'm getting along better. I have less shortness of breath and I can do more activities. The last few weeks before the surgery were rough," said the patient, breathing every few words.

"Any fever? Or chest pains?" Kate fished out the stethoscope from her purse. She placed it on the man's chest and listened, but it was his eyes she came to analyze.

"No. Doing really good," he said. Their eyes connected, giving him a sense of security and well-being, knowing he was being cared for. The connection gave Kate a sense of frustration and disappointment. This was not the monster. She placed the stethoscope back in her purse. Underneath the medical instrument, Kate felt the instrument of death. The revolver remained undisturbed. After some chitchat, Kate exited the home, returned to the Honda, and made an entry on the infamous patient list. Exasperated, she pulled off her blond wig and threw it on the passenger seat. A deep sigh.

"Next!" she said out loud to no one there.

49

Jack was due in court the next day. A preparatory meeting with his attorney was in the cards for today. The guards came to his cell and escorted Jack to the visitation room. His lawyer was waiting. They shook hands but remained silent until the officers departed, leaving them to strategize.

"How are they treating you, Jack?" started Lee.

"Okay. This place is growing on me," lied Jack. "I discovered the library and gym. What else could somebody want or need? As long as you get me out of here by the Soccer World Cup next summer, I'll be fine." Both laughed.

"Jack, I've been thinking. How did Lagrange know where to find you when you were flying back home the day he tried to kill you in the air?" asked Lee.

"There's an Internet program called www.FlightAware.com that allows tracking of airplanes. I'm sure that's how he knew where I was and my route. Why do you ask?" Jack replied.

"Can we use that to flush him out somehow?"

"No, right now he's too sick to fly. If he could fly, we wouldn't know which airplane he's using and—" Jack paused pensively. "I don't think he owns an airplane, so he probably rented." Another contemplative pause. "I have contacts at the airport that can help us. Maybe we can prove I am innocent, if he's been seen there while supposedly being dead. Or maybe we can identify his alias. Let me think about it. What else do we need to consider getting ready for tomorrow's court appearance?" Jack was excited with this new avenue of investigation.

The two men conversed strategy and tribunal decorum for two hours. Soon after Lee Chappell departed, Claire arrived. Jack had remained in the visitation room, scheming, writing notes on a legal pad left behind by his lawyer, after approval by the guards.

"Hi, sweetheart," said Claire, kissing him then sitting down.

"Here's an idea I just got from Lee. Lagrange was flying a fast airplane. I can't be sure, but it looked like a Piper Meridian. Will you go to see Steve Peski at the Evansville Airport and show him Lagrange's picture? See if he recognizes him. Maybe he's seen him at the airport recently, while he was supposed to be heartless and dead." The hope in Jack's voice was palpable. And infectious. Claire felt rejuvenated and recharged with his words.

"That would be great. I'll take care of it right away. Maybe I can have some information by tomorrow's court time. I can't wait to have you home again. You don't deserve this, Jack."

"Neither do you. Or Nick."

"I have pictures of Baby Sean Michael." More invigorating news. "Both mamma and baby are doing fantastic." Jack looked through several photos of Susan and the newly arrived baby boy. He smiled. She smiled. For several minutes, all their troubles vanished.

"It's time for chow, doc," announced one of the prison guards, pulling Jack and Claire back to reality.

Claire called Susan as soon as she was in the parking lot. She informed her of Jack's condition and idea. Claire drove straight to the airport and soon was in front of Steve Peski, the shift supervisor. She explained the situation. He knew most of it from the news reports. He had seen Lagrange but didn't know his pseudonym. He had not seen the man in the photo in about three months, he recalled. He knew the man didn't own his own airplane but was aware that he had rented airplanes from plane owners at the airport. When Claire mentioned the possibility of a Piper Meridian, Steve's face brightened.

"There is a person by the name of Eli Johnston who owns one," he recalled. "Eli rents it out from time to time." Steve made a call and soon Claire was on her way to the Johnston Dairy Farm, armed with Lagrange's photo.

"Do you recognize this face?" she asked after introductions.

"Yeah, that's the guy I rented my Meridian to. The last time was about a month and a half ago, at least, if not longer. His name is Warren McGrath."

50

"Warren McGrath," said Kate, alone in the Honda, reading the next patient's name. "Number 6." She reread her preliminary notes. "This guy is fifty-eight and had his transplant about eight weeks ago. His last outpatient clinic appointment was five days ago and was progressing well postoperatively." She entered the patient's address on her GPS. Despite her youth and characteristic vigor, sleepless exhaustion had started to surface. Kate had been at this for over a week. Although she had rented a hotel room a few nights, mostly she slept in her car, in between gathering intelligence and sipping Starbucks.

She arrived and parked under a large oak tree, approximately thirty-five yards up the street from the small house. She waited. Several hours went by. Nothing. As it started to get darker, she decided to stretch her legs. She placed the wig on her head and exited the Honda. Her usual first move was to walk by the home, trespassing, as if to cut across the property to get to the street behind. There was no fence, visible or invisible. There were few windows. No dogs were detected. As she walked past, she saw no one indoors. Inside the home, things were neatly arranged, from the little bit she could see. The furnishings were sparse. No vehicle in the small attached garage. No overtly demonstrable cameras on or by the house. So far, so good. She would take about fifteen minutes on foot around the streets behind the property, then return via the same path to the street in front, all along making firsthand observations. She returned to her car. About thirty minutes later, a car drove into the driveway. The garage door opened and the vehicle entered. As the door descended gradually, one older man exited the car hesitantly, obvious signs of discomfort demonstrable throughout the process.

By the time the garage door obscured the view totally, Kate had formed a mental and visual picture of Warren McGrath. The chances that the man in the car was the monster were rather high. Unlike all the other transplant patients she'd visited at home, this one was alone. No family or friends to help ease his pain caused by using his arms and chest muscles exiting his car, and so soon after having his thorax cracked open. Kate knew the agony that being alone caused, having dealt with post-open-heart-surgery patients. She would now wait. Kate grabbed her purse and felt for her revolver, its cool steel providing some comfort. She was terrified, but the fury and rage in her heart prevailed. Realizing she was probably only thirty or forty yards from the monster gave her pause. Thoughts of whether she could really finish the job she came to do surfaced.

Could I really pull the trigger and kill him? I thought I could. Just this morning, I was sure I could. But would I? She began to feel sick to her stomach as the reality of the situation and the time for her to pull the trigger and rob a monster of his life neared. Drips of sweat appeared faintly on her forehead. Her hands shook, adrenaline pulses rushing through her veins. *I don't think I can do it!* Kate thought, sobbing at first, then bursting into tears. "I can't do this," she wailed. She whimpered somberly, shaking her head. "I can't do this. Sorry, Amelia. I can't do this." She was exhausted. "I can't do this," she cried repeatedly until she fell asleep.

Later that evening, when a blanket of pitch-darkness covered the neighborhood, Kate felt a sudden eerie feeling. The howling wind whistled right outside her car, swaying it gently, like a crib. Kate heard a noise just to her right and behind. The sound of footsteps on dry leaves and fallen tree limbs, perhaps? She strained to hear it again but now there was only silence. The Honda rocked soothingly, influenced by the passing breeze. Kate looked outside the car, but the visibility was nil, her world shrouded in an opaque mist. Out of the blue, a flashlight shone intensely on her face, blinding her vision. She looked downward to avert her eyes from the sudden painful brightness, but her gaze stopped at her own chest, a red dot flittering on her shirt. She heard a muted thump followed in milliseconds by shattering glass then a hard thwack, a bullet puncturing her skin, all this appearing to occur in slow motion. A mild discomfort appeared at the site. A slight burning sensation. Minimal awareness. A few seconds later, blood spewed from the hole in her thorax as Kate realized she'd been shot. She could now start to appreciate a progressive difficulty in catching her breath. Still in a haze, she fumbled for the door, unlocked it, and pushed it open with her foot. She looked at her right hand, now completely covered in crimson. The man smiled at first, then laughed loudly. The monster she could have assassinated earlier had pulled the trigger. Kate felt her life departing her body. She was too weak to stand up by herself. She grabbed onto Lagrange. The monster stood right outside the Honda, amused by the situation. Now nearly lifeless, Kate slid down the killer's body, leaving behind a trail of her own blood. The man guffawed with obvious glee, his hands, shirt, and pants now painted with crimson tracks. Kate prepared to take her last breath, gasping loudly. This woke her up from the awful nightmare. She sat up straight, breathing a mile a minute. Her heart hammered vigorously inside her chest. Still somewhat confused, Kate felt her upper body. She wasn't shot. Her shirt was clean. Wrinkled, but not bloodied. Sweating profusely, she needed some air. She opened up her car door and stepped outside. She was alive. *It was all a nightmare*, she repeated over and over in her mind, now starting to emerge from the dream fog. The ding, ding, ding of the open-door warning was cheering and slowly, little by little, Kate began to connect with reality. The cool breeze felt magnificently. She leaned on the Honda. She brought her hands to her line of sight. They were shaking uncontrollably. Tremors of contentment. *Dead hands don't tremble*, reasoned Kate, another indisputable sign that she was okay. *It was just a nightmare.*

She stood there for a long moment, feeling the draft hit her face, easing her distress.

She looked at her watch. It was almost five in the morning. She didn't have much time. Clandestinely, she walked toward the back of the garage and stood underneath a window.

51

Kate could not help feeling her recent accomplishments swell her head. Now, in front of Detective Brad Mills, she was about to offer incontrovertible proof that Dr. Jack Norris was innocent. She delineated her actions of the last few weeks in Indianapolis, the result of which was to discover the whereabouts of Simon Lagrange, whom all considered dead. She had his address in the capital, his home away from home. She had seen him with her own two eyes.

After hearing it all and studying the copied documents from the outpatient clinic in Indianapolis, Detective Mills decided Kate's efforts deserved further evaluation. The truth was, when he first learned he had to deal with Jack Norris, he assumed the man would be the typical almighty doctor—pompous and full of himself. His first inclination was to be hard on the physician. Show him who's boss right from the outset. He felt he needed to take control and give him a short leash. As time went on, however, the detective began to get a different feeling. Jack was actually a nice person. He was decent and down-to-earth. By then, the tough-guy appearance had to persist, so Brad had continued to be his usual hard-ass self, acting much like he always did around criminals. As he was beginning to notice that Jack was different, the heart showed up in his car, derailing Brad's feelings toward the doctor. The foregone conclusion was that Jack killed Lagrange. Nevertheless, at each interview, every fiber in the detective's body declared loudly that Jack had to be innocent. He did not fit the profile; it wouldn't have made sense for Jack to kill Lagrange, despite all that Lagrange had put him through. Despite the overwhelming evidence against Jack, Brad was starting to have serious doubts about his guilt. Kate's accounts and observations would give him an excuse to delve deeper into the situation. *Let the light of truth shine brightly and illuminate the way*, he thought. A call to the Indy Metro Police and a trip to the capital were in order. For good measure, he would also alert the FBI and bring them into the search. With the proper channels of legal action secured, the house would be painstakingly searched and DNA evidence collected. Hopefully, if all this panned out, Lagrange would be arrested and an innocent man set free.

Kate was sworn in and asked to affirm that she was not an agent of the police. That her services had not been solicited to search for Lagrange. All was properly transcribed and signed. All the proverbial legal t's were crossed and i's dotted.

"Luckily, Kate, you didn't enter the Lagrange home, so there won't be any questions later of evidence contamination or tampering," commented Julius Washington, the Evansville district attorney, a distinguished African-American man in his fifties, wearing a pin-striped blue suit. He was both dapper and well-spoken. Kate forced a smile and nodded.

"So, what happens now? Does Dr. Norris go free?" asked the young nurse.

"What you've told us is intriguing, but we'll have to corroborate it. Once we have incontestable proof that Lagrange is alive, then yes, Dr. Norris will be set free," stated Mr. Washington. "We'll also corroborate your findings that Lagrange, alias Warren McGrath, had heart transplantation. And that he had an outpatient clinic appointment with Dr. Buhler in Indy five days ago. We'll also search for the heart removed from him and see if, in fact, it is missing."

"I understand. I'm sure you'll work as fast as possible so an innocent man doesn't have to stay in prison any longer than necessary," said Kate with contempt in her voice.

"We'll work as fast as we can. I hope we will have some answers within seventy-two hours. Sooner, with some luck," said Mr. Washington.

And so it was. The authorities searched the house in Indy. A cell phone company statement indicated Lagrange's address in Evansville; that home was explored meticulously. An inhaler-type instrument was later tested and found to have remnants of Rat Poison, though in weak quantities. DNA from a hair follicle discovered on a comb matched precisely to the tissue in the heart. Prior DNA evidence conclusively proved that McGrath and Lagrange were the same person. The medical records showed that Lagrange had visited the clinic alive when he was supposed to have been dead. And the sick heart removed from Lagrange had been stolen from the laboratory several days before. All this proved that Jack Norris was innocent and would soon be released. Simon Lagrange, however, remained at large and on the FBI's Most Wanted List.

Detective Mills insisted on being the one to inform Dr. Norris of the decision to release him from jail. Timidly, the gumshoe approached the physician's cell.

"Hi, Dr. Norris," he said, holding on to the thick metal bars that isolated Jack from the outside world, "We—huh. I owe you an apology."

"An apology?" asked Jack.

"We now know beyond the shadow of any doubt that you are innocent. I'm here to set you free. Ms. Fanning has been very busy securing evidence to prove your innocence."

"Not a second too soon," said Jack cheerfully. One of the two prison guards that accompanied Mills unlocked the cage and the detective entered the cell. "You don't owe me an apology," continued Jack. "You were just doing your job. By the way, did you ever find the guy I chased home? The light blue car?" asked Jack, getting up from the small uncomfortable cot that had served as his bed for the last many nights.

"Thanks for understanding, Dr. Norris. And yes, I finally caught up to him. He had been out of town and lives alone. Nobody seemed to know where he was, around his neighborhood. But he did come home yesterday and did confirm your story," said the detective somberly, his right hand extended, their eyes locked. Mills had learned to trust his intuition. All good cops have it. When, so often, one has to act based on conjecture and uncertainty, the good cops learn to analyze those with whom they deal for clues from the soul. To look into the soul, you have to study the gaze. Peeking into Jack's soul through his eyes, Mills had long seen strength, sincerity, honesty, and decency.

"You can call me Jack," said the doctor jovially.

"Thank you. You can call me Brad," he said. The two shook hands. "I should have trusted Susan Quentin," he continued, his gaze still locked on Jack's. "Susan has been through a lot with you and your wife. Susan trusts you both implicitly, and I should have as well. She had no doubt whatsoever throughout all this about your virtues, despite the overwhelming evidence against you."

"It's not over yet, not even close. Lagrange is still out there. I think we need to continue to work together, and trusting each other will become more and more important, going forward," said Jack.

"Well put. We'll catch Lagrange." The two men smiled and walked out of the small compartment.

"So this is how the other half lives?" said Jack with a sigh of relief, looking back at the empty prison cell, a smirk illuminating his face. "It's a great feeling to be freed," he continued, walking alongside the police detective. "It feels so great to be liberated, I'm thinking of spending a week in prison once or twice a year, just to experience this exhilarating feeling."

"Isn't that a lot like running headfirst into the wall several times, because it feels so good when you stop?" asked Mills. The two laughed, Jack nodding yes.

52

Kate fired up her computer. Patiently she waited as the machine booted up, a grin on her face.

"Where are you, monster?" she spoke to herself, no one else in the Honda. Within minutes, the screen came alive with a map of the United States. A red dot came alive in Tennessee. She zoomed in. *Just north of Nashville. Probably on your way to Mexico*, she mused. *You are mine now, Lagrange.* She inputted Nashville, Tennessee, in her GPS and headed her car southward.

Her cell phone rang. She looked at the caller ID. It was Claire Norris. She was obviously concerned with Kate's absence of several days incommunicado. Her mobile also displayed several calls from Frank Hanes and Susan Quentin. Once the voice message icon appeared, she dialed and listened.

"Kate, it's Claire. We are all worried about you. Please call me back and let me know what you are up to. We are all in this together and we want to help. You shouldn't do this alone. Jack wants to see you and thank you personally for all you've done to prove his innocence. We all want to thank you, but please, let us in on your plans. We're a team. We want to help you get Lagrange. Please call me back. Please!"

Stubbornly, Kate deleted the message and threw her cell phone into her purse, sitting on the passenger's seat adjacent to her computer. The red speck on the screen was motionless, just north of Nashville. *He's probably having lunch.* She drove on, in silence, a wicked grin on her face. Lagrange abducted her little sister, forever scarring her life. *Lagrange, you are mine.* She drove on.

Within six hours, the dot corresponding to Kate's position was close to that of Lagrange's.

"Come to mamma, monster," said Kate, spying the computer. "Come to Kate."

It was getting dark, as nightfall approached. Lagrange was heading south on Interstate 24 almost to Chattanooga, Tennessee. He was making slow progress with frequent stops. The blip's progress stalled once more. Kate would arrive there in approximately ten minutes. The fervor with which Kate pursued the monster had blinded her from reality. For all the hours of pursuit, just now did her thoughts turn to the hows and wheres. The whys had consumed her every reflection—revenge what the monster did to Amelia. And Jack. And her.

"I will make you pay dearly. You mess with the Fannings, buddy, you get payback," she repeated to herself. Now that revenge was nearing, how would she do it? *Will I just kill him in cold blood?* she thought. *Run him off the road? Bullet to the head? Tie him to my bumper and drag his sorry ass up and down Interstate 24? Squeeze the life out of him?* snarled Kate, adrenaline burning her insides like acid. Lagrange's car was just up ahead a couple of miles. The GPS blip corresponding to his car had stopped on the side of the road. A sign announced a rest area coming up in two miles and Kate recognized Lagrange had made a pit stop there. She slowed down and eventually turned onto the ramp exiting the highway. It was dark out. A small building in the area was poorly illuminated. A placard indicated that there were vending machines and bathrooms within. There was only one vehicle in the parking lot. *It's too dark to be sure, but this has to be Lagrange's car,* she pondered. Watchfully, Kate pulled into one of the stalls, about thirty yards from the parked vehicle. She turned off her car and its lights dimmed rapidly into darkness. There was no one visible inside the other vehicle. *He may be asleep and out of sight,* she speculated. She felt for her gun and fished it out of her purse, her eyes still scanning outside her car. The world was still, except for sporadic, slight movements of tree limbs. Kate placed the gun inside the back pocket of her jeans and unhurriedly exited the Honda. All was quiet and still. She closed her car door soundlessly. Distant noises from the interstate signaled the paucity of traffic at this late time of the evening. Like a commando in the night, Kate took several slow steps toward the building, her eyes partially on the parked vehicle. A loud racket coming from several feet of the desolate building interrupted her next step. Her heart dropped to her feet then pounded in her chest. There was a sudden twist in her stomach, as if the wind was pounded out of her, forcing her to lose her breath. Panicky, her eyes honed in toward the source of the clamor. A raccoon, as shocked as Kate was, fled the garbage cans on which it feasted and disappeared into the night. Kate took a deep breath, feeling calmness unsuccessfully attempt to outrival her unraveled nerves. Her hands trembled, her gaze back on the other vehicle. It had remained undisturbed throughout this nerve-wrenching ordeal. She approached unhurriedly.

Nearing the automobile, now about ten yards away, Kate could now see a man. He was face down on the passenger seat. A blanket covered most of his body, which was moving up and down slightly. There were moans now barely audible.

Is this Lagrange? Can't be him. This man is having—Kate started to have doubts, her previous confidence waning. *He's in there with someone, having sex. It can't be Lagrange.* Kate retreated to avoid embarrassment. She would return to her car and recheck the computer for the GPS bug. As she walked away, now approximately twenty yards from the car, she had a thought. She pulled out her cell phone and dialed a number. Within seconds, a familiar ringtone radiated from the auto.

It is *him. I can't believe I fell for that trick*, she thought as she turned toward the vehicle. *I'll never fall for your tricks, about having sex, or otherwise.*

Unexpectedly, the car came alive and its lights came on, illuminating the small forest surrounding the stop area. The car backup light came on. The vehicle was in reverse, suddenly in motion. Kate pulled out her gun and aimed at the back tires. She pulled the trigger. A direct hit to the right rear tire caused it to go flat. The car veered to the right for a few beats then straightened out. Despite her shaking hands, Kate aimed at the right front tire and squeezed the trigger. Direct hit. Uncontrollably, the car's drunkenlike forward staggering swerved off the road and collided with a large tree. Kate took several fast steps toward the fallen vehicle. The driver, now clearly Lagrange, opened the driver's door and attempted to escape the wrath of Kate.

"Don't even think about it, scumbag," she threatened, her revolver held by outstretched hands. "Freeze or I'll shoot you like the dog you are, Lagrange."

53

It was 22:00 on the fourteenth day of September, exactly one hour before commencing the execution of the plan.

Remember 9142300. Commit it to memory. Don't write it down, recalled the prisoner, lying on the bed in the infirmary. The reason for his protracted vomiting over the last twenty-four hours had overwhelmed the good prison doctor's diagnostic acumen, but time heals everything. Sure enough, prisoner Mike Ganz was on the mend with some good supportive care. He had stabilized and, more than likely, would be able to return to his maximum-security cellblock by morning. Another one saved.

Mike rehearsed the plan in his head. The moment he had been anticipating for months was now here.

At 22:25, Mike called for the nurse. She arrived three minutes later. Mike begged to go to the bathroom. A prison guard would have to accompany Mike out of the infirmary and into the facilities. One arrived at 22:46. So far so good. Handcuffs and ankle shackles positioned, Mike waddled toward the men's room.

"Come on, Tony. Can *you* piss with handcuffs on? Come on, man. I'm sick, give me a break, huh?"

"Okay, Mike. Don't let me down," said the guard removing the handcuffs.

"Thank you, Tony. You're all right." Hands free, Mike shuffled toward the urinals. The guard removed a cigarette from his pocket and lit one up. He pulled hard, inhaling, holding his breath.

"Want one?" asked the guard.

"I thought you'd never ask," said Mike appreciatively. As the officer approached, Mike punched his face with as much might as he could muster. As his knuckles struck the face and temple, the guard's head snapped hard away from the blow, blood spewing from the nose and mouth. The man fell on the bathroom tile like a bag of potatoes. With a crumb of consciousness left, the guard attempted to get on his feet. Mike punched him again in the back of the head, causing his nose to hit the floor. A pool of blood expanded under the man. Now dazed from the repeated concussions, the guard stumbled slowly to his feet. Mike grabbed his head and pushed the guard face-first toward the large mirror. The glass shattered into pieces, bloodstains embedded throughout. The guard collapsed into unconsciousness, hitting the tile with a loud thump. Almost in unison, a loud explosion from right outside the bathroom shook the building. It was 23:00. Mike searched the guard for a key and undid his ankle shackles. Taking large steps, something he had not been permitted for the last three years, Mike leapt toward the back of the infirmary, where the deafening blast arose. The explosion had smashed the wall that separated Mike from the human race. With a grin and utter satisfaction, Mike stepped into the world.

As promised, about fifty yards due west of the explosion site, a mature oak tree stood proudly. In its trunk, there was a large natural opening covered by bark, a most suitable hiding place. In the hole, Mike fumbled for a bag, which he found readily. He exchanged his orange clothes for a pair of dark jeans and a black shirt. As planned, in the right pocket, there was a key. A car key, its vehicle parked in a street adjacent to the wooded area separating the prison from the city of Terre Haute. Mike heard the familiar chime as he pushed the keyless entry remote. He drove off.

Meanwhile in the prison proper, the relatively small explosion of the infirmary was overpowered by a salvo of three much louder blasts, all occurring at precisely 23:00. The other detonations had created significant damage to the walls of block C, the maximum-security wing, allowing several inmates to escape into the yard in front of the prison. All available officers were dispatched to that location to retrieve the escapees. Bright lights dumped sunlike illumination onto the yard. The commotion persisted for several minutes and distracted the prison staff's attention from the posterior portion of the building. Only the nurse on duty in the infirmary noticed Mike's escape. One other patient with a broken pelvis and right femur needed her presence. She dialed multiple extension numbers, but her calls would not be answered for over thirty minutes. By then, Mike would be long gone.

Inside the glove compartment of the small Toyota, Simon Lagrange left a cell phone programmed with the number for the voice message retrieving system. This was reached by pressing and holding the V key. The P key would dial Simon's cell phone, P for papa. There was also a key and directions to the house outside Evansville. While entering Route 41 South, Mike pressed P. The mobile rang six times; then a generic message instructed the caller that the number dialed could not be answered at this time and that a message could be left.

"Papa, where are you? I can't wait to see you. The plan worked marvelously. I'm on my way to Evansville. I'll call you soon, if you don't call me first. See you soon," said Mike into the receiver after the beep. Mike hung up. He pushed the V key.

"Michel. Ganzo. If you are hearing this message, that means you are out. But it also means I didn't answer the phone when you called me. So the police may have me. If this is the case, I want you to leave the country. Don't worry about me. I left you money and clothes as well as disguises in the house. Take everything and leave. Be happy, Ganzo. Have a great life." The words made Mike's eyes well up with tears. He drove on. Then he made another call.

"Hi, baby. It's me, Mike," he said into the phone. "I'm finally out." A pause. "Yes, I escaped. Just like I told you I would. We can now be together, forever." Another pause. "I love you too. I can't wait to see you." Silence again. "No, I can't tell you. If the cops arrest you for any reason, I don't want you to be able to tell them where I am. There are still some crucial things I have to do. I will call you as soon as I can." A pause. "We'll be together soon. I promise."

54

The deserted barn was balmy, the sun's rays slapping on its walls and rooftop. Several small high windows with broken panes allowed beams of light into the structure, proclaiming daytime outside. Here and there, there were piles of dried-up hay, remembrances of bygone days when the farm building was home to many barn animals. Nowadays, this side of the large farm was deserted, given its location in a floodplain. On the south side, the land remained uncultivated, allowing for trees of many shapes, heights, and maturity, home to coyotes, deer, and many other wild critters. The north side, many miles away and with a separate access road, was home to Kate's grandparents and the barnyard animals to which they attended.

The ride to the deserted barn had been difficult, given the lack of passable roads. Kate's Honda was parked underneath several large trees, out of sight. She and her guest had to walk about two hundred yards to reach the structure. For most of that, Kate had to support Simon, his right arm over her shoulder and his body nearly flaccid. The two stumbled for what seemed to be an eternity but finally reached the barn. Inside, three long thick poles supported the ceiling, which was surprisingly intact. Next to the center pole, Lagrange sat on a chair, his muscle strength still spent from the previous long walk. A rope securely attached his body and his seat to the pole, preventing his escape. Now that Lagrange was restrained, Kate took some time to clear a passageway to allow vehicles to reach the dilapidated barn. Having done so, she drove and parked close to the structure.

Simon Lagrange felt weak and defeated. Facing the real prospect of his own imminent death, and so soon after his heart transplantation with the promise of a new life. Simon, too late realized that maybe all of this had been for naught. The inner rage produced by having Mike on death row and Ian in the grave at the hand of Jack Norris had fueled his yearning for revenge. In the midst of the process, his own heart betrayed him. Miraculously, a cardiac donor was secured and a new pump implanted in his chest. A new life. A time to put all of it behind him. Forgive. Live and let live. But he had not been able to stop. Despite it all, he had followed his inner demons, and now, he was about to die, the barrel of a small handgun about to be pointed at his forehead, as Kate reentered the barn carrying a revolver.

"How does it feel to be the prisoner?" snarled Kate angrily, her double-barrel gaze locked on the criminal's eyes. "How does it feel, huh? You monster. You bastard." The young woman spoke furiously, pacing back and forth like a caged animal about to strike. The man remained silent. "You don't know how much pain you've caused all of us, Lagrange. Or maybe you do." Kate was fuming. "Maybe that's the whole appeal. To cause pain." Kate's heart was thumping, her breath quickened. She raised her right arm, the gun now at Simon's eye level. "Let's see how you like it, you son of a bitch." Kate pointed the revolver at the man's forehead and began to squeeze the trigger. Beads of sweat tracked downwards on their faces, both hot and scared. Kate held her position for several seconds, then put the gun down. She felt rage. Disgust. Repugnance. Why was she put in this position? She needed to make the monster pay. She would pull the trigger and shoot him dead. Right here. Right now. She raised the gun again and again, aimed it at the man's forehead. Kate took a deep breath. She held the shooting position and mentally prepared to assassinate the assassin. It would be no different from a Coke bottle or empty aluminum can. She breathed out. Then in. Steadying her hands, Kate prepared to dispatch the monster to the afterlife. Click, click, click. One more click and it would all be over. Lagrange took a deep breath and looked at the gun's muzzle aimed directly at his forehead. *This is it*, thought Lagrange. *At least it'll be quick and—*

"I can't do it." Kate exhaled forcibly, her revolver again pointing to the ground just in front of her. "I can't do it, Lagrange. I can't be like you. I can't," she sobbed. Deflated. Eyes puffy. Kate deposited the gun back in her pocket and fished out a tissue from her purse. "I'll let you self-destruct, instead." She blew her nose. She walked to a nearby pile of hay and picked up the paper bag perched on it. "Let's see how your new heart does without these rejection medications. Without your heart pills." She looked at the pharmaceutical bottles inside the bag. She tossed the bag back on the hay, and then tossed a grin at Lagrange. "I don't have to kill you. You'll kill yourself for me. How long will you last without these little magic pills?"

55

As Jack entered the building, he first noticed the nothingness of the creepy silence in the waiting room. That there were no patients yet waiting was no surprise. From this location, typically he would hear the noises of the busy outpatient clinic as it accelerated into game-time readiness. There would be nurses and secretaries bustling about, copiers and fax machines rushing to come alive, computers booting up online, and phones ringing off the hook. Intrigued by the silence, Jack sauntered deeper into the building, toward his office.

"Surprise!" yelled many voices as he entered his space. "Welcome back to work, Dr. Norris." Smiling faces approached, hugged him, and shook his hand. Behind the crowd and perched on his desk, there was a large chocolate cake.

"If I knew I was getting this much attention, I would have asked to stay in jail a few more days," said Jack bashfully.

"You're not fooling anyone, Dr. Norris. We know you love attention," asserted Shalyn. "And you deserve it. So enjoy." She smiled. "Now, you have to promise not to eat the cake until lunchtime. This is to share with all of us, you know."

"I make no such promise." Jack smiled. "Thank you, everybody, for this wonderful welcome." Little by little, his office emptied out and soon he was alone, piles of charts stacked up high in the *To Do* tray.

"Dr. Norris, do you have a moment?" asked Frank Hanes warily.

"Sure, Frank. Come on in. Sit down." Jack pointed to a chair as he made himself comfortable in his captain's chair behind his desk.

"I haven't seen Kate in several days. I'm worried about her. She's not answering most of my phone calls, and when she does, she is aloof. Distant."

"She's been through a lot, Frank. You need to give her some time. Give her some room."

"I'm just worried. This isn't like her at all," agonized Frank.

"Hi, Dr. Norris. Hi, Frank," said a young woman's voice at the door as she knocked lightly on the door. "I don't mean to eavesdrop, but I overheard you two talking about Kate. I'm worried about her too. I haven't seen or heard from her in days. Is she okay?" asked the medical assistant, worried.

"I don't know. I'm worried about her too, Shelley. She hasn't answered my calls," answered Jack.

"Dr. Norris, I have a patient to discuss with you, please," said a voice from outside the office. It was one of the cardiology fellows.

"Sure, Maria. I'll be right there," dismissed Jack. "Hopefully, she'll contact one of us when she's ready. I think she needs some time by herself." The three remained pensively in silence, contemplating the possibility that the young nurse was merely taking some time off from the world and not in any trouble. "Let's be positive." With a forced smile, the small group dispersed, each returning to daily chores.

Jack felt good to be back to work. The quotidian routines were therapeutic. Of course, just about anything was therapeutic after one is released from being unjustly incarcerated. He coached the resident and fellows as they attended to the patients visiting the Cardiology Outpatient Clinic.

It was a little past five o'clock, and the bustle of the office had died down considerably. Jack was in his office reviewing charts when his cell phone rang. It was Kate.

"Hi, Kate. We're all worried about you," answered Jack enthusiastically.

"I have Lagrange," said the nurse, sobbing. "I tried to kill him but I can't. I need your help to figure out what to do," she continued, tears flowing down her cheeks.

"There's only one thing you can do. You have to give him to the authorities. He'll pay for his crimes. Tell me where he is and I'll take care of everything," offered Jack.

"No, I want him to suffer," exclaimed Kate, venom punctuating her words. "If I don't give him his rejection medications, he'll self-destruct. He'll suffer like Amelia did. I want him to feel me in control of his life."

"Don't do it, Kate. If you allow him to die like that, you will never forgive yourself later. You'll become like him. And you're not like that. You're nothing like Lagrange. You are kind and compassionate. Don't let yourself become like him."

"I need time to think."

"Sure. Think this through. I can help you do that, just like you helped me when I was in trouble. Because of you, I'm out of jail. Let me help you, Kate. Please," pleaded the doctor. A moment of silence ensued. Jack heard Kate's sorrowful whimpers. He knew she was confused and overwhelmed and direly in need of his direction.

"Okay," said Kate softly when she regained her ability to speak between sobs.

"Tell me the whole story. Tell me everything."

And so she did. She explained how she tracked down Simon Lagrange and found him in Tennessee. His car was still at a rest stop. After several minutes of conversation, Jack and Kate decided the next logical step was to tell the police about the car. Let them search it for further incriminating evidence against the monster.

"I'll call Detective Mills and take care of everything." A pause. "And, Kate."

"Yes," came a soft reply.

"You have to give your patient his meds. Will you please think about doing that? For me?" supplicated Jack. "Let me come over and help you. Bring you both food." Silence. A wordless hush ensued, which seemed to last an eternity.

"Okay," finally returned a defeated voice.

56

"Hi. Thanks for coming in," said Brad Mills as Jack entered the Office of Detectives. "The GPS coordinates you gave us were precise and took us right to the vehicle."

"No problem. I'm glad to help," remarked the young doctor. "So, what did you find of interest in Lagrange's car?"

"It was full of evidence. His cell phone was in the car. Our people have done their electronic magic. We have the messages he sent to another cell phone. I'd like for you to listen to the messages and see what you can glean from them," said the cop.

"Sure, no problem," said Jack.

"Then I want you to tell me where you got all this information. You said you'd come clean after we retrieved the car. We have," added the policeman.

"I know. Let's hear the messages first."

"Please sit down. Want some coffee?" offered the officer.

"No thanks. I'm fine," said Jack, sitting.

"*Michel. Ganzo. If you are hearing this message, that means you are out,*" started the voice as the detective clicked the Play button on his computer, the program designed to replay the retrieved messages from Simon Lagrange's mobile phone. "*But it also means I didn't answer the phone when you called me. So the police may have me.*" Seeing the bewilderment in Jack's face, the detective clicked on the Pause button.

"Mike Ganz, alias Michel Lagrange, escaped from prison, whereabouts unknown," he told Jack.

"Mike Ganz is Ganzo and Simon Lagrange's son? I didn't see that coming. When did he escape?"

"Yesterday. He's on the way here to meet Simon Lagrange. We have every cop looking for him."

"So, if that's the case, I want you to leave the country. Don't worry about me. I left you money and clothes as well as disguises in the house in Terre Haute. Take everything and leave. Be happy, Ganzo. Have a great life."

"Here's another message," said Brad Mills.

"I hope you found the keys, the car, and the notes," continued the recovered recording. *"And I hope you are well and safe. But, if you can't get a hold of me, it may be that the cops have me in jail. In that case, listen to me carefully, Ganzo. I want you to leave the country. Go back to France and never come back. I left you some money in the house. Use it to change your appearance and leave."*

"There's another one. Here it is," said the detective, clicking on another document on the computer screen.

"Ganzo, I've been found out. The cops searched my houses in Evansville and Indy. I'm on the run, going down to Florida for a while. Call me when you get this message."

"Here's the last message." Jack continued to listen intently.

"I'm in Tennessee. I don't think I'm being followed. I'll call you in the morning, if I can. If I don't call, that means I've been nubbed. Leave the country."

"Here's a message he received from Mike Ganz."

"Papa, where are you? I can't wait to see you. The plan worked marvelously. I'm on my way to Evansville. I'll call you soon, if you don't call me first. See you soon."

"And that's it. No calls in or out after that. It's as if Simon was apprehended. Except we don't have him. So, where is he?" asked the detective.

"I know where Simon is," said Jack.

"I figured as much. Where is he?" inquired the cop perplexedly.

"Kate has him in a deserted barn. She has a lot of rage inside and wants to kill him. I got her to agree to let me come over. I don't think she'll kill him now. But she needs help," said Jack compassionately.

"Well, you figure this out and quickly. We need to take over the prisoner. Now!"

57

"I can't wait to return to work," said Susan.

"I know. I can't imagine what it's like to not go to work every day," said the babysitter from the kitchen, placing the infant back in his crib. She was mixing up baby formula, while Susan got ready in the master bedroom.

"I'm happy you're starting slowly, little by little. This meeting will get your feet wet. When is the meeting?" asked the babysitter. Dave entered the kitchen from the garage and poured himself a cup of coffee. "Need more java, Susan?" he yelled out to her.

"No thanks. I've had too much already," answered Susan. "There are two meetings, the first at ten this morning and the second at five this afternoon. It'll feel weird entering police headquarters after all this time off, but I'm excited about it." Susan arrived in the kitchen sporting a pantsuit, her blond hair up and beautifully manicured.

"You don't drink coffee, right, Shelley?"

"No, thanks, don't touch the stuff," said the sitter.

"And yet you live," asked Susan rhetorically.

"If you can call that living," smiled Dave. "We can't live without it."

"Shelley, thank you for your help today. Dave has to travel for work and won't be back until tomorrow morning."

"It's my pleasure. I love to babysit and I don't have to be at work until the afternoon today. It worked out well. At least you're not breast-feeding."

"I wanted to breast-feed, but I dried out pretty quickly. Too bad! My parents will be home by later this morning. You have directions to their house, right, Shelley?"

"I'm all set. I'll take the baby there before going to work later today. What time will you be home?" asked Shelley.

"My meeting will be a couple of hours, so I should be home by one or so. I'll come home and work on some paperwork and go back for the five o'clock meeting. I'll be home by six or six thirty."

"Are you picking up the baby then?" asked the sitter.

"No, I have another meeting at eight in the morning tomorrow. So, my parents will keep Sean tonight. It'll work out well, thanks to you. Hey, tell Dr. Norris we said hello when you see him at work later today."

"I sure will," said Shelley, shoveling green goo with a baby spoon.

Susan kissed her husband and her baby, grabbed her purse, and left, waving goodbye to Shelley. Dave followed Susan out to the garage, gesturing adios. They entered their cars and departed.

"I'll be right with you, little guy," said Shelley to the infant in the crib. She walked away and entered the laundry room. She first looked out into the backyard. All was quiet, no one around. She unlocked the window and opened it all the way up. The window slid up in its track with little effort. She closed the window, making sure she left the latch unlocked. Then exited the laundry room and shut the door behind her.

58

It felt good to be in the adult world, as Detective Susan Quentin put it. Two official meetings today began to place Susan back into her groove. She was sitting quietly at her desk at home, reviewing police policies. With no crying baby interrupting every minute, no high-maintenance husband demanding her attention, she was able to submerse herself in her work. She wore comfortable workout clothes and periodically sipped from her water glass. In the background, soft music from Lou Rawls filled the void. All was good.

A few miles away, the Norris family was watching cartoons, an after-dinner, prebedtime rite. It was gloomy outside, a blanket of moonless darkness awning the area.

"Let's go upstairs and read books," stated Jack, a fatherly tone in his voice, when Dora and Diego, the explorers, said their goodbyes. This expression signaled it was time to begin the slumber-time routine. The animation DVR show was deleted, giving way to live TV. As the three took the steps upstairs, in the distance and inaudibly, a newscaster reported on the escapee, Mike Ganz, the once FBI agent turned criminal. As the anchor spoke, the murderer's picture was displayed prominently on the screen. Upstairs, the Norris clan proceeded with the evening bedtime ceremony. A chart of magnets proudly announced Nick's good deeds of the day—he had not whined, hit, or been disobedient, and he had gotten dressed, brushed his teeth, and consistently used his thank-yous and pleases. All squares of the matrix were filled, proclaiming Nick's excellent behavior. Swollen with pride, Nick entered his bed already half-asleep. Jack and Claire turned off the light in the bedroom and tiptoed downstairs. The couple sat on the couch holding hands.

About twenty minutes later, Trinity barked lightly at first, then again with more rancor, her ears up in the air, scanning side to side.

"What is it, girl? Hear something?" asked Jack, getting up, his interest piqued. "Stay," commanded Jack as he looked out his front windows. All seemed quiet and still. He returned to Claire's side.

Outside, a dark figure ambulated unhurriedly, protected by shadows. He viewed the inside of the house through the window. He had remained undetected.

Detective Susan Quentin analyzed the paperwork in front of her relentlessly. She had reviewed several of the policies on her desk, but more work was required before she would retire for the evening. Her home was quiet. Soft Lou Rawls music filled the background. Occasionally, she sipped from a glass of water.

Back at the Norris' homestead, Trinity, first resting at Jack's side, once again rose up, all senses on alert. She stared at the front door and growled. Jack put a leash on the dog and walked out the front door, spying in all directions. All was tranquil. The tree branches and leaves swayed side to side, ever so slowly, gently persuaded by a light breeze.

"Anybody out here?" asked Jack of no one there. No response.

Unnoticed by the world, a mysterious man clandestinely moved past one window, ducking down to avoid being detected by the home dwellers. He remained undetected. In silence, he stirred delicately like a serpent in the dark.

"Trinity, you're hearing things, girl. Settle down," said Jack, pointing to the floor right next to the couch. He kissed Claire and sat down next to her. She was reading a book and sipping on a glass of wine. He raised his goblet and drank of the merlot. He put his drink down and picked up his book. The TV was off. The house was submersed in peaceful silence.

The trespasser tried multiple windows in the back of the home. He knew one of them would be unlocked, but was unsure as to which one. He tried one by one. One by one. One by one, until the one permitted his entrance into the domicile. Like an evil ninja in the night, he stepped inside the house into an unlit room. He shut the window, then put his ear to the door and listened. He strained to hear sounds from beyond the wood.

Restless, the dog whined again. She stared at the outside of the residence, as if her eyesight could penetrate the walls and doors.

"Settle down, Trinity. Settle down," softly spoke Jack, hoping to reassure and calm the canine. The words seemed to have tranquilized the dog, at least for now. "It's okay, Trinity. Settle down." A long moment later, Jack put his book down. Claire looked at him as he stood up.

"I'm going to the bathroom. Be right back," he said to Claire. "Stay," he continued, pointing at the floor, his gaze on the dog.

Jack walked toward the back of the house, some of the wooden boards under his feet creaking as he passed. Passing by a window, Jack took the opportunity to look outside. All seemed quiet and calm.

Susan picked up the glass on the table to take a sip of water. The glass was empty. She made a face and got on her feet, taking the opportunity to stretch her aching muscles. She walked to the kitchen and filled up her glass with tap water. She walked out of the kitchen and noticed the bathroom, its door ajar. She placed the cup of water on a decorative table just outside the restroom. The door closed after she entered the small space.

Jack closed the blinds and adjusted the curtains around the window and continued his journey to the toilet.

The figure in the darkened room patiently awaited his opportunity to pounce on his prey. Hearing steps in his direction, he made final preparation for the ambush. Someone entered the room next door. It was the downstairs bathroom. As the toilet flushed a few moments later, Mike took the occasion to open the door and silently tiptoed into the unilluminated hall. He stood in silence. The person in the bathroom was now at the sink, hand washing.

This may be the last time you wash your hands, he mused. The door opened, dumping bright light into the area.

It was then that Detective Susan Quentin realized her plight. Mike Ganz worked brilliantly fast, jumping out from the dark, rag of chloroform in hand, which he put to her nose and mouth. In the process, he caused the glass of water perched on the nearby table to fall on the wooden floor and shatter into pieces. She struggled with all her might, but her strength and resolve diminished rapidly as the brain numbness overwhelmed her senses. A few breaths of the anesthetizing gas blanketed her into unconsciousness as she fell lifelessly into Mike Ganz's arms.

"Thanks, Shelley," said Mike, no one listening. As he prepared to carry Susan's out-cold body to the car outside, he briefly glanced back into his entry room. It was the laundry room.

59

"Hello, Dr. Norris. Do you recognize me?" said a familiar voice as Jack answered his cell phone.

"Ex-FBI agent Mike Ganz," answered Jack. "I've been waiting for your call. Are you ready to return to your cage, where you belong?"

"Very funny, Jack. Very funny. Let's see if you're still funny after looking at the Web page I'm sending you right now." The phone call suddenly went dead, as did Jack's grin, his eyes focused on the developing screen. His system revolted with a sick feeling in his stomach. The Internet address was *www.SeeSusanDie.com*. As the picture unfolded, Jack observed Detective Susan Quentin on top of a large block. Her wrists were tied up behind her back. Her ankles were bound, her feet resting on a wide platform, atop a large cube. Behind the large block on which Susan stood, there was a gallows, a rope and noose around her neck. Susan seemed to be recovering from being barely conscious as her struggle to free herself augmented with the increasing awareness of her surroundings. Her tussle would remain futile. Jack's trance of horror as he viewed his cell phone screen was briskly interrupted by an incoming call.

"So, funny man. Are you still laughing?" asked the man.

"What have you done, Mike?" said Jack when he could speak, the horrific images still garroting his voice.

"You're seeing Susan die. She's standing on a block of ice. The ice is melting and as it does, her noose will become tighter and tighter until—" A pause. "Well, you get my drift."

"Please stop this, Mike. What do you want from me?" asked Jack excitedly.

"You have Simon Lagrange. Give him back. Even exchange."

"I don't have him, Mike," uttered Jack.

"Well, you get him. But work fast. It's pretty hot. That block will be melting all the way down pretty soon. I'd say you have a couple of hours, at most."

"Okay. I'll see what I can do. How do we do this?"

"You tell me where Simon is and I tell you where Susan is. It's that easy!" The criminal spoke confidently. "You have my cell phone number on your caller ID. Personally, I wouldn't bother with the police. Believe me, they'll just slow you down with their questions and procedures. And, Jack, time's not on Susan's side. Contact me when you have Simon's location."

"Wait, Mike. Wait!" yelled Jack into a disconnected call. As his mobile screen swapped back to the Internet mode, the doctor viewed his friend, panic and horror congesting her eyes as she squirmed about on the large ice cube. His gaze zeroed in on the noose around Susan's neck.

60

Jack called Kate. He knew he had to work fast. It was a moderately warm day. He wasn't sure how long it would take until the platform on which Susan stood would be too short to support her weight, at which point she would be hanged. He may have one, two, at most three hours. His action had to be multipronged. He had to set up a swap between Simon Lagrange and Susan Quentin. But he realized he was dealing with crooks. He wasn't naïve enough to think that it was a sure thing. Chances were good that Mike would not keep his word. After all, he, like his father, was looking for revenge. Revenge from Susan. Mike and Susan had been an item three years ago. The relationship suffered a sudden death when she stopped him from leaving the country and placed him under arrest for murder. Three long years of incarceration made him very bitter and bent on revenge.

"Hi, Kate," said Jack anxiously as she answered her cell phone. "Simon Lagrange's son, Mike Ganz, alias Michel Lagrange, abducted Susan."

"Mike Ganz is in prison," interrupted the nurse.

"No, he escaped. He's got Susan and will kill her if we don't work fast to swap her for Lagrange. Does your cell phone give you Internet coverage?"

"Yes."

"I'm sending you a web link. It's www.SeeSusanDie.com," explained the doctor breathlessly.

"Wow," said Kate after a few moments. "What is she standing on?"

"It's a block of ice. She won't have enough rope for long," began Jack. "It's a warm day and—"

"Let's swap them," interrupted Kate nervously. "Let's do it quickly. How do we do it?"

"I'll call Mike and tell him where you are. I need you to do me a big favor," said Jack.

"Sure, anything."

"I don't want you to be there when he arrives. He's a very dangerous man. But I want you to go get a bottle of champagne and some plastic flutes."

"Did you say champagne and flutes?" asked Kate incredulously.

"Yes. If you can't find champagne easily and quickly, any good wine or bubbly will do. We'll tell Lagrange you and I are planning to celebrate putting him in prison. Don't tell him about Mike or the swap," remarked Jack. "I don't have time to explain now. Trust me. And hurry up." He disconnected the call. Then he called Detective Mills and explained the whole situation. The police were already on maximal alert for the fugitive, but they would focus their efforts in the Evansville area. When Jack hung up with the detective, he dialed Claire's cell phone.

"Will you please call Dave, her husband?" he solicited once he explained the whole situation. "Maybe her parents too."

"Sure, I'll do that. No problem. What else can I do?" asked Claire.

"Where does one get a huge block of ice?" posed Jack, intrigue all over his face.

"I'll find out. For that matter, how do you transport it, to use it as a platform of death?" continued Claire. "I'll find out the answer to these questions."

"Get back to me as soon as you can. I have to go steal some medications from the pharmacy at the hospital."

Jack drove like a madman to Newton Memorial Hospital. There was no time to waste. He looked at his mobile phone's screen and glimpsed at the surmounting horror in Susan's face. The noose was still loose, but already he could perceive the hanging rope had less slack in it. The ice block height was diminishing. With much resolve, he drove on.

"Hey, Nelson. Buddy. I need a huge favor," he asked the head of pharmacy at the hospital.

"Sure, Dr. Norris, anything," agreed the pharmacist. "What can I do for you?"

"I need Antabuse," said the hurried doctor, "and I need it quickly. Do you have some in stock?"

"I'll look. We don't use it much at all. I may have some. I'll be right back," said Nelson, disappearing deep into the belly of the pharmacy. He returned a few minutes later, what seemed to be an eternity. In his right hand, Nelson carried a vial containing a few tablets, which Jack whisked in a heartbeat.

"Great! Thanks," said Jack, running away with it.

"Wait—," the pharmacist started to say but in a flash, the doctor was gone.

Jack drove to the barn and entered hurriedly. He beat Kate to the destiny.

"Simon Lagrange, we meet again," said Jack, approaching the older man tied up to a chair. "I have good news for you. I convinced Kate to give you your medications. I have them for you." Jack placed three tablets in the man's mouth. "Here's some water," added Jack, helping the prisoner take the medications.

"Thanks," said the criminal appreciatively.

"You are welcome." There was a long awkward moment of silence. "Did you swallow your medications?" asked Jack.

"Yes. Thank you. I'm glad you convinced her to give me my meds even after what I tried to do to you," said Simon, a hint of remorse in his voice.

"I also have some food and water for you to drink. I'll get it. It's in my car outside. Are you hungry?"

"I'm starved."

Jack walked toward the outside door and disappeared from sight. He had used this excuse to speak with Kate, whose car he had heard approaching the barn. He waited until she parked nearby.

"Let's follow the plan like we discussed before. I'm going inside with the food. You come in and join us in a few minutes. Bring in the champagne and glasses and we'll pretend we're going to celebrate his capture," said Jack. "We'll leave the booze and the flutes in the barn in plain sight when we leave.

"Okay," said Kate, sitting back into her car seat anxiously.

Jack entered the barn with a bag of burgers, enticing smells escaping from the sac.

"If you'll behave, I'll free your right hand so you can eat by yourself. Deal?"

"Sure, Jack. I'm too sick to run away," agreed Simon with a grin.

Jack freed up his right hand and Simon took on the burger ferociously. A few minutes later, Kate walked in.

"Let's celebrate capturing Simon Lagrange," stated Kate as rehearsed, placing the bottle and flutes on a table near the exit.

"Not yet, Kate. Let's celebrate after we deliver him to the authorities."

"It just so happens, I brought a bag of ice. It's in the car," she walked toward the front door. "I'll be right back." She disappeared beyond the barn door. A few minutes later, Jack's cell phone rang. As it did, Kate entered and Jack exited the farm building. Kate set up the champagne on the bucket of ice and arranged the two flutes nearby. A few minutes later, Jack reemerged, a concerned look on his face.

"Kate," started Jack. "I just received a call from Mike Ganz." These words lit up Lagrange's face, who, nonetheless, remained silent. "He has Susan Quentin and will kill her if we don't give him our prisoner." Jack paused. "We have no choice. I told him how to get here. He agreed to call me when he takes Simon to tell me where Susan is. An even exchange." There was a long pause.

"Okay. I don't see that we have any alternatives," agreed Kate. Jack retied Simon's hand behind the chair and soon Simon Lagrange was alone again.

61

The rope was starting to cause Susan some discomfort. She was alone. Her feet and legs were becoming increasingly cold. She was wearing tube socks and sweat pants with a thin, flimsy Columbus Crew jersey Jack had given her for her birthday last year, together with tickets to one of their soccer games. Her feet were tied together painfully, with little give. She had tried to move her feet, hoping to loosen up the rope that forcibly united her ankles. Under her feet was a large tray, separating her socks from the actual ice cube. Her wrists were tightly bound behind her back. Efforts to slacken the ties had been fruitless. She could still stand straight on the cold platform under her feet, but she realized the platform was lowering itself little by little. Around her neck, there was a noose attached to a rope. The idea was plain to see. As the ice block underneath her shrunk to the effects of the ambient temperature, the neck noose would cause her hanging. How much longer would she have? She pondered fearfully. Who was looking for her? Would she be rescued? The place was dim, but Susan was aware of what appeared to be a camera, maybe two, pointing at her. Were there microphones? Who was watching? Who was listening? Anybody out there?

Suddenly, she felt her body fall toward the ground a few inches, causing the discomfort around her neck to intensify. With difficulty, Susan directed her gaze downwardly. Around the block of ice, there was an increasing pool of water, which was steaming up toward the ceiling. She swallowed some saliva that had accumulated in her mouth. Swallowing caused slight discomfort, but Susan realized this was going to become quite painful in the near future, as the choker around her neck tightened.

Susan's thoughts shifted to David and Sean. How happy she had been since meeting her husband and giving birth to their first child. Would she be deprived of this happiness forevermore? Was this the end of her life? Who would raise Sean? She had to think of something to get herself out of this predicament. But what?

62

The large barn was hot, humid, and quiet. In the center, tied up to a chair, which was securely attached to a supporting pole, waited Simon Lagrange. Cautiously, a car approached and parked, the driver carefully spying all around to make sure he wasn't being set up. Satisfied, Mike Ganz exited the vehicle, a gun drawn. All remained quiet and still. Mike entered the barn.

"Papa," he said, enthusiastically running to Simon's side. He quickly freed him and the two hugged. "How are you? Are you hurt?"

"No, I'm fine. Let's get out of here, Ganzo," said Simon, hurriedly rushing out toward the door, Mike in his wake.

"Wait," paused Mike, noticing the champagne perched in the small ice bucket. "We'll take this. We need to celebrate, and liquor stores are out of the question for us for a while." He smiled at Simon, confiscating the bottle and the two flutes. Soon the two fugitives were sitting in Mike's car, speeding away from the farm.

"You have Simon. Where's Susan, Mike?" asked the caller as the car sped faster and faster.

"I do have Simon, Jack. Thanks for taking such good care of my father."

"Okay. Where's Susan?" repeated Jack.

"You really think I'm going to tell you, Jack?"

"You gave your word, Mike. Tell me where she is. Please."

"Bad guys don't have to keep their word. Only good guys." The car sped on. The call went silent, a smile on both prisoners' faces as they briefly looked at each other.

"Where is Susan?" yelled Jack into his cell phone even after he realized there was no one on the other side to listen to him. Frustrated, Jack hit the steering wheel with the palm of his right hand then dialed another number.

"Claire, what have you found out?" asked Jack.

"I got a lot of information. I'm still processing it. I'll have some answers for you in a few minutes. What did you find out?" asked Claire.

"Mike has Simon. They drove away from the barn. But Mike's not telling us where Susan is," said Jack despondently.

"We need to work fast. How is Susan doing? Did you call the police?" asked Claire.

"I'll check on Susan as soon as I'm done filling in Detective Mills. Get a hold of me when you have any clues or ideas about the ice block."

"Where's Kate?" inquired Claire.

"She's driving her car right behind me. We'll be at your location in a few."

63

Jack called Detective Brad Mills and delineated all the details of the recent events, catching the cop up with the most up-to-date activities.

"Brad, place undercover policemen at all the emergency departments. The Lagranges will be showing up at one of them over the next few hours," forecasted Jack. "I'll explain later. I have to join forces with Claire and find out where Susan is. She doesn't have much time left."

Once the call terminated, Jack returned to www.SeeSusanDie.com and witnessed his friend squirming uncomfortably on his screen, the noose on her neck increasingly tense. Although no sound paralleled the live image, the facts were plain to see. Susan was getting in trouble and would probably not have much longer. They would have to find her. And soon. Jack could also determine that she was freezing, noticing her body shivering uncontrollably, a plume of breath visible as she exhaled.

"Where are you, Susan?" deliberated Jack aloud. "What type of room are you in?" He gawked attentively at the screen. "What kind of walls are those? They look weird. Are there any windows? How far are you from the door?" The image quality was purposefully poor to prevent derivation of clues. Jack could not discern any windows or doors. The walls were devoid of pictures or paint. Just dull gray drab. There were no furnishings, other than the dreaded gallows apparatus and the diminishing ice block platform. *It must be very cold in there*, reflected Jack, observing the thickness of Susan's breath. "At least I can see you're breathing. Hang in there, Susan. We're coming for you. We'll get you out of there," resolved Jack, doubt amassing in his words to himself.

64

By the time Jack and Kate reached Claire's location, she had a plan.

"Okay, we know Susan's on a block of ice," began Claire. I looked up places here in Evansville where you could buy those. There are three places. The next issue is, how do you transport the block of ice? It's huge and weighs a ton. A refrigerator truck. I found a place in Evansville that sells ice blocks that big, and as it so happens, they reported a stolen refrigerator truck this morning. Detective Mills helped me with that. I have a picture of the truck. It is gray and huge." Claire removed a large picture from the backseat of her van. "The police have disseminated the picture to all the patrolling officers, and they have an APB out for Mike and Simon, not only in Evansville but also in surrounding towns and counties. The local police and the FBI are doing all they can to locate the Lagranges, but so far, they have not had any luck," said Claire.

"Can we use GPS to locate the missing truck?" asked Jack.

"Unfortunately, this company doesn't place GPS tags on its vehicles, so we can't use that to locate the truck. I don't think there's anything else we can do besides wait." Claire sounded defeated.

"Excellent work," said Kate encouragingly. "There's got to be something else we can do. For one thing, we can drive around and look for the truck as well. I'll call everybody at work and send them a picture of the truck. The more eyes we have looking, the better the chance of—"

"Wait a minute. That's a great idea, Kate," interrupted Jack, looking heavenward. "A wonderful idea." Jack had an optimistic look on his face. Enthusiastically, he fished out his cell phone from his pocket and dialed.

While Jack retreated to make his call, the women typed in their mobile devices: www.SeeSusanDie.com. On the screen, Susan was now standing on her tiptoes, the noose around her neck and rope stretched tightly. She was beginning to have significant respiratory distress, the breath moisture coming in spurts. The melting process was slightly uneven, and Susan was struggling awkwardly to stand on the right side of the block, the higher ground. She shivered uncomfortably.

"She doesn't have much time, does she?" asked Kate, fear and frustration obvious in her voice.

"I don't think so," answered Claire, losing hope. "I don't think so."

"I can't stand to watch her and I can't stand not to watch her," finally said Kate after a long pause.

"Come on, ladies. We have to get to a fax machine quickly. Who wants to drive?" asked Jack, returning to where the women were standing, his voice excited and eager.

65

The Emergency Department at the small hospital in Vincennes was quiet. One man lay on a gurney in room 3 watching TV, his wife sitting at his bedside. He had presented two hours earlier with chest pains. So far, the evaluation had not revealed a heart attack. It would be a waiting game for a few more hours before a determination would be made as to whether he could go home or would needed to be observed in the hospital overnight.

Fifty minutes earlier, a woman brought in her seventeen-year-old son who had suffered a concussion while playing football at the local high school. He was in room 4. Interestingly, the head trauma transpired during a well-executed and legal play. Cody rested comfortably, now aware of his surroundings. A splitting headache was still present but manageably so. The initial nausea and dizziness waxed and waned, but for now, he was at ease. The beep, beep, beep of Cody's heart monitor competed musically with the older man's in the room next door.

"No, I don't like football. American football, that is. I love real football as played all over the world—soccer," said Dr. Robertson.

"Come on, Doc. Football is exciting; I love to watch the pros on TV," disagreed Cody.

"Exciting, yes, if you like commercials." A short pause for effect. "Look, you watch an hour game for three plus hours. So, there are three minutes of commercials to every minute of football. Of that hour of football, there is action for only about twenty minutes. The rest of the time, we're watching the clock tick. Competing for those twenty minutes of playing action, there are three teams per team—offense, defense, and special teams. So each player, on average, sees about two to three minutes of actual action, right?" asked the ER doctor.

"Yeah," said the boy.

"And then the number of injuries in football far exceeds that of just about any other sport," continued Dr. Robertson. "You're a good example. Let me put it this way: The average American lives about seventy-seven years. Do you know what the average life span of an NFL player is?"

"No, what?"

"It's only fifty-five, fifty-three for linemen."

"Wow! Really?"

"I'm not kidding. Do a Google search when you get home. That's where I got my information."

"I told you and your father that football is a barbaric and dangerous sport and I didn't want you playing it," interjected Cody's mother, sitting in a chair at the bedside.

"This is how I see it: you need very expensive gear, during the games you sit for over three hours to play less than five minutes, and you put yourself at a much higher chance of serious injuries than just about any other sport. Fortunately, soccer is growing at an incredibly fast rate in this country and, hopefully, more and more kids will continue to choose soccer and stay away from football." Cody and his mother remained silent, in thought. "We'll watch you a little bit longer. I'm still waiting on the neurologist to call us back. So stay in bed for now. Call the nurse, if you need anything." Dr. Robertson left the small cubicle.

Two nurses and two techs conversed about their ordinary personal lives. A hospital security guard and a township undercover police officer had joined in the banter. Suddenly, the large doors to the emergency vehicle bay swung open. *An unannounced ambulance? Why hadn't they radioed in?* all mused, everyone's eyes gazing toward the opening. From the shadows beyond the threshold, two dark figures appeared. A man assisted another, who was bent slightly at the waist, into the building. He was in obvious misery, stopping occasionally heaving dryly. The older man was obviously weak, anguish written all over his face. The younger of the two appeared anxious and restless. The ER staff got up from their perches and rushed to the newly arrived.

"Get Dr. Robertson," said the older nurse to the younger one. She complied. "Get a stretcher, Jon," she continued, looking at one of the techs. Soon the distressed man was on a bed and in room 1. The doctor arrived and, with the rest of the crew, disappeared into the small cubicle.

"Let me get some information from you, sir," demanded one of the techs, of the departing younger man.

"Sure. I'll be right back. I need to go park my car," said the younger man, leaving the locale hurriedly.

All the while, the Vincennes undercover officer sat back in his chair, observing. He had carried from his car a clipboard, which he placed on the counter. Trying to remain inconspicuous, he nonchalantly spied the two large pictures. The pictures of the two men he was dispatched to this location to seek.

"He won't be coming back," he told the hospital security guard. "Come with me, Milo," he continued walking to room 1, the other guard in tow. He opened the door to the examination cubicle. A nurse was holding a large puke tray and the patient was unloading pieces of his hamburger lunch into it.

"Can you please wait out there?" asked the nurse.

"No, I'm sorry. I can't," said the policeman. "This is Mr. Simon Lagrange, a most wanted man by the FBI. He is dangerous. I need to frisk him for weapons for your protection and place him under arrest." And so he did. He searched him quickly and thoroughly then cuffed the prisoner to the stretcher. "He's clean," said the cop, making a face while wiping his hands from vomit on the bedsheet. "Well, sort of clean. No weapons, at least. Milo, you're in charge until my men come in. Let the doc and nurses do their thing, but don't let this man out of your sight for any reason. Okay?"

"Fine," responded the security guard, one hand on his revolver, holstered on his belt. "I'll take care of it." The cop departed the room swiftly.

"Four-seven to headquarters," said the officer into his microphone as he pursued Michel Lagrange's vehicle out of the parking lot.

"Go ahead, 4-7," came the reply.

"I'm in an unmarked car following one of the men on that APB you sent out earlier. The other one is under arrest at the ER. Send a car there to stay with him and bring him in when able. The man is in room 1 and is pretty sick right now. I'll give you a plate number on this vehicle, as soon as I am able. The car is a Chevy Impala, black. Inform Detective Mills of the Evansville PD and have him call me on my cell ASAP." The inconspicuous pursuit continued heading south on Route 41. Unobtrusively, the cop kept the vehicle in sight, staying back about three cars. A few minutes later, his mobile phone vibrated.

"He may be going to her location now. Don't let him see you," demanded Brad Mills after giving the Vincennes officer the background information. "He's our only lead to find my detective. If he knows we're following him, he'll escape and we'll have no way to find her."

66

Her eyes were puffy from the tears. But they were not tears of defeat; they were tears of rage. She would endure. It was becoming very difficult to breathe, her choke collar increasingly suffocating her. Standing on an icy platform had caused her core temperature to become glacial. Her body obliged her to unconsciously accelerate her respiratory rate and depth, deepening her agony. Stretching her body and toes was still giving her enough support, but it wouldn't be long until her windpipe would collapse completely, giving to the weight of her own body. The good news was that the ambient temperature had dropped significantly, given the small quarters. This had created a refrigerator effect, and decreased the rate of melting of the huge ice block. Susan feared losing consciousness. If this happened, her full body weight would cause her cervical spine and airway to crumple, garroting her to death. To gather strength, Susan thought of Dave and Sean, her boys. Right now, they provided Susan with much-needed resolute stoicism. To stay awake and generate body heat, Susan danced like a ballerina on the frigid stage. She knew she would not last much longer. She sang to herself and pranced about, tippytoeing on her little scaffold. *"You are my sunshine, my only sunshine. You make me happy when skies are gray,"* she chanted in silence, smiling at the reflection of her baby son. *"You'll never know, dear, how much I love you, so please don't take my sunshine away."* The tune gave her the strength she required at this time to stay alive. Her love for her son would see her through this ordeal. *"The other night, dear, as I lay sleeping, I dreamed I held you in my arms. When I awoke, dear, I was mistaken. And I held my head and cried."* Someone will come for me. There must be hundreds of people searching for me. *"You are my sunshine, my only sunshine,"* continued Susan, shivering, her mind still singing, *"You make me happy when skies are gray."* Her consciousness was slipping into oblivion. She couldn't allow that. She would fight. Fight and sing. *"You'll never know, dear, how much I love—"* she leapt from toe to toe. Stay awake. Don't give up. *"How much I love you. Don't take my sunshine—"* a pause, a slow agonizing swallow. "Away," she managed to say aloud, her word merely a whisper, raspy and slurred.

67

"Sweetheart, I don't want you around me for now. I just rescued my father from the police but I had to take him to the ER. He got sick to his stomach. I couldn't care for him alone." He paused while the other person spoke.

"This is too hot right now. You stay away from me. I'll call you when things settle down," he commanded authoritatively, then paused to hear. "Yes, I have her. Remember where I told you I would meet you one day, if ever I escaped?" A break in the conversation, while Mike listened. "Yes. She's there. They'll never find her in time." Mike drove on, ascertaining that his driving was lawful and impeccable, lest he be stopped for speeding and ruin his chances of escaping. "On TV, really? Already? I figure every cop in the district is looking for her. And us." The conversation went on for several minutes.

As Mike hung up the call, his thoughts were of his father. He was too sick and taking him to the ER was his only salvation. With his recent heart surgery, being this sick could kill him. *At least he's in a small ER. I'll come back for him tomorrow.* But how opportune it all was.

I rescue him from Jack Norris and he begins to throw up violently with waves of dizziness, mused the assassin, now thinking more like an FBI agent, his previous paying job. *I thought it was the champagne, but Papa has had champagne many times before. And I had even more champagne and I didn't get sick at all.* Mike drove on, more and more suspicious of foul play. *Jack did it to us again.* A pause. A moment to process. *That son of a*—His thoughts were interrupted as he became acutely aware of his situation. He looked in the rearview mirror, then side to side, suspicious of all things. He turned right at the next light, barely tapping the brakes to slow down. *Voila!* he said aloud to himself. *I'm being followed.* He was now sure of it as a vehicle struggled to turn right from the highway at a fast speed, surprised by the sudden change in direction. Mike stood on the accelerator, picking up speed. His phone vibrated in his pocket again.

"I can't speak now." He put the caller on speakerphone as he would require both hands to drive fast and away from his pursuer. "Let me call you in a—" He was interrupted.

"Mike, I just turned on the TV. Your father is all over the news. He's under arrest in the ER at Vincennes. The newscaster says you fled and that they're pursuing you," said an excited woman's voice.

"It's true. I'm trying to escape now from an unmarked cop car who's right on my tail. What else are they saying?" yelled Mike so as to be heard over the roaring engine. Mike took a sharp left and reentered the highway. He gunned the Chevy.

"Your father is stable in police custody and will be released from the ER later today to jail here in Evansville," continued the keyed-up voice on the other side of the call.

"Okay, keep me informed of what you learn. I'm going to try to lose this bozo behind me. Call me—" Mike's sentence was cut short by the loud sound of a helicopter overhead.

"I hear it too. Mike, I see your car on TV. The chopper is giving a live feed." The woman yelled frantically into her phone, competing with the background noise. "There are several other police cars coming your way," she shouted. "From all directions."

Mike's car swerved left, again exiting the interstate. He entered a small country road, his foot depressing the accelerator to the metal. The helicopter hovered overhead, like the proverbial black cloud. Two cruisers rushed in his direction from the west, three others from the south and one on his tail, the chase clearly displayed on the television.

"Mike, turn north," roared the woman into the microphone, realizing all other roads were occupied with wall-to-wall cop cars.

"Thanks, babe," screeched Mike, turning his steering hard. The car skidded for several yards and collided with a sturdy oak tree head-on. Smoke burst from the front of the crashed automobile.

"Mike! Mike!" yelled the woman. "Mike, can you hear me?" she cried. "Mike, are you all right?" Her screams became chocked with emotion as her realization of the terrible accident sharpened, her brain still in shock. "Mike! Mike," bawled the voice from within the wreckage, the cell phone still on speakerphone.

The live feed on TV cut to a newsman, who for the umpteenth time recounted the events of the last several minutes. Horrified, the woman would soon hear the cops declare the fugitive was DOA right through her own phone.

68

Several miles to the south, Jack looked up at the skies. It had been an eternity since his last phone call, and he was starting to get worried. The heavens were clear of clouds, the visibility as long as the eye could see.

"There they are," announced Jack to the women, pointing to the blue above. "Can you hear them?" A few more seconds passed when multiple aircraft started to appear, patrolling the county, all pilots with a picture of a large ice truck. Jack dialed a phone number on his cell.

"Steve, how many do you have up there?" he asked. Jack placed the mobile or speakerphone to allow the ladies to follow the conversation.

"There are nine airplanes and two helicopters. I'm coordinating from here, at the airport. I created a grid of the surrounding counties. They're all looking for—" his words were interrupted by a radio transmission in the background. "Hang on, Jack." Steve Peskie placed his phone on the desk and picked up the radio microphone.

"Go ahead, 72-foxtrot-bravo," he replied.

"Steve, I see a truck that perfectly resembles the one in the picture. It's on a farm, twelve miles from Pocket City VOR on the 290 radial," proclaimed the private pilot assigned to fly southwest of the Evansville airport, the thrill of discovery evident in his voice.

"What's a Pocket City VOR?" asked Kate. Claire shrugged her shoulders.

"Pocket City is the name of a transmitting beacon referred to as a very high frequency omnidirectional radio or VOR. It's located to the west of the city, used for navigation for incoming and departing flights. According to the pilot's report, the truck is located twelve miles in the direction given from that point in space."

"Here it is!" exclaimed Steve. "I looked up that area on Google Earth in my computer. I'm sending the Google map info to your cell phone right now."

"Got it," said Jack a few moments later. "Thanks, buddy. I owe you one," said Jack.

"No, no! For all of this, you owe me at least three flights on your Bonanza. You know how much I love your airplane," said Steve.

"You got it. Steve, give the pilot my cell number and text me his cell number. That way we can both communicate with each other easier."

"Will do," said Steve.

"Thanks, man." Jack terminated the call as the three entered the car. While Jack drove like a maniac, Kate informed Detective Mills of the recent events and the location of the scene.

Once he received the pilot's cell number, Jack called him to ascertain that communication was feasible. The pilot provided a thorough description of the area surrounding the large truck. The vehicle was located on a small unattended farm. Close to the small country road serving the location, there was a house and three barns of different sizes, all in disrepair. The truck had been parked farther back into the property, near a ravine overlooking the Ohio River, meandering far below. A futile attempt had been made to obscure the corpulent vehicle from view by large trees, but its sheer size made that task unfeasible. Jack drove on, but his ETA to the scene was twelve more minutes, with eight miles to go, according to the GPS. Jack vowed he'd make it in ten minutes.

Two squad cars arrived first and parked in front of the main farmhouse. The officers, guns drawn, had taken the immediate task of searching each structure, going room by room, clearing each as they progressed. Detective Mills' unmarked vehicle and four other police cars arrived. They added their efforts to the search within the barns, which had remained fruitless.

69

Jack drove like a madman. Claire looked intently at her cell phone, viewing www.SeeSusanDie.com. Claire's face was distorted with agony and pain she felt for her friend. Kate looked on, horrified. Helpless.

"Come on, Jack. Get there," the ladies would yell from time to time, their nerves unraveled by the images.

Susan was now just about completely suspended by her neck, her toes barely touching the platform over the shrinking ice cube. Her breaths were shallow and labored. Occasionally, she swallowed saliva from her mouth, but painfully.

"Hurry up, Jack," agonized Claire, her heart aching. As their car approached the area, the red and white emergency lights of the multiple police vehicles gave testimony of the unfolding crisis. Hurriedly, Jack put the Lexus in park and all exited.

"No, she's in the truck. Down there! In the truck," yelled Jack excitedly at the crowd of police officers, pointing down toward the ravine and the ice truck. "She's dying in the truck."

As Kate exited the car, her attention was immediately drawn to one of the police vehicles. Kate gawked inside, spying a rifle resting on a gun rack. She opened up the door and quickly removed the firearm. She analyzed the weapon—it was loaded. On top of it, a telescope was mounted. *Sweet,* she thought. *You might come in handy.* Unnoticed by the busy officers, Kate carried the rifle along.

"Did you just take that from the police car?" asked Jack, noticing the nurse was now carrying a long weapon.

"Yes. It may come in handy," said Kate.

"Do you know how to use that?" inquired Jack, not sure what to think.

"Yes. My father taught me how to shoot. I've been around shotguns and rifles all my life. I've won many trophies in contests." Jack gave a nod of understanding, and the two joined the others, who remained unaware of the weapon.

The road was not passable by the types of vehicles present, with multiple fallen trees in the way, the whole property neglected by the passing years.

"Someone bring blankets, oxygen, and a knife to cut the ropes. Call for an ambulance," yelled Jack, beginning to sprint.

"Have EMS approach from the south. They won't be able to reach the truck either if they come in the way we did," ordered Detective Mills. One of the cops nodded in agreement and retreated slightly to communicate to headquarters with his radio.

The truck was parked sideways, the back of it facing away from the spectators. The back door was ajar. As Jack and the others began to run toward the truck, their hearts suddenly paused. Frozen by the developing horror, they stopped in their tracks. To their dismay, the truck quivered to life, a puff of smoke blowing out a pipe over the cab. Someone exited the cab and walked rapidly toward the back of the vehicle. A woman, perhaps. It was too far to be sure. The person entered the ice truck through the back door. Instinctually, Claire glimpsed at her cell phone; the atrocity of her friend's suffering continued unfolding in front of her eyes. Unlike before, Susan now had a visitor, seen on the Web page. The woman touched a button, and the screen developed a voice. In the foreground appeared a young woman's face, her hair disheveled, her eyes swollen.

"You killed Mike, the love of my life," she screamed, tears rolling down her cheeks. "Now, I'll kill your friend," she continued, bawling loudly.

Jack, Claire, and Kate looked at one another in disbelief, realizing who the crazed young woman was.

"It's Shelley," murmured Jack to those around him. "It's Shelley from the office." He couldn't believe his eyes. "Don't do this. Let us help you. Please," yelled Jack, begging of his office assistant, though nothing would carry his words into the truck far down the hill. He felt betrayed, a dagger through his heart, adding to the melancholy of the already gloomy occasion.

"Shelley. Let us help you. We're your friends," screamed Kate, now continuing her trot, following all others.

Shelley disappeared into the background, Susan becoming again the main feature on the Web page, the noose around her neck unyielding. The truck quivered more forcibly, a thicker plume of smoke exiting from its exhaust pipe, then began moving forward, slowly at first, shaking as it did. The group accelerated their run toward the moving vehicle, which was gathering speed, gaining forward momentum. Jack's phone vibrated. He answered the call, running.

"The truck's moving toward a huge cliff. An abyss. It's going to dive into the Ohio River below," exclaimed an excited man's voice. Jack looked up and saw a Cessna 172 circling over the farm. "I can see the whole area and it ain't good," continued the aviator. "It's gotta be about a three-hundred-foot fall, maybe more. At present speed, the truck will be at the edge in about fifteen maybe twenty seconds."

After thanking the pilot for the information, Jack hung up the call so he could concentrate on his dash. The truck was now moving away from the group, its back door allowing a view of Susan, now suspended by her neck, her hands tied behind her back. Despite their run, it would be unlikely the group would reach the truck before it dove into the river below. For that matter, it would be doubtful that Susan could survive another moment hanging in the moving vehicle.

"Everybody, stop," yelled Kate from amidst the advancing cadre. "Get out of the way!" All eyes turned to her as they stopped in their tracks. Kate had ceased to dart, seeing its futility, and had assumed a rifle-shooting position, one knee on the ground supporting her arm holding up the weapon. "I can do this," she stated softly and calmly to the cops, Claire and Jack nearby. Detective Mills instinctively advanced toward the girl and placed a hand on the body of the firearm, ready to yank it out of Kate's possession.

"Let her shoot," uttered Jack firmly, his eyes locked on Mills'. "Trust me," he said, nodding slowly. "We have nothing to lose. We can't reach the truck in time." Mills acquiesced and released his grip on the weapon, his instincts chillingly beseeching him to do so. Kate steadied herself as she peered through the telescope, visualizing inside the cargo area of the escaping truck. Through the expanding cloud of dust and smoke trailing behind the moving vehicle, Kate continued to steady her hands, hoping for nothing short of pinpoint accuracy. The hanging rope tied to the noose around Susan's neck swayed in and out of the crosshairs of the rifle as the object moved farther and farther away, more and more by each passing tick of the clock. The gallows now supported Susan's weight, 100 percent of it. She balanced precariously on the fence separating this world from that beyond. Her only source of oxygen now was the meager amounts already in her bloodstream, allowing Susan less than twenty or thirty seconds before succumbing to asphyxiation. As moribund as this notion was, if Kate's efforts did not free Susan from the scaffold, she would have less than ten seconds to live, fastened to the diving ton of metal, the truck likely to explode on impact with the terrain hundreds of feet below.

The gap between the advancing massive vehicle and the edge of the abyss closed with each passing heartbeat. Kate's breaths became slow and rhythmic, as she had done thousands of time when she was a younger girl, on the farm with her dad. *Sturdy and balanced. No rush*, she heard her father's calming voice say in her ear, distancing her from the chaos. *Here goes*, she thought, pulling the trigger. Double shots in quick succession resonated through the canyon. A few seconds later, the ice truck became airborne and disappeared into the chasm, leaving behind a thick plume of dust and smoke. A moment later, a loud explosion pierced through the peaceful afternoon, massively disrupting it. Paralyzed by the unfolding tragedy, the rescuers stood for a moment, aghast and in shock. Then, they resumed their rapid procession toward the place where the truck disappeared. The dust began to clear, allowing the group to see the path taken by the large vehicle. Multiple thoughts swirled around their minds: *Did anybody escape? Is Susan dead? Did the two women perish in the explosion, as the truck dove into the gorge? Did the rifle shots free up Susan, and if so, was she able to jump off the truck in time?* As anticipation swelled, tears began to sprout in the rescuers' eyes, all early signs pointing to a bad outcome. Through the dissipating haze, a distorted image appeared to have moved several yards in front of them. The group persisted with their unrelenting scuttle. A poorly defined mass within the smog had definitely moved, ever so slightly, but surely. As they approached, the body of a woman could now be appreciated, the dust clearing further. Definite movement—slightly at first, then a fruitless attempt to stand up. It was Susan. Detective Susan Quentin was alive, a severed frayed short rope still attached to the noose around her neck, a rope and noose previously destined to suffocate the life out of the detective. As the group arrived at her side, Jack knelt next to her.

"Susan, you're going to be all right. We're here with you," said Jack repeatedly. Susan was freezing cold, shivering uncontrollably. The noose around her neck had caused a painful deep groove surrounded by swollen tissue. Susan still struggled to breathe. Jack carried her in his arms, first alone, then others rushed to help.

"Let's get her away from this dust. Where's the oxygen? We need warm clothes and blankets," yelled Jack. Little by little, the concerned look on Jack's face began to fade, replaced by hope and optimism. "I think she'll be okay. Susan, you're going to be okay." The noose was gently slashed, allowing her to pass air and saliva through her mouth and nose, improving her color drastically.

"Thank y—," she slurred, a smile barely forming on her face. "Thank you," she repeated, her teeth chattering, her jaws quivering, from the cold. Near-frozen tears dared to flood her eyes. Relieved, Susan's brain began to mercifully disconnect as she slowly slipped into unconsciousness, all along her mind still singing, *"Don't take my sunshine away!"*

Epilogue

A year and a half later

The indoor soccer game was full of excitement. The Heartbeats were playing their nemesis, the Old & Arthritic, a team they were yet to beat. Jack, the captain of the Heartbeats, had rallied the troops before the game, hoping the psychology of it all would give his team the advantage. And it had. Somehow, the Heartbeats were up 2-0 as the buzzer sounded, announcing halftime. There would be a ten-minute interval before resuming play.

"I figured it out, Dr. Norris," screamed a voice from the spectator seats, adjacent to the indoor field.

"What did you say, Frank?" shouted Jack from the indoor soccer field.

"I know how to move the wolf, the rabbit, and the carrot," yell Frank. Jack walked back to the net separating the audience from the players.

"Okay, tell me."

"The first trip you take the rabbit across the river. The second trip you take the wolf, but bring the rabbit back. The third trip you take the carrot to the wolf. Last trip, you come back for the rabbit."

"You got it, grasshopper," said Jack, smiling. Claire, Susan, and Kate looked on, a bemused look on their faces. Jack winked at the group and returned to his teammates for the halftime rituals.

"What was that all about?" asked Kate.

Frank began to explain the riddle posed by Jack. As the words were spoken, Claire's mind drifted, her thoughts shifting to the well-being of her friends and family, reflections she'd experience on and off since the ordeal. The horrors they had endured had left deep scars that would imprint on their lives and psyches forever.

The psychology of a groupie intrigued and fascinated Claire. *What would make a young woman with a long, healthy, happy life ahead of her fall in love with a convicted assassin, serving a life sentence while the courts determined if he should be put to death prematurely?* she thought. *Shelley Simms could have had any man she wanted. She was interesting, intelligent, vibrant, and beautiful. Why Mike Ganz? What was he to her? The bad boy persona?* Claire had researched the literature and attended several conferences on the subject, but remained highly intrigued and troubled by it all, uncertain if she would ever understand the phenomenon sufficiently well. *Shelley had given her life to revenge a man she hardly knew,* she couldn't help thinking. *What promises could he have made her? What enchantments could he have imposed on the young woman that made her choose the path she chose? A path that led to her senseless death.*

Clearing her mind from this never-ending enigma, Claire attempted to hone in on some other thoughts. She smiled. *Kate's wedding was beautiful,* she mused, now furtively glancing at the young couple sitting on the bleachers a few feet away. They were both now standing up, cheering on the Heartbeats. *The union between two people in love serves as an anchor of strength to us all,* she heard her mind whisper. The two lovebirds were looking at a life of happiness, vowing never to look back at the atrocities of yesteryear. After a long, drawn-out battle in court, twelve of Kate's peers finally declared that her license to practice nursing in the State of Indiana should be suspended indefinitely. *I don't even know what to think about that one,* contemplated Claire. *A young woman under extreme duress, fearing for her sister's life, and her own, is commanded by a man*—Claire nodded her head faintly. *Sure, this is sad and regrettable, to say the least, but why did they have to strip her of her license? How is that serving justice? The greater good?* Amelia and Kate's other family members had resumed what appeared to be complete normalcy, but Claire understood that appearances and reality often diverge. The scars would probably heal completely, but not for a long while. *Keep on keeping on*, she mused, a smidgeon of sadness now on her face.

Beyond the net, Jack kicked the soccer ball around the midfield to one of his forwards.

"Come on, Dad. Score one more goal. You can do it," yelled Nick, seeing his father run by, goal-bound. A moment later, a bad pass and a bit of bad luck caused the Heartbeats to lose ball possession. "Ugh! Come on, Heartbeats!" screeched Nick disappointedly, getting up on his feet. Sean imitated the older boy.

Lance Lantz, continued Claire musingly, a faint smile back on her face. *Now, there's an unusual chap.* The lab technician had sought Claire's advice as a clinical psychologist and, at her beseech, eventually came clean with Kate, professing his undying love for her. In turn, Kate introduced him to one of her girlfriends. The matchmaking scheme had promptly returned dividends as Lance and Lucy took to each other like pigs to mud. *Well, they are engaged to be engaged*, thought Claire, an expression of doubt punctuating her idea, an unnoticeable wrinkle on her forehead. Lance had since become a successful professional photographer, proudly displaying his artwork at a thriving gallery. Given Lucy's influence, he made his living nowadays selling his "masterpieces," some of which were actually quite good. Lance's most precious photos, however, would probably remain hidden forevermore. Several close-ups of Nurse Kate still hung in a secret room of his studio, concealed from Lucy, obscured from the world. *Maybe one day, he'll share them. Maybe not.* Claire smirked imperceptibly as these thoughts came and went.

On the field, the two rival teams continued to battle for goals. Well-executed passes between the players had resulted in multiple fruitless attempts to score, given impeccable defense on both sides of the court. Both teams were playing exceptionally well and both deserved to win.

Claire smiled again. *What about my Jack?* she reflected. Jack was busy at work. And soccer. And flying. In other words, getting back to normal. He vowed to use the past only to be better in the future. Thoughts of coulda, shoulda, woulda had surfaced now and again, but Claire steered him away from them. *You can't second-guess yourself after the fact. You do the best you can with the information you have at the time.* He claimed he made a mistake by not taking his family away from Evansville initially and moved to another city. That would have made it more difficult for Lagrange to locate them. But Evansville was where his heart belonged. Besides, Lagrange would have found him anywhere. *Why make old mistakes twice when there are so many new mistakes you could be making?* Learn from your mistakes and move on. Jack seemed to be handling things well. The nightmares would come and go, but they were less devastating and fewer these days.

The lawsuits. Ah, the lawsuits. Claire continued in deep thought, now shaking her head slowly and inconspicuously. *Now the hospital is involved too. I can't believe some of the lawsuits are still pending. People totally disregard their aging parents until they die. Then, the love suddenly returns as they think they can get a buck for it. Human nature. Funny, really, when you think about it. Despite all the facts in the cases, that some lawyers were still after Jack's insurance money is—*

"No!" exclaimed Nick mournfully. "Mom, they scored on our team." He squealed loudly in her ear, interrupting her thoughts. Several moments later, with the game once again afoot, Claire returned to her reflections.

Simon Lagrange was sentenced to death, but appeals were underway. *Not sure how he's taking it, but, who cares? You made your bed, now lie in it,* contemplated Claire. Retrospectively, she had been utterly amazed by how much Nai Trepur had initially provided reassurance and encouragement to her and Jack, for that matter, to the townsfolk. Hiring him as the head of security had endowed the hospital and all who worked within it with a sense of safety, the healing grace that became the vehicle to begin the curative process. *And all was going so well, until—what a terrifying betrayal,* she thought, reflecting on how Nai had been transformed from hero to villain in a blink of an eye. The dreadful feelings engendered in Claire and Jack by this monster had been perhaps the most damaging. *How can we have fallen for this duplicity? Can we ever find a way deep in our hearts to trust anyone?* she paused, reflecting. *We'll just have to find a way.*

"Mom, they scored on us again," yelled Nick, jumping in place next to Claire, momentarily pausing her musing. "They scored, Mom. The score is tied at 2, Mom," he repeated, sensing that Claire's mind wasn't on the match. The game resumed, and so did Claire's contemplative state.

Sitting next to Nick was Sean; the boys had become good pals, almost brotherlike, both highly interested in soccer. *Nick loved to play and watch soccer very much. It doesn't fall far from the tree.* Thankfully, the two boys had been too young and removed from the catastrophes. They had no consequences from the events that tormented their families.

"Oh no!" exclaimed Sean and Nick. "They scored again. This one was Dad's fault. He's going to be so mad at himself," shouted Nick, exasperated.

"I think he can handle it, Nick. Please settle down. I don't want you to fall off the bleachers. Now settle down," said Claire authoritatively. She locked eyes with Susan, winking at her, grinning, each reading one another's minds.

Susan was back to being a detective with the Evansville Police Department, promoted to lieutenant. *She's a great mom. And my best friend.* Was her trauma all forgotten? There were scars, deep inside in the soul and on the skin. Her neck was forever etched with the inscription of the noose that almost stole her life. Susan wore it proudly as a constant reminder of how precious life is and how easily it can be poached. *Live every day as if it could be your last.* Every night, even now, Susan confessed to Claire, when she goes to bed, she passes by her son's bedroom and peeks inside. Looking at his ensconced, slumbering, growing little body warms her heart, a much-needed remedy. Susan still sings the song that represents her strong love for Sean, stronger than the very rope that choked her breath away. The melody had kept her alive during the ice truck ordeal: *"You are my sunshine, my only sunshine. You make me happy when skies are gray. You'll never know, dear, how much I love you, so please don't take my sunshine away."*

CPSIA information can be obtained at www.ICGtesting.com
Printed in the USA
LVOW11s2105130614

389982LV00001B/203/P